I0681383

# A DARK FICTION LITERARY ANTHOLOGY

Volume 9

Guest Editor
## Stacey Longo

**Dark Alley Press**

# INK STAINS ANTHOLOGY
## Volume 9

ISBN 13: 978-1-946050-13-7

© 2018 by Dark Alley Press
Individual stories copyright by authors

**Dark Alley Press**
http://www.darkalleypress.com

An imprint of Vagabondage Press LLC
PO Box 3563
Apollo Beach, Florida 33572
http://www.vagabondagepress.com

First edition printed in the United States of America and the United Kingdom, July 2018

10 9 8 7 6 5 4 3 2 1

# INK STAINS

## A DARK FICTION LITERARY ANTHOLOGY

# INTRODUCTION

W hen I first agreed to editing this issue of *Ink Stains*, I had a few questions: Would there be fame and glory involved? (Unlikely.) Did the publishers think I could handle that sort of fame? (Yes.) And most importantly, what was the theme of the issue?

"We like to let the theme develop organically," N. Apythia Morges assured me. "Just start reading, and pick the stories that speak to you."

*Organically?* Was she serious?

You see, I've been a copyeditor most of my adult career. Every time *The Chicago Manual of Style* publishes a new edition, I read the whole thing again for fun. I like rules. Directions. Guidelines. I like themes. Give me a theme, and by golly, I'll find the best darn stories to fit it. But Ms. Morges was asking me, in essence, to wing it.

I will neither confirm nor deny questioning her sanity. But she was in charge. I opened the submissions folder and started reading.

My first selections could've fallen into a few categories: monsters, for example. Or birds. Could've gone either way. I kept reading, kept finding some stories I really liked, but was still positively stumped regarding the whole theme thing. Roadkill? Cthulhu? Death? Nothing seemed to fit *all* the tales I was selecting.

Then I read Adam Michael Nicks's "After Kurt." The tale of a young man trapped in a mental facility, obsessed with Kurt Cobain…I loved it. But there was not a monster nor a bird to be found. But there was something so engaging and curious about the story, I couldn't let it go. I mean, this kid was messed up. Funny and charming and depressed, but seriously, his relationship with Cobain was—and that's when it struck me.

I looked over what I had. A Lovecraftian, otherworldly monster in a love triangle. One messed up marriage. The worst sort of sibling rivalry, two father/son relationships from hell, a man who could only have a real relationship in his dreams. An insane troop leader. Two scavenging girls who didn't seem to like each other very much. Some more innocent: a mother looking for her missing child, a man losing his job after decades with the same company. And one guy who collected roadkill.

All of the stories I'd earmarked as my favorites *did* have one thing in common: they all featured dysfunctional relationships, be it with a parent, a friend, a would-be lover, or Kurt Cobain.

*My goodness*, I thought. *I do believe what we have here is a bona-fide, organically developed theme.*

So welcome to this edition of *Ink Stains*, in which we explore some of the most fantastic, frightening, and fascinating dysfunctional relationships ever put down in ink.

Some thanks, of course: to N. Apythia Morges, for having faith this theme would develop (and in me); to my editing partner, Rob Smales, who helped out when I was bumping up awfully close to deadline on first edits; and to the authors, who delighted me with their twisted tales.

I'm happy to report that among all the people I just mentioned above, I had not one single dysfunctional relationship in the bunch.

*Stacey Longo*
*March 2018*

# TABLE OF CONTENTS

# THE CHILD'S ROOM

Bobbi Thomas

Some people complained about the coffee at the meetings, but not Emily Branch; she thought it tasted like sorrow, and that was just fine with her.

"Hey, you don't have to do that."

Emily turned, still holding the big, old-fashioned coffee urn. Paul Painter waved from where he'd begun folding chairs: seating for the past hour for a group of sad, confused, and sometimes angry parents.

"I don't mind," said Emily, bustling toward the kitchen. She was a little short, and a little plump, and going a little gray, and seemed practically built for bustling. "I want to help. You do a lot for us, Paul, running these meetings, helping us all cope. You deserve a hand every once in a while."

"That's what The Child's Room is all about." Paul folded a chair to stack with the others. "Coping and hoping. They're our kids, Em. There's always the chance they'll be found or come home." He took up another chair. "The one thing that *does* seem hopeless is my coffee. I'll never get the hang of that big pot thing of theirs. Sorry."

Emily had to smile at that. "It's just fine," she called back as she entered the kitchen.

"I'm parked over here." Paul pointed to the right when they reached the top of the stairs, the last two people to leave the Devon Community Center basement, where The Child's Room met Wednesday nights.

"I'm that way." Emily pointed left. "I guess I'll see you next week?"

He spread his hands. "If you need us, we'll be here. There's always the chance of a miracle between now and then, but we'll be here."

With a wave, Emily bustled toward her car, low, sensible heels clack-clacking through the November night. She paused beneath a streetlight, squinting at one of the faces staring out from the handbills festooning the wooden pole, each bearing a different picture but captioned with the same stark message: MISSING.

*Getting a bit tattered*, she thought. *I'll come back tomorrow and replace it. It's time I replaced all of them. I'll—*

"Excuse me?"

A shape stepped into the cone of light beneath the streetlamp, ratty sneakers silent on the sidewalk. Emily's gasp—just a little more air to fuel a scream, if needed—came out in a tentative sigh as she took in the figure: well-worn jeans clung to slender legs, giving away the slimness hidden by the threadbare, oversized hoodie, and though the bill of the Red Sox cap left the face in shadow, the stranger was no taller than she. And that voice had been female, and high, and…

*A girl?*

"Yes?" Emily said.

"Can you spare a dollar?" The hat tipped back, lamplight spilling across a hopeful smile. "I just want to buy a hot chocolate, I promise."

Emily's gasp this time wasn't a quick startled inhale, but a deep inrush of air spawned by shock. Christ, Paul had *just* mentioned a miracle, but this—

"Jenny?"

Now the girl looked startled. "No…it's Jesse, but how did you… have we met before?"

Emily stared from the poster to Jesse and back. No, now that she was really looking it was obvious they weren't the same girl. But still, the resemblance was striking, with the fair skin and blue eyes and the blonde hair sticking out from under the cap, and seeing her quickly, under the streetlamp like that—

"No," Emily said. "Sorry, you just…reminded me of someone, that's all."

"Oh." Jesse wrinkled her nose. "Weird. Well, would you have given *her* a dollar?"

Despite her racing heart, Emily snorted. "Are you kidding? I gave her money all the time."

"Well then," said Jesse. "Can I have a dollar? For cocoa. It's getting colder at night, and I still have to find a shelter or something."

Emily glanced at Jenny's picture again. *There's always the chance they'll be found or come home*, she thought. *Have I found someone here?*

"Jesse, are you a runaway?"

Her bluntness surprised even her—she really should have phrased it differently, but things were moving too fast in her head—and the girl fumbled for an answer. "Let's just say I'm on my own," she finally said, but in that awkward pause, Emily had come to a decision of her own.

"Forget the dollar. We'll get hot chocolate on the way home."

"Huh?"

"Forget the shelter. You're staying with me tonight."

The girl put up her hands, backing away. "No, hey, look, all I wanted was—"

"No argument. It's getting cold, like you said, and I have room. I've got heat, and a bed, and a kitchen full of food—how long's it been since you had a good meal?—and it's just for the night if you want. No strings."

Jesse'd stopped retreating at the mention of food. "Seriously? You mean it?"

"I mean it."

"No strings? No cops, anything like that?"

"I promise."

Without waiting for an answer, Emily hooked an arm through Jesse's and started walking her toward the car, throwing a glance toward the notice-covered pole. "You can stay in my daughter's room. She's…not using it right now."

Rhonda looked around the foyer, admiring the architecture of the big house—and taking note of the security panel beside the door.

"Just give me a minute to hang our coats," said Emily, fingers flying over the alarm keypad, "and we can check out the kitchen. Or would you rather see Jenny's—I mean, your room?"

"Whatever works for you," Rhonda said, not surprised by the slip. She'd heard all about Jenny on the ride, Mrs. Branch obviously unable to help herself. Rhonda had just let her chatter, confirming things she already knew: Jennifer Branch had gone missing, long enough ago that her parents had split up over it—separated or divorced, Rhonda really didn't care—and Mrs. Branch refused to give up on her daughter. Now she lived alone in a great big house, and was, in Rhonda's considerable opinion, just about as vulnerable as it got.

*This shit is so damn easy*, she thought, tugging the hoodie over her head and handing it to her host.

It worked every time. Roll into a new town and check out the community center, library, or go online and read the local *Patch*. Find a support group for parents of lost or missing children and scope it out. See who comes alone, who stays late, who tends religiously to the posters they've plastered all over the place. Rhonda was twenty, but looked fifteen without makeup. Thirteen with. And she was good with makeup; give her a picture to work from—a MISSING poster, perhaps—and an *uncanny resemblance* was easy enough. Dress like a street kid, give them a name like the one on the poster—she could be *Jesse* for now, no problem—and what wounded, hopeful parent of a runaway *wouldn't* invite her in for a bit?

Mrs. Branch closed the wide closet door. "Ready to raid the fridge?"

"Sure," said Rhonda—*Jesse*, she reminded herself, *your name is Jesse*—"but can I use the bathroom first?"

"Of course," said the older woman, leading the way through a spacious living room filled with enough expensive-looking furniture and tchotchkes—Rhonda wasn't sure exactly what a tchotchke *was*, but at least *one* of these gold-plated doodads had to fit the bill—to make her stomach tingle. "The downstairs bath is right here, and I'll be in the kitchen, through that doorway there, when you come out."

*We just got here, and she's already leaving me alone?* Rhonda thought, shutting the bathroom door and sitting on the closed toilet lid. *This is going to be easier than usual!* She pulled out her phone and thumbed in a brief text:

*I'm in*

Then she started a new memo, typing in the four-digit code she'd just watched Emily Branch punch into her security panel. She didn't want any trouble remembering it when it was time to let Gary in.

)(O)(O)(

Dinner was leftover roast, potatoes, carrots, and corn, all microwaved back into a semblance of warm perfection. "And there's apple pie for dessert," Emily said.

"I thought you said you lived all alone here?" said Jesse, picking up a fork and digging in—which was good, Emily thought. She'd lost too much weight.

"I do," Emily said, fixing her own plate. "Tom couldn't deal with the house. Everything in it reminded him of Jenny. But I couldn't leave. What if she came back and found us gone? What would she think?" Just imagining her daughter coming home to find someone else living there, like she and Tom had simply moved on with their lives, broke her heart.

Jesse's fork swung in a short arc, indicating the table and everything on it. "So you make all *this*, just for you?"

Emily looked at the spread, easily dinner for four—five in a pinch—and shrugged. "I guess I'm still used to cooking for a family."

Jesse stared at her. "Still used to…how long has it been?"

"Since Tom moved out? Oh…" she had to pause and do the math. Sometimes the Valium Dr. Botolo had put her on made everything drag by, but sometimes she lost whole days, depending on how much she took, and even she had to admit she sometimes took a lot; time had become a somewhat fluid thing in the life of Emily Branch. "Four years," she said, finally.

"Four years?" Jesse echoed.

"He moved out the year after Jenny…left."

"And you still—"

"Don't worry about that right now," Emily interrupted. She had the vague sense she might have been embarrassed at this conversation about her cooking habits, but honestly, it was just so *good* to have a child in the house again, to have Jenny's seat at the table filled again. Nothing else seemed to matter. "You just eat up. Clean your plate and there's pie, remember? We'll get some meat back on those bones—then I'll show you your room."

XOXOX

"Wow, uh, great room," was all Rhonda could think to say. The woman hadn't let her leave the table without a second helping, then pie, insisting Rhonda was too skinny. All Rhonda had wanted to do was get to bed—to get *Emily* to go to bed—though she had no intention of sleeping. Not for hours yet. So she'd feigned exhaustion to cut the conversation short. They'd gone back through that living room that just *smelled* of money and up a sweeping staircase, Rhonda trying to mentally catalogue everything so they'd know right where to go once Gary pulled the van in. The less time spent with a strange vehicle in the driveway, the better; the police drove through the neighborhood on a regular schedule—they'd timed it last night, once an hour, like clockwork—but they couldn't rule out a nosy neighbor.

She was still making a shopping list—*that's a seventy-inch flatscreen, a Bose stereo, that breakfront displaying the china must have the good silver, those figurines on the mantle looked old and collectible, and if that clock up there with them isn't an antique I'll eat it*—when Emily had opened a door and ushered her through.

The room was pink. It was frilly. The dollhouse in the corner was huge and intricate, as opposed to the canopied bed, which was a twin at most. The desk was neat—a place for everything and everything in its place—but small, maybe half-sized. She scanned the low bookcase set beneath the window, and even from a distance made out several books from her own childhood; the Nancy Drew series was all right, but Magic Treehouse?

*This is a* kid's *room,* she thought, scrabbling about for something else to say. *But the girl on the poster was at least fourteen, fifteen easy.*

"Yep, this is…something," she finally said.

Emily beamed. "I've kept it just the way you left it."

Still stunned by the room she almost missed it, but Emily's words managed a fingerhold on Rhonda's attention as they flew by. "Wait—how *I* left—"

But her host was holding a fistful of material toward her. "Here, put on this nightgown, and I can put those clothes in the wash. The bathroom's through there."

"No, you don't have to—"

"I insist," said Emily, and there was steel in the older woman's voice that hadn't been there before. "Besides, you'll be more comfortable if you're not wearing all that, won't you?" It didn't sound like a question, the way she said it. It reminded Rhonda of some teachers she'd had; *ordering you politely* was how one of them had explained it.

"Fine." She took the nightgown—pink, of course, and was that a faded Minnie Mouse on the front?—just wanting the woman to leave her alone and go to sleep, so she could explore the house a little before giving Gary the all clear. She marched through the doorway Emily had indicated and stopped. The first thing she noticed was the pass-through door into the next room: a notably *adult* bedroom. The second thing she noticed was the toothbrush holder over the sink, in which rested three toothbrushes: two full-sized, blue and red, the third child-sized and bright, bright pink.

She almost didn't hear Emily, closing the door behind Rhonda: "Besides, that's your favorite nightgown."

On her way back from the laundry room, Emily stopped to check that the front door was locked and the alarm on. She'd had quite a time getting the girl to give up *all* her clothes, including the underwear. But what kind of girl didn't change her underwear for two days? That Emily *knew* of—it might have been more.

The door was tight and the alarm set. *Good*, she thought. *Have to keep the girl safe. The poor thing's been on the street too long. I can tell. Not to worry.* She mounted the stairs. *Sleep in a good bed, get a few good meals into her, make sure she's got clean underwear, and my Jenny will be right as rain in no time.*

*This woman is crazy*, Rhonda thought, lying in a bed surrounded by stuffed animals and clutching her phone like a lifeline. The plush bears, puppies, horses, and other, less-identifiable creatures stared rather creepily at her in the glow of a night-light shaped like a fluffy little chick. *Yes*, that stare seemed to say. *She's crazy, we're crazy, and it's just a matter of time for you...*

She'd heard of parents who never wanted their kids to grow up. She'd seen something about it on TV once. Had it been on *Maury*? Jerry Springer? Didn't matter.

*No wonder the kid ran away. I would have, too.*

She waited two full hours before sneaking out of bed and crossing to the door, twice as long as she usually did. She wasn't afraid of the woman, exactly; hell, she was a chubby forty-something who reminded Rhonda of a librarian; what was she going to do, get physical? But something about the way Emily had slipped up a couple of times, referring to it as *her* room, calling her Jenny once without even realizing it…it had her on edge.

She crept past Emily's bedroom and down the stairs, pausing at the foot to send Gary a quick message. *Starting my walkaround. Let me know when you're on the way in.*

*Got it*, he sent back. *Gimme a few.*

The TV and stereo were givens, and the keys for the Mercedes Emily had driven were on the side table in the foyer; they'd be taking that, too. She checked the figurines: the mark on the bottoms said *Dresden*, which was something she'd heard of, so it *must* be good. She didn't find a maker's mark on the clock, but she was in a hurry, and the thing still looked older than Christ. The china in the breakfront looked even older than the clock, and the silver—thick, heavy pieces smelling of polish—were right in the drawer where she'd suspected. The center of the breakfront, though, right above the drawers, was a pair of locked wooden doors.

*The silver's not locked up, but whatever's in there* is?

The doors might be secured, but people were people, so Rhonda checked the silver drawer again, using the flashlight in her phone. There, tucked in a back corner, was a small antique key.

It fit the lock.

*Too easy.*

Her phone vibrated with an incoming text: *On my way.*

*Just have time to check this shit out*, Rhonda thought, turning the key with a quiet click and swinging both doors wide, revealing a thick vase.

*What is this, one of those Ming Dynasty things, like in the movies?*

She played the light across the vase, and her nerves, already a-jangle from that weird woman and her bedroom, went numb. The engraving read:

Jennifer Anne Branch
1997–2012
Beloved Forever

*What the fuck?* Rhonda had trouble catching her breath. *Ming nothing—this is an urn! The kid didn't run away, she's fucking* dead! *This lady really* is *crazy!*

A tiny, choked scream erupted from her lips as the lights came on.

"Sneaking around again. I should have known."

Rhonda whirled. Emily stood at the foot of the stairs, hand on the light switch, face filled with sorrow.

"Why do you fight me on everything?"

"What?" Rhonda whispered, then, louder: "What are you talking about?"

"Why?" Emily went on, as if she hadn't heard, voice as sad as her eyes. "Why have you always wanted to grow up so fast? Mother knows best—can't you see that now?"

"I'm not your daughter," Rhonda said, edging sideways, toward the front door, never taking her eyes from the madwoman at the stairs.

"You left us. Left us to be on your own, all grown up—but here you are, five years later, homeless and in dirty clothes. And you're so skinny, Jenny."

"I'm not Jenny," Rhonda shouted, and the woman flinched. "I'm not her!" She pointed toward the cabinet, and the urn. "Your Jenny's gone! She's dead!"

Emily's face hardened, eyes furious. "Christ, I know that! Don't you think I know that? I *found* her!" The hard eyes softened. "My baby, just dangling…why? But that won't happen again—there's no rope in the house now. None." She thrust one hand in her dressing gown pocket, the other pointed upstairs. "Now go to your room, young lady. Now!"

"Fuck this, crazy lady." Rhonda spun for the door. "I'm outta here!"

"Don't you go," Emily wailed behind her. "Not again! Not again!"

Rhonda flipped the deadbolt and tore the door open; the alarm shrieked. Gary rushed in through the gap, eyes wide with shock, looking around wildly at the noise.

"What the fuck?"

Beyond him, in the driveway, stood salvation: the van. All they had to do was drive away from this madhouse and never look back. "We gotta go!" Rhonda yelled.

But Gary couldn't hear her over the howling alarm, and in his confusion he'd clasped her upper arms; small as she was, she couldn't just break his grip and step around him. "What's going on?" he shouted.

"We got to *go!*" she screamed up at him—and Gary's left eye disappeared in a clap of thunder. He spun, still holding her arms, and bore her to the floor. On her back, pinned beneath Gary's hundred and eighty pounds, she saw Emily Branch loom in the foyer doorway, a pistol gripped in one hand.

*She shot him! Jesus fuck, she shot him!*

Over the unwavering eye of the gun barrel, Emily's eyes were hard as, deafened by the gunshot and alarm, Rhonda read her clearly enunciating lips.

"Not again."

"Just this," Emily said to the cashier.

"Emily?"

She turned to see Paul Painter entering the convenience store. "Hi. Long time, no see."

"I'll say! We haven't seen you at The Child's Room in, what, almost six months?"

"Just about," she agreed.

"Is everything...okay?" he said, cautiously.

"Actually, yeah," she said. "Everything's better than it's been for a long time."

"Glad to hear it!" He pointed at the counter between her and the cashier. "I didn't know you smoked."

"I don't," she said, scooping up the carton of Marlboros and walking out the door.

"How are they treating you?" Emily asked, sliding two packs of Marlboros across the table, but keeping her grip on them, not letting go quite yet. The guards had checked them out thoroughly, and pronounced them safe enough.

"How long we gonna keep doing this?" Rhonda asked.

"Until we deem you grown up enough to be out on your own. Which you're obviously not. I mean, look at you. Your hair's a mess, and I've told you orange just isn't your color. But you've never listened to me before; why would you start now? So"—that unlikely steel crept back into her voice—"how are they treating you?"

"Same as they were when you asked last week." Rhonda leaned forward and tugged on the smokes. They stayed put. She sighed and gave in. "Mom."

Emily's fingers sprang open, freeing the cigarettes. Her other hand held up a crisp twenty. "Visiting once a week doesn't seem like enough to me. We have five years of catching up to do. I want you to start writing two letters a week."

The smokes and cash could buy her favors in here, and with Gary dead it wasn't like anyone else was going to bring her anything. Rhonda gritted her teeth. "Two letters. Okay, Mom, whatever you say."

The twenty slid across the table. "Thank you, dear. Mother knows what's best, after all. You know I love you."

*I'm up for parole in two and a half years.* Rhonda thought of a pink, frilly room, and a rope. *Just two and a half years and I'm out from under this woman's thumb.*

*I can't fucking wait.*

XOXOX XOXOX XOXOX X

# About the Author

Bobbi Thomas is a long-time fan of character-driven dark fiction. Hailing from Eastern Massachusetts, she spends her days trapped in a third-floor corporate cube farm lit by computer screens and smoldering human souls, and her nights reading with her husband, son, two dogs, and a three-legged chinchilla named Ferdinand. "The Child's Room" will be her first published story.

# THE GULLS

Matt Meyer

The world is flat.

Its edge is just over Killy Bridge. When people leave Killdeer Key, they fall off.

Nobody ever comes back. Not a damn one.

At least that's what Bobby Cullen said.

And as far back as Wayne Pilsen could remember in his miserable thirty-one years of life, Bobby was right.

Wayne sat on the old floral couch his mama had picked out before she died—how long had it been now? Ten? Eleven years?—and deep, drunk thoughts had gotten the best of him.

Blues had faded to grays, greens to yellows, and the pinks to dirty whites. The bamboo armrests were chipped, gouged, and even burned. Daddy wasn't always the ashtray type. It smelled of skin and use, and every once in a while (like tonight), he swore he could smell his mama.

Hurricane season was a bitch. Rain and wind hammered the aluminum double-wide like a drunken steel drummer. Quite literally everything had to be bolted down and cheesy lawn ornaments (flamingos, gnomes in bikinis, parrots a-fucking-plenty) hidden in garages—or in the Pilsen's case, their living room. The two cracked and faded flamingos the family had come to know as Gertrude and Burp (the children named them separately) sat on lawn chairs, their post-legs sticking through the crisscrossed nylon straps. They eyed Wayne with black beady orbs that bore no emotion.

The storm's only upside was it forced folks to huddle up inside with a few good books (and ample amounts of booze) until Mother

Nature decided to stop giving it good and hard to the Florida Keys. Wayne Pilsen lived for it (especially those years it closed up Daddy's shop for days and even weeks), and made the most of it these last two nights. He'd been on a bender for more than a day, sleeping little the night before, and waking with what felt like an ice pick through his hindbrain. Ibuprofen didn't take, but hair of the dog seemed to work just fine.

Drinking wasn't normally one of Wayne Pilsen's pastimes; in fact, he rarely touched the stuff. Maybe a beer here, a beer there, but it was a rarity he'd have even two in one sitting. After seeing what it did to his daddy every day, the appeal was lost on him.

But after work yesterday, in their linoleum-covered kitchen from decades past, he was in dire need of a numbing agent. And not a physical one from one of Daddy's temper tantrums that left him bruised and aching. This was a deeper need…a need to numb life.

He'd gone to the freezer to ice a swollen cheek that'd begun to purple into another bruise, the latest of many he'd received from his daddy for doing something wrong or not looking at him the right way or breathing too loud or—

Wayne couldn't keep track anymore.

It was then the rusting old Frigidaire spoke. *I've got what you need, Wayney. Pull a few from the back. Daddy will never know.*

One became two, two became five, and five became thirteen, an unlucky number that Daddy would surely notice. He sat on the floral couch with a dime-store book he'd picked up the other day: a short yarn about a gunslinger chasing a devil across the desert. When the words got too fuzzy, a yodeling Dwight Yoakam from the crackly cassette deck in the corner kept him company instead as the cheap beer went down like water.

Wayne even danced a bit for his flamingo audience.

"*Gee-tars, Cadillacs…*" he slurred at the birds and winked. "*Hillbilly music!*" He stumbled as he took a long swig and smiled devilishly at his pink friends. "My, my! You ladies look delightful tonight. And *woo-wee* those pink skirts—you're all legs!"

He'd expected his daddy to come stumbling through the door any minute, drunk and ready to talk business with his knuckles. *Didn't I tell you not to read any more of them stories?* or *What you doin' dancing around like some kind of queer?* or *What the hell did you do with my beer you little sack of shit?* Or all of the above.

Probably all of the above.

But lucky for Wayney, Daddy'd never made it home last night. He'd finished up work after Wayne, driven over to Coconutz to drink with Sheriff Sutton, met a visiting optometrist from Miami, and spent the night in her parent's vacation home she'd inherited after they croaked up in Vermont.

*Don't expect me home 'til Sunday. Keep outta fuckin' trouble.*

So Wayne drank to his heart's content. It was Saturday mid-afternoon that dams began to break, thoughts and contrition seeping through widening cracks. Wayne began contemplating his existence—something Daddy would surely call *hippie bullshit*—and what the hell he was still doing on Killdeer Key. Living with his daddy. Eating a shit sandwich day in, day out.

The booze had numbed his inhibitions, all right. It had given him the C4 to blow open his brain-bunker's ceiling hatch. Sunlight poured in as he climbed the ladder into a field of flowers, free thinking, and regret.

He loathed working for his daddy at the fish market, Land Lubber's, the hole-in-the-wall, grade-A shithole Willy Pilsen owned. He even hated that stupid fucking name. Daddy'd taken to hitting him at the counter lately, even in front of the customers. Most recently, in front of Mary Gilespie, his high school crush from an age long past, prehistoric even.

But she was still so beautiful—still so creamy and perfect—he couldn't help but gawk. Two kids from some jerk who'd done and left her hadn't affected that soft, skinny frame, and he still longed for her. He'd felt an erection coming on like all the uncontrollable pork swords he'd popped in his adolescent years. Full salute. God, she hadn't aged a day. Wayne's eyes met hers, and she smiled. Daddy noticed this small, utterly rare moment of bliss and, as always, rained on Wayne's parade with a hard clout across the ear.

Mary gasped, frozen. Wayne froze, too. Blood worked its way into his face from the pain but mostly sheer embarrassment. She frowned. There was pity in that frown. Pity for such a pathetic specimen as Wayne Pilsen. She abandoned the seasoning salt on the wrong shelf just to get the hell out of there, turning her back to Wayne for perhaps the final time. And with every little step of those petite Keds, his anger tweaked higher, like dragging a stick up a xylophone.

He turned to his daddy, face purple and irate. All Willy Pilsen did was smile.

"What are you gonna do? Hit me?" His yellowy, tar-stained teeth beamed. His purple gums had receded to the roots. "You're a chicken-shit pussy, little Wayney. You don't have the balls."

And he didn't. Wayne turned away, ashamed. It was the closest he'd come in his god-forsaken life to fighting back—hitting back—and it wasn't even *that* close. Instead, he shrank into a corpuscle of shame and embarrassment as he always did. His daddy hit him again, then took him by the back of his shirt.

"You can fuck her if you want, Wayney," Daddy said, leaning in real close. Wayne smelled the stale beer on his breath at two in the afternoon. "But don't think for one second you're leaving Willy Pilsen.

"*Nobody* leaves Willy Pilsen."

He had no friends anymore to confide in. No one to bitch to even a little bit. Didn't have time for them, working 6 a.m. to 8 p.m. at that dump of a shop. A young waiter, Bobby Cullen, was the only person who took time out of their day to chat with him when Wayne delivered fish to Coconutz. The friends he once had were long gone. Curtis Lee, his best childhood buddy, had packed up his orange Camaro shortly after Wayne's sister had flown the coop, headed for the mainland to work for the state of Florida, and that was before his mama passed. In other words, a long-ass time ago.

When it rains, it pours. And in Wayne's prequel to his first weekend bender, it *poured*. When you know the outcome, prequels suck.

ХОХОХ

Now, it had grown dark on night two of his time in Pissville. Rain pattered against the roof, and blowing palm shadows danced across the walls. Leonard Cohen spoke his dirges in the darkened room from the cassette deck's radio on a station Wayne had never been able to pick up before. The couch smelled strongly of his mother.

There was no moonlight, but his truck seemed to glow in the driveway. Much like the old Frigidaire, it called to him and invited action. He brimmed with a deepened need. Purpose.

*Act, Wayney...*

These were the kind of fleeting thoughts that meant everything in the moment, utterly bright and brilliant and *deep*; they united ideas and lives and worlds with cosmic glue. Come morning, though, they were the kind that lost their magnificent glow, broken up in dull fragments, extinguished in the aching, stale coming of sobriety.

*Act now.*


So he drove like hell. If Bobby was right, and there was a cliff at the end of the world, he was going to take it at well over eighty miles per hour with a goddamn beer in his hand.

Because anywhere—even getting sucked into a big black fuckin' hole in space—was better than Killdeer.

*Halle-fucking-lujah.*

In the short time between his drunken premonition and climbing into the truck, he cleaned out his daddy's sock drawer, stole six more cans of liquid courage out of the fridge, and took his daddy's .44 Magnum. Two empty cans already rolled and clamored in the bed not a quarter of a mile out of the Pilsen's driveway on Tortuga Lane.

*Redneck wind chimes guide me, for this is my last day on Killdeer-fucking-Key.*

When that truck started, his courage started. Turning the key took every ounce of his frail being, but once it turned over, so did Wayne Pilsen. This would mark his last Saturday in their shitty old double-wide.

Memories, old souls, and the forgotten swirled. Clots melted away. It was like smelling things of the past all at once.

*Smells ring bells, oh yes.*

One smell wafted oldest and truest: there'd always been something very off about the key he sought to flee. Kids ran off and never came back. As far as he knew, nobody even cared to go looking for them. They were rarely mentioned again, and if a lost soul came up in a conversation, eyes flitted back and forth and said subject was changed in haste.

His sister was one of these escapees. The year-rounders lived with a kind of passive ignorance that almost implied they feared discussing such occurrences; they feared Killdeer Key was listening.

*Nobody leaves Willy Pilsen*…and yet, she had.

Hadn't she? Surely there was hope for him, a grown man with a bit more knowledge of the world than a bunch of runaway kids.

He glanced in the rearview mirror, and two bloodshot eyes stared back. They sank into a pallid face. An *old* pallid face. Puffy dark bags pulled at his lower lids with the weight of too many years and too many beatings from Daddy dearest. He'd had dreams of college and building a life for himself outside of this hellhole, but those dreams seemed more and more dead as they faded into youthful obscurity.

Wayne had been an imaginative child, full of whimsy and adventure. His dime-store books provided worlds outside his own. His daddy never liked them and eventually forbade them.

"Puttin' too many liberal ideas in that noggin' of yours," he'd slurred.

*Nobody leaves Willy Pilsen.*

Now he could only read after his drunken daddy had passed out. They still gave him a form of escape, but the exciting boyish fantasies of *really* escaping seemed to pass with his mother. The monotony of life on Killdeer Key wore him down to a nub, and his father all but extinguished his sense of self.

Bob Seger screamed and rasped from the speakers.

Was there still time? Or was he damned to working behind the counter at Land Lubber's with his drunk daddy until the old bastard finally gave in to a cancer that surely must be coming his way?

How cruel the world was. How fucked a world was that still allowed sadistic old fucks to *prosper*. Daddy drank and smoked like the devil, made a boatload of money from the fish market (the pun made Wayne groan), and somehow his poor mama bit the dust first—a woman who didn't even have the tolerance to finish a glass of wine, a woman who'd never smoked a cigarette in her life and gotten cancer anyway.

Wayne could only hope once he stared across Killy Bridge, he'd have the courage to look his future in the face, and he prayed to a God he doubted knew the name *Wayne Pilsen* that his daddy wouldn't come after him if he did.

If Willy came looking or got Sheriff Sutton to radio the north keys for help, his current escape would be short-lived and the grandest of beatings would come his way…

*Nobody leaves Willy Pilsen.*

The air conditioner cut through the humidity with a cool mildew stink. Something in the dashboard rattled persistently, a constant reminder of just how many miles had been acquired on the old Chevy Silverado. Florida could keep a car alive years, sometimes decades longer than the colder states that saw rust and rot with snow and salt.

Cars could last, but dreams, under the bullshit guise of carefree happiness the Keys were known for, could not.

The wind and rain had continued for nearly two days straight, waterlogging everything. Water crept up onto low spots in the road, becoming more pond than puddle as Mother Nature continued to bawl.

Wayne rounded the north end of Killdeer to the west side and took the puddles well over the speed limit, feeling the Chevy hydroplane on one side or the other when she hit the big ones. If it wasn't the overgrown puddles, it was downed branches and sticks. He rolled over them, and they crunched like wooden bones. If they sought to stand in his way, they did so in brittle vain.

Each snap and crunch gave him a kind of weird satisfaction that fueled the intention of never going back—like he was trampling this dark place, breaking the witch-knuckled Gumbo Limbos and writhing Banyans that reached out on all sides to halt his escape.

Soon those witch-knuckled trees shrank back as he came upon Killdeer Village. His daddy's fish market was a quarter mile up on the left, and he felt it coming. Oh, how he hated that fucking fish market. Between it and his daddy, they'd robbed him of the best years of his life. Or at least what was supposed to be, according to his books.

*Books are my only friends.*

How pathetic that sounded. His knuckles went white on the steering wheel.

With headlights reaching out like desperate feelers in the night, he drove down Parrot Parkway through the heart of town toward the boundary of his known world. Optimistic thoughts of life outside, maybe even a late start in college, crept into the forefront of mind.

"College is a scam for liberal fucking yuppies," Daddy had once said. "'Sides, I need you sellin' meat at the store. Someday, if you don't piss me off too much, I might leave it for ya."

The thought of owning the establishment could not have been more repulsive. Wayne passed the dimly lit *Land Lubber's* sign on the right without a glance, fearing eye contact with the fish market might suck the courage from him, shrivel up his balls, and send him back home. It was a place of sadness and evil. Even at nearly fifty miles per hour, time slowed, and he slogged by it at a glacial pace.

*Look at me, Wayney. Look at me! I've sucked the years out of you but I'm still hungry. Still soooo hungry Wayney. Look at me!*

He refused. Instead, he sucked back the remaining beer in the can and tossed it through the window into the truck bed before opening another, drowning the sobering nags of the place before it could put dark sensibilities in his head.

Even though it was Saturday, and Land Lubber's was closed for the weekend, Monday morning was a heaping, stinking precipice you could smell from any day of the week. By Sunday evening, the stench was full on, a constant reminder of the cyclical hell that would come by morning.

Wayne longed to be rid of that feeling. Longed to escape Sundays ruined by Monday's wafted rot. He longed to be rid of the beatings. Longed to never hear the screeching gulls out back of their double-wide on Tortuga Lane ever again. Longed to get the fuck out of the Dodge that was Killdeer Key.

Most of all, he longed to be rid of his daddy. *Why couldn't he have gone first?* Mama had died more than ten years ago from cancer that'd spread through her lungs and guts. It had been just the two of them since.

Daddy beat her almost as hard as he beat Wayne, but she had it worse. Daddy made her his receptacle for everything horrible, mostly when he was tanked. Trouble was, Daddy was always tanked.

She was a loudmouth bitch for talking on the phone, a dirty whore for wearing just about anything outside the house, and a cunt-if-he-ever-saw-one for running out of beer—all of which were offenses that had gotten her cuffed and bloodied.

One dysfunctional little memory stuck out worst…one at the rotted root of his childhood. Every day Daddy'd bring home raw fish that had passed its time of freshness—sometimes considerably so—from Land Lubber's to feed the gulls out back.

The smell was unbearable. The sack sat out back each night, and the breeze often brought in the sickening smell to Wayne's room.

Once, when Momma had cooked grouper that wasn't to his daddy's liking, he went out back, brought in a piece of the spoiled gull food, forced it into her mouth and made her chew it.

He grabbed her by the jaw while she cried and dry-heaved, half the piece of rotting meat dangling from lips, and said, "If you ever cook like shit for me again, I'll make you eat the whole fucking bag." She ended up in the bathroom on her knees, vomiting for most the night.

When Daddy looked in on her later, after the Marlins were down 0-6 in the bottom of the eighth, he'd said, "Don't you dare think about leaving me, Delores. *Nobody* leaves Willy Pilsen."

As he did whenever she cried, Wayne brought her an old pink washcloth with seashells to dry her tears. There were no tissues in the house (an extravagance Willy Pilsen found unnecessary, because he wasn't going to bring up faggots or crybabies) and toilet paper seemed less than chivalrous; the pink washcloth had become the magic wipe for Mama's tears.

"Here you go, Mama," he whispered.

She took it and smiled. "Someday," she'd said. "Someday."

Her words were lost on Wayne until he'd gotten old enough. She'd wanted out of hell, and planned to take her kiddies with her. Away from Willy Pilsen.

But it never happened.

The road began curving. To his left, a gull stood at the side of the road. He heard it scream even over the nearly floored engine.

It looked at him through the windshield as he roared by. A black dread spread up from his gut. A ridiculous thought popped into head: *Daddy might be watching me through those black little eyes...does he know already?*

Nobody asked Willy Pilsen why he fed the disgusting things. Nobody asked Daddy much of anything, out of fear of the obvious.

Every night after work, he'd walk out back of the house with that lumpy feed bag and just the sight of him would drive the gulls into a frenzy. Daddy'd feed them half then and half the next morning. It amazed Wayne they never tore the bag open while the humans slept. They waited—waited for their master to feed them rot for breakfast.

The following day, he'd set down his coffee with a cigarette pursed between his lips, pick up the bag, and fling a piece with his bare hands out into the lot of them, usually twenty to thirty gulls in all. One night in the hot, humid air multiplied the rotty stink tenfold.

There was fighting, screeching, and the flutter of dirtied wings. The single piece of meat probably passed between ten different beaks before one of them finally managed to down it.

They looked ratty and discolored, more so than those you'd see in a textbook, and much older than they should. As much as Daddy fed them, they should've be a healthy white and more patient about their food.

But they were always ravenous. Always ready to rip at meat as if it'd been days—or weeks—since they'd last gotten a decent meal.

Then they'd all look back to Daddy for more.

Begging.

Screeching.

And the worst part? If you listened to them enough—let them really work their way into your ears—they'd begin to sound human.

Daddy flipped the pieces one at a time, always watching with tempered amusement.

And it *stank*. But that didn't bother Daddy. He'd smoke his cigarette with the same fingers that flung each rancid piece, a closeness to the birds that always made Wayne's stomach curdle.

"He gets off to it," Bev, Wayne's sister, had once told him. "I've seen the stiffy in his coveralls when he does it. He feels power when they fight over scraps, just like he feels power over us when he takes out his fists. The only difference is he loves those sickening birds more than he loves us."

As the bulk of trials and tribulations came to light on that old floral couch just hours before, the worst memory of all made him consider ending his troubles by sucking on the long end of his daddy's .44 and serving the wall a helping of brain pudding.

Instead, after careful deliberation, the .44 rode in the glovebox, and he'd made it his mission to find his sister, the only Pilsen who got the fuck out of Dodge.

*Find Bevvy and live happily ever after. Never see this place again.*
*Oh, Bevvy Smells ring bells,*


Beverly Pilsen was the prettiest girl in school. Boys chased after her like the paparazzi stalk movie starlets. Girls loved and loathed her for her looks, as all girls normally do. Perhaps, because of this beauty, it made the night her face was broken that much harder.

She and Wayne had been close. Very close. She was six years older, and the age gap was enough to dispel most fights and rivalries siblings had. As broken as Mama had become, Bevvy was the closest thing he'd had to a hero.

They listened to Mama's Eagles records in Bev's room, watched Johnny Carson together when Daddy passed out early, and she even gave Wayne his first cigarette. He'd coughed until he really thought his lungs might end up on the front lawn. She'd laughed and said *That'll teach you to go near these*. He hadn't since.

She'd given him his first sex talk, his first dance lesson, and his first driving lesson; his first swig of beer, his first double-dog-dare, and his first real encouragement to be whatever the fuck he wanted to be. Bevvy looked out for Wayne, and Wayne thought Bevvy was *it*. It didn't get much better for siblings. In fact, he knew it didn't. She was perfect.

So why had she'd gotten it bad? So, so undeservingly bad? Especially the very last time.

And his father had made him watch.

*All of it. Oh, God…all of it.*


The night it happened, a couple years before his mama died, Daddy threw open Wayne's door and caught him reading in bed: *The Haunting of Hill House* by Shirley Jackson.

"Those goddamn books of yers. Why can't you go out and shoot shit with your BB gun, or beat your meat like normal boys yer age when their door is closed?"

Wayne elected to say nothing. Nothing good came from speaking.

"Put that faggot trash down and come with me," Daddy slurred, beer in hand. "We're gonna sit a while."

Wayne followed, and they sat on the new floral sofa in dark silence, the only sound the wet sucking of beer out the can and heavy gulps. Wayne knew better than to ask what was going on. Daddy's cigarette glowed a bright orange every time he took a heavy drag.

Wayne was sure something awful was coming.

They sat like that for almost an hour. It all became clearer when Jasper Higgins pulled up, the boy Bevvy was seeing, and Willy told Wayne, "You're gonna learn tonight how to treat a woman who don't mind you."

Wayne had begun to sweat. He clutched the edge of the couch, his knuckles a ghostly white, helpless to warn her, as they often did when Daddy was pissed at one of them. He couldn't do shit but sit and wait.

Bev bounded up the walkway, drunk as a skunk, all smiles in the moonlight. They watched her fiddle with the door handle as quietly as she could, hoping she was in the clear for her curfew two hours past. Daddy slowly got up and moved to intercept her. Her tardy slip came in the form of a fist.

A reminder about who really owned the place. Owned *them*.

Daddy flipped the lights on and broke her nose, did God-knows-what to her swollen cheekbone, and busted two of her front teeth. She ended up swallowing both.

As she lay on the floor, a broken mess in a puddle of her own blood and spit, all he said was, "Look at what you made me do."

He grabbed her by the hair and whispered, "No daughter of mine is gon' be driving around town and gettin' knocked up by some bumblefuck from the Higgins family." Spittle hung from his lips. "And don't dare thinking about leaving me, Bevvy. *Nobody* leaves Willy Pilsen."

He finished his beer, crumpled the can, and threw it at her. He turned to Wayne, flashed that drunk, yellowy sadistic smile they knew, and said, "I hope you learned somethin' here tonight, Wayney." His eyes looked black. Black as death.

Daddy then went to the bedroom, told Mama she had a whore of a daughter, slammed the door, then did God-knows-what to a woman with stage three cancer.

Wayne had heard it all from within the walls of his room in the double-wide over the course of his thirty-one years. His dime-store used books helped turn down the volume, but it still played in the background. He'd often read horror and not know it; the terror of home ripped the guts out of anything trying to be scary.

What happened to Bev was the scariest story he'd come across, even after all those afternoons picking through bins of musty old books. So scary, and so questioning of one's mortality, it played over and over in mind to this day, freezing him in time as it did that night.

Once the muffled cries of his mother had quieted, and Daddy entered the dead world of drunken slumber, Wayne tore himself from shock that had reached its fingers deep into his stomach. He'd helped Bev off the doormat and into the kitchen. He was scared for her; it was the most blood he'd seen come out of a living thing.

"I'm getting out, Wayne," she'd sobbed. Blood had run down her black pleather jacket and even some into her pretty blonde hair. "I'm getting out. I have to."

She'd paused and took his hand.

"I'm pregnant and it's Jasper's and I can't have it here. I just can't! Not around *him*. I hate to leave Mama, but I just can't have it here with Daddy. I won't!"

She pulled him in close and cried into the nape of his neck. The blood was warm, but the tears were hot.

"Come with me," she'd said later that night, standing at the door with a packed bag.

But he hadn't. He'd cowered as he always did. Jasper picked her up in his hand-me-down Ford Pinto. She stood at the front door, her face nearly swollen shut, and tried smiling. She raised a weak, limp hand as a goodbye.

"I'll come back to save you from hell, Wayney."

*I'll come back…*

He thought about Bev as he drove, struggling to stay between the lines. Hoped she'd gone somewhere safe. Made a life for herself. Raised his nephew in a way Willy Pilsen was incapable of. But he hadn't heard from her since the night he let her go—a night that had passed almost eleven years ago.

It stung.

That morning Bev left, Daddy woke up, poured his coffee, and went out back to feed the gulls like he always did.

It was like that every morning. But the morning Bev left had been different.

His father'd said nothing. He walked past the coffee maker and his box of cigs on the counter and straight out the back door. The gulls watched him walk out, and they stood silently.

No swarming, screeching or clawing. No fluttering, no hopping, no movement whatsoever. They'd all stared up at him like a congregation stares at a pastor in church, motionless and brooding, awaiting some dark benediction.

There was some kind of perverted understanding there: an unnatural connection between man and his island pets.

Daddy'd looked them all over with admiration at the corners of his mouth and walked back inside.

"They're full this morning," he'd said, touching Wayne on the shoulder gently as he walked past to the front door. The screen door clanged shut, Daddy's truck backfired, and he'd gone to work.

Wayne had looked out the back sliding doors at them. And they'd looked back, unmoving.

He hated them. Every fucking one.

After Bev left, Wayne's mother declined quickly. In the months before she died, she could no longer walk and had bad spells daily. Senility had come knocking. She'd call for people who weren't there, long dead or unknown to Wayne. Eventually, Daddy couldn't take her "*loco* bullshit" any longer, so he moved her into Bevvy's old room. Wayne handled the cleaning and rubdowns to keep away infections and bed sores. He cooked her meals (which soon came in the form of an IV bag) and sat with her, reading her his dime-store fantasy books, though he doubted much of it stuck at the time.

She was reduced skin and bone, helpless as the flowering mutations in her body devoured her from the inside out. It got to the point where she required constant attention, and Daddy refused to pay for hospice care, so he left Wayne home with her. Wayne didn't mind. It kept him out of Daddy's store. He could do without seeing her lady parts, but eventually so much of her shrank down, it was more like bathing a corpse than a woman.

She did a lot of rambling and had very few moments of lucidity. Her last moment, the day before she passed, Mama took his hand and said, "Your daddy was the handsomest boy in school. I used to drown in those big blue eyes…but this place changed him. Killdeer," she spat. "I drowned in those eyes, Wayne. Don't let them drown you, too."

He'd been the one to discover his mother the next day, after the cancer finally took her. The window had been left open, and three gulls had found their way inside, picking at her face. The skin on her cheek stretched and snapped like a rubber band in one bird's beak.

To see the wretched thing touch her like she was the same decrepit meat Daddy fed them drove Wayne into a blind rage.

He closed the window, cutting off any means of escape, and killed all three with his bare hands. Their necks snapped easily. Satisfaction surged through him as he ended their disgusting lives. He tossed their bodies back out the window and watched their friends peck and mutilated their limp bodies.

Screeching.

Snapping.

*Tearing.*

Wayne went to her, knelt beside the bed, and moved to hold her hand one last time. He found it under the cover, and in it, she clutched the pink washcloth.

He took it from her lifeless hand and wept into it fiercely.

Wayne decided the thought of living his mother's dream of escaping Willy Pilsen and seeing Bevvy again was what had shattered his prison walls on that old floral couch. Being drunk often allowed one to give retroactive definitions to acts of spontaneity in any old way one chose.

He shuddered and held back tears, surprised he had any left after shedding so many into his depleted state of hydration. Wayne realized it'd been more than a day since he'd had any water. Head throbbing, he picked up a fourth can of Pabst from the passenger seat, cracked it, and took a long, gratifying swig, silencing his internal need a bit longer.

Eventually the road hit an intersection where he turned left, a straight shot to Route 1, the concrete white whale he'd finally worked up the courage to hunt. His Chevy was the *Pequod* and he'd accepted the role of Ahab. His only hope was that his new obsession wouldn't be the end of him and his truck.

Although Wayne was solidly plastered, he was thinking more clearly than he ever had. Pings of realization so thought-provoking and clear had opened the dusty, dirt-covered window to the outside world that he was finally able to see, and it told him he'd been a prisoner of this key for far too long.

Through some awakened omniscient power that broke down the walls of denial, he determined something seemingly impossible: not in his thirty-one years of life had he set foot off the island. Not to the mainland, not another key, not even a single footstep on Route 1, which his daddy'd forbidden him to glance upon.

"Ain't nothin' out there 'cept hurt and false hopes," Daddy had said. "Your place is here." He'd slapped Wayne hard in the ear and leaned in close to push his trademark line through his teeth.

"Nobody leaves Willy Pilsen."

In his stupor, the blindness had been lifted and only questions remained. *How in hell does a person go more than thirty fucking years without ever leaving their birthplace?* He was guilty of the same passive ignorance his fellow sheep were, and to his recollection, his parents had never left either. Not even once.

Born, raised, and poised to die.

*Stick a needle in my eye.*

He hummed like a machine processing hard and obvious truths and knew nothing was as it seemed in Killdeer Key. His vision now saw farther than it ever had, its boundaries uninhibited. His fear of the world beyond, if there was one, made him anxious and excited.

Was there a wall at Killy Bridge that he'd hit, crumpling his car? Tourists came and went like flies in the summer heat, but the townsfolk…they were a different story. Perhaps a big fucking troll stood guard with a lever, trap door flipping open as the unworthy drove over it, dumping shitty trucks into the wet darkness of the sea below.

*One way to find out*, he thought, pushing the accelerator closer to the floor.

Wayne had an experiment in mind; he planned to hit Killy Bridge at full speed, shattering whatever magical barrier might be there blocking his way out.

It had to work, didn't it? After all, he'd read it in a book once, and he was due his storybook moment.

Supposing his gallant departure indeed worked, he'd drive down south for another drink and grab a hotel for the night, maybe in Marathon, revel in his escape and plan his future. Maybe even a stop at the Hemingway house in the coming days. Then he'd surely flee north to the mainland.

No more ocean for Wayne Pilsen. Only earth. A world of opportunity and *dirt* existed out north of here, and it sat there brimming with untapped potential.

He slowed to a stop at the base of Killdeer Bridge (Killy Bridge to those who joked folks fell off) that ran perpendicular into US Route 1, just past a big blue *Come back soon!* sign with a smiling cartoon sun that looked relatively new, tropical colors beaming, friendly and touristy without any hint of the hell anyone was truly leaving. It mocked him and he felt pangs of anger.

The rain made it impossible to see much farther than the sign, thick pounding droplets splattering on the windshield, the blades whipping back and forth in vain as he increased their speed, the downpour too heavy to keep up with. The rain grew audibly stronger as he considered driving forward, revving the engine, wishing his courage could be throttled in the same fashion.

A fear of driving off into the black waters consumed him, and he questioned whether he'd be able to break free of the car should he take the plunge. Irrational fear coupled with being straight-up drunk was beginning to twist reality. Nervousness swelled.

*It's all a crock of shit. Tourists come and go as they goddamn please.* And yet…

There was no shaking that this might very well be the end of the world, flat as pancake with nothing but the skin-searing griddle of hell off its brown and battered edge.

He surprised himself and opened the truck door. Rain pelted him, cold and hard, and he was immediately soaked. Plodding forward in his drunken stupor, dizziness took hold. He moved to the sidewalk along the bridge, gripping the circular guardrail as a guide, thinking it best to stay out of the road in case someone sped around his truck.

Looking back, he saw a similar sign on the opposite side with the same fat, cartoon sun.

*Welcome to Killdeer Key!*

He turned back to the task at hand, squinting, but the static of rain allowed him to see very little, making the dizziness worse, even with the car's headlights at his back. The beams reflected and bounced hopelessly off the rain, leaving him face to face with the unknown.

*Man up, Wayne. You can get the hell out of here or stand at the edge and look down into the eyes of nothingness.*

*In nothingness, there's peace.*

*Win-win.*

Walking somewhat earnestly, adrenaline began pumping at the premise of a new world—or the end of it—now within reach. Should it be the latter, he'd already decided he was going to throw himself off, meet the cold vacuum of space. Or maybe a Martian or two.

The car was quite some distance behind him now, headlights growing less and less visible as he looked back, until the curve of Killy Bridge covered them.

He walked for some time. Much farther than he thought he should based on the map he dug out of his glove box. A wet darkness had encircled him: the only things visible were the guardrail to his right and cement squares as he crossed them.

*I'm doing it! I'm really doing it!* He couldn't help grinning, elation washing over him as if from the rain itself.

Five steps later, the feeling gave out and a sudden onset of nausea and vertigo took its place. His head felt like his brain had been spun around in his skull. He stumbled back a step, then forward a dozen, until he steadied himself on the guardrail.

As quickly as the wave of queasiness came, it disappeared, and his mind righted itself. But there was no longer elation in its place.

*Was that the barrier? Am I through?*

A faint pair of lit orbs came into view, slightly to the left as they passed, hovering there like Japanese lanterns in the middle of a storm. Moving closer, he realized it was another vehicle approaching in the opposite lane.

Why this drove him to sprint, he didn't know. His boots squished, his T-shirt weighed a thousand pounds, and the rain pelted his widened, unblinking eyeballs. He ran to the outsider's car like he'd run into his mother's arms all throughout childhood when she'd return from work, ecstatic in the moment that someone new and *safe* had entered his day.

In that moment, it felt right.

Using his peripheral view of the guardrail as a reference, he maintained a straight line on the sidewalk before adrenaline reached its climax, and he moved onto the road. He'd gone at least five hundred yards, and Wayne knew he must be approaching the base of the bridge at Route 1. There'd been no magical barrier or sudden pit, no dark boundary or cliff off the end of the earth.

He'd gone far enough to know he'd gone far enough.

*I'll flag it down and ask for a ride back, then drive on out of here.*

It was soon after the thought, that he realized the car should've been upon him by now, but it moved much too lethargically. As he slowed to a jog and then a walk, it became apparent the car wasn't moving at all.

Wayne's run had become a sullen plod once more, the excitement falling off. The rain slowed, and he could see more clearly now. It was indeed stopped. Was it broken down? Where there should be traffic lights at the intersection of Parrot Parkway and Route 1, he saw only darkness. Perhaps the lights had been shorted by lightning, and this car was here to help coordinate traffic?

He doubted the latter scenario because there was no illumination other than the headlights to guide other vehicles, and they were pointed away from the intersection back toward the Key. The prior was disproven by the hum of the engine.

He raised his arm in what was barely a wave, attempting to signal the driver he was friendly, and, though he expected the flashing of headlights or a short honk of the horn, the truck sat motionless.

As he came within ten feet of the hood, he knew its owner immediately.

Nothing had ever driven the hope from Wayne entirely. Not the death of his mother, not Bev leaving, not even the almost daily beatings. Sometimes it was more hidden, sulking deeper on dark days, but he still clung to some kind of hope that he could get out of Killdeer for good.

At least he had, until the full view of the truck tore it from him. Tore out his bleeding soul.

Wayne approached the grill and rested his hands on the hood, eyes wide with disbelief, needing touch it to make it real. He raised his shaking fingers to his mouth and backed away in impossible fear.

"No…" he muttered. "No, no, no…"

His body shook uncontrollably. The fumes he'd been riding on had combusted all at once, singing his insides as he looked upon his idling Chevy. It sat there, the silver grill frowning in dismay.

*Sorry, Wayney. We can't leave. Ol' Killdeer won't let us.*

He looked past the car to the back of the sign he'd parked beyond, its mocking signage crudely painted on wood that was deader than dead.

Welcome to Killdeer Key!

Three wretched-looking gulls sat atop the sign, watching him with great interest. Four more had perched along the railing at his back. They sat silently, screeching and squawking none of their usual cackles. Their eyes were voids boring out of their white faces that cried something black.

*None of this can be right,* he thought. *I've gone mad.*

Wayne got in and revved the old engine. There was no magical barrier. No edge at the end of the word. This was hell. He was in hell.

Not to be so quickly undone, he thought of his book, *Silver Lightning*, the story of a car that had a taken on its old owner's spirit. It was a story he'd read at the age of ten and again in the days after Bev had left. Danny Carson had escaped the demonic, dimension-traveling circus by hitting the gas, telling the Silver Lightning that he loved him, and crashing through the ringleader Amon Fulp's Magic Mirror to Nowhere. It shattered instead of sending them to Nowhere as intended, and the shards rained chaos down on Fulp and his evil circus.

Wayne's foot found the accelerator and his hand the gearshift.

"I love you," he whispered to the old truck. Wayne thought he'd immediately feel foolish, but it turned out to be the most warmingly brilliant thing he'd ever said. He punched the gas to the floor.

At first, nothing happened; it took the old girl a bit to wake up and her purr to become a roar. Tires squealed, the air stank almost immediately of gas and rubber, and he was off. She thrummed and glided as if new, just off the lot. Adrenaline and a fresh sense of purpose surged through Wayne. He found himself smiling almost maniacally.

Short-lived. Everything on Killdeer was short-lived except your time there. You could extinguish the fires of hell with a bucket, but with an endless supply of gas and enough crazies around to throw matches, hell always resumed.

Hell resumed with blue flame. Willy Pilsen stood there in the road with a bag of guts and what looked to be a gull on his shoulder like the old pirates who hunted key deer on the island and gave it the stupidly crude name.

Wayne's own Mirror to Nowhere was his daddy, and for a moment Wayne had every intention of running him down, dragging his body as far the truck would take it, and leaving him a ragged mess atop Killdeer Key.

Sadly, kindness and innocence have a way of getting the best of you at the most inopportune of times. He swerved at nearly seventy miles per hour, jumped up over the sidewalk, and punched into the guardrail like a rock through papier-mâché.

The truck seemed to float. Everything slowed as it hung in the air for an eternity.

Time clicked back on, and his Silver Lightning hit black ocean with a force that drove him painfully into the steering wheel, cracking ribs and exploding the air from his lungs, air he'd desperately need far under the surface of Killdeer Bay.

Ballooning black spots filled his vision, and the darkness took him. When he came to, the truck was almost completely submerged, and once it dipped below the surface, it sank like a stone.

Water rushed into the Chevy through the dash and the back window, cold and sobering. His first thought was to get through the opening that served as a hole for his empty beers, but it was too small for his grown body.

The door wouldn't open. The handle moved as it should, but water pressure held the door shut: Killdeer Key wanted him to drown deep down in its guts.

Panic overtook him.

This was it. He was born on Killdeer to die on Killdeer. A cruel joke, it seemed: the suffering, the abandonment, and the beatings were all he was meant for.

He tried thinking of those who passed on with even less. Like those starving, abused kids in Africa his momma always talked about to make him feel guilty enough to finish his dinner. But it didn't help. His respiration stayed rampant, his heart drumming against his ruined ribs. Trying to calm himself with deep breaths that sent jolts of pain through his chest, he recalled a book he'd once read about escaping a sinking car.

*Wait.*

Wait?

*Wait.*

Pressure had to equalize.

The truck hit bottom with its front bumper first, the back tires finding the seafloor a moment later. The Chevy's headlights cut through the deep—and shone on a watery cemetery. The tombstones were vehicles. Dozens of them.

Trucks, cars, bikes, mopeds, even a battered and slimy orange Camaro a few cars to the left…but it was the nearest grave that caught his attention.

A Ford Pinto.

It was covered in muck, sea algae growing off the roof. The algae danced and writhed back and forth in the headlights as if in some seafloor Broadway musical.

There was a single bullet hole through the windshield on the driver's side. In the driver's seat sat the skeleton of Jasper Higgins, a hole through his exposed skull above his right eye. He leaned slightly toward the center console, as if to peer around the hole in the glass and smile his lipless teeth.

Wayne thought of the gun—the same gun that probably put that hole in Jasper's forehead. Reaching under the rising pool, he opened the glove box, found the gun, tucked it into his waistband, and hoped to God it still worked.

Water had nearly filled the cabin and he pushed up against the roof to get one last good look through the top of the windshield.

No one appeared to be in the passenger seat.

*Bevvy?*

Once completely submerged, he tried the door handle again, doing his best not to panic. His ears popped painfully as the door moved in liquid slow motion.

With one last look at the empty passenger's seat, he got his feet up on the roof of his truck and pushed off. After what felt like an eternity moving up through Killdeer's dark stomach, he surfaced and greedily sucked in the humid air.

He swam to the base of the bridge, ribs screaming in agony with each stroke. Large rocks made up a jagged seawall down from the road, ugly little bushes sprouting between them. Wayne hoisted himself onto one of the flatter stones and made his way upward.

The rain had nearly halted. *Welcome to Killdeer Key* mocked him from above. Daddy and his own Chevy truck were under the sign now, along with more gulls than Wayne had ever seen. He was tempted to run back to town, but Daddy would just as easily catch him. *It all ends tonight,* he told himself, and began plodding toward the lot of them.

When Wayne got close enough, the gulls looked at him and screamed in unison, crying tears of oil from their blackened eyes.

The sound was deafening.

Human.

Daddy had a devilish grin across his face, his own eyes pools of dark matter, seeping black malice like the gulls.

*Oozing. What happened to my daddy?*

He flashed back to his mother's words: "Your daddy was the handsomest boy in school. I used to drown in those eye…"

And she did. Over and over. Whoever Daddy was now, he wasn't the same person. This place had done something to him.

*Don't let them drown you, too.*

"Look like you seen a ghost, boy." Daddy lit a cigarette.

"Bevvy—" Wayne's voice cracked. "Bevvy wasn't down there."

"Your sister Bevvy crawled outta the bay like you did just now." Daddy smiled as he took another drag. "Tough little shits I raised."

"What did you do with her?" Wayne sounded more like a child than a grown man.

"You got a 'preciation for the arts. What'd you think of my work down there?"

"*What did you do with her?*"

Another drag. "I gave her a choice like I'm 'bout to give you." He exhaled. "You can get in this fucking truck, we'll go home, and I'll give you the beating you fucking deserve—"

Drag.

"—or I'll break your kneecaps and cut your hands off right 'ere on this fucking bridge." He looked down at the bag of fish guts, then back at Wayne. "So long as yer covered in guts, these fellas won't know the diff'rence 'tween you and old meat. They'll eat it *all*."

The gulls chirped and glucked in excitement.

Wayne managed ragged breaths, his heart thrumming painfully. He was terrified but would not be kept from knowing the truth.

"What happened to *Bevvy*?"

Daddy laughed. "You really wanna know?" Drag. Long exhale. "I shot her in her pregger little tummy right about where you're standing. They ate her guts out while she was still alive, 'cludin' that peckerhead's little tyke she had growing inside her. Tossed it around like a chew toy."

"You're a fucking *liar*!" he wailed. "I don't believe you." He thought—*hoped*—the disgusting thing he called *Daddy* was lying, but in his sinking heart, he knew he spoke dark truths.

"Some little son of a bitch took my gun tonight, so I went with plan B," he smiled, giving the bag a couple loving taps. "It's mostly innards. They stay stuck on a bit better. And when yer covered in 'em, my friends here won't know the difference 'tween fish guts and Wayne guts."

He threw his head back and howled. The gulls laughed with him with sickening little glucks.

The smile left his face. "Didn't I tell you, boy? Nobody leaves Willy Pilsen."

*Drag.*

"Nobody leaves *Killdeer Key*."

Willy laughed, but this time, the laugh wasn't his. It was wet and deep, like something or someone else coming through.

Something *old*.

"Say, boy, I don't think I ever told you how much money I saved skippin' your momma's funeral." He gestured to the gulls and chuckled. His voice was changing now, too. "You didn't think that feed bag was *always* fish, did you?"

Wayne felt sick. Shocked. Infuriated.

He pulled the gun out from his waistband and brought it around, trained on Daddy.

The gulls screamed again. Some began to take flight.

No, not Daddy.

No more Daddy.

Only Willy-fucking-Pilsen. Or whatever the fuck he was now. Maybe always was.

Willy maintained that evil grin. "Go 'head and kill your dear old daddy. But you'll never know how to get outta this place." He took two steps toward Wayne. "Do it!" he screamed. "I didn't raise no fucking pussies. *Do it*!"

The magnum wavered. Wayne's sweaty hand couldn't hold it still. *End it,* he thought. *End it now.*

Willy Pilsen took a step closer. "Last chance, boy."

His finger rested against a trigger that weighted a thousand pounds, but Wayne managed to pull it anyway.

*Click.*

Willy laughed, syrupy and *wrong*. "Shells a bit wet, boy?" He lurched closer.

The gun trained on Daddy's head, Wayne pulled the trigger again. *Click.*

And again and again.

*Click. Click.*

Willy hoisted the bag a little higher and opened the top with his free hand.

One of the more ravenous-looking gulls, gray and worn, dove at Wayne, screeching and flapping something furious. One talon sank deep into the side of his scalp, and the warmth of trickling blood was immediate. He pistol-whipped the bird as hard as he could, to the crunch of breaking bones; it flopped dead on the pavement.

Two more took flight directly at him, for his face, screeching, their talons drawn like hawks diving for prey. He clubbed one, nearly taking off its wing, but the other got its talons into Wayne's cheek and forehead. It pulled out a chunk of his hair. More blood. He managed to grab it by the tail feathers, pulled as hard as he could, and slammed it down into the road. He stomped it with his boot, sending a small spray of insides out its anus. It screamed and died.

All the while, Willy casually walked closer, smoking and smiling and laughing, his voice no longer something of this world. Soon those rancid guts would cover Wayne, and this would all be over. Birds would peck the life from him.

The .44 was trained on Willy Pilsen's head one last time until an idea took him.

*Plan B.*

His aim dropped down to the bag. Willy's smile melted; he hesitated a moment and drew back a step.

*Please God oh please God oh please God . . .*

"You little fuck—"

Willy's words were silenced with a *click-boom* as the Magnum erupted. The bullet hit the feed bag and Willy Pilsen's arm, sufficiently exploding both.

And another. *click-boom.* The bottom of the bag tore open, along with what was once Willy's lower rib cage, and emptied down his leg and onto his boots.

The smells of gunpowder and decaying meat filled the air. It had grown completely silent; no gull made a peep. Wayne's daddy stood there dumbfounded, much of him covered in dark, curdled guts, mouth agape, brow furrowed in confusion.

The vile things only looked at their master, their *alpha.* Many looked again at Wayne and back at Willy, their little heads flicking back and forth as if watching a game of ping-pong. Confused. Utterly confused.

Two made the decision for the group, took flight and dove, screeching wildly, at Willy. He raised his good arm to defend himself, and they latched onto it like feeding perch. Three more joined them, snapping at whatever they could manage.

Some took to the bag, but most were on Willy. Slashing…
flapping…tearing. Within moments, he'd fallen to his back on the
pavement. He screamed in that otherworldly tone, over and over,
until it grew faint—became his own harrowing shrieks. There were
at least a hundred gulls waiting their turns. Within moments, the
most he could manage was a wet gurgle. Then only the ripping of
flesh and insides.

Then, perhaps silence forever from Willy Pilsen.

*Silence forever from Daddy.*

 The rain started pouring again, gently rippling the pooling blood
with each drop that hit the expanding black mass. The gulls carried
on mercilessly for what felt like hours, but Wayne was entranced.
As he watched, a strange hunger befell him. He felt Killdeer. Its
dark, maddening fingers wrapped themselves around his heart and
squeezed.

After they'd picked most of Willy Pilsen clean—both skin and
guts—he witnessed something most amazing; a group of the winged
vermin wrapped their talons around fleshy bones, flapped their wings
and took slow flight with the carcass. A flap of hairy scalp and the
smaller toes and fingers were the only parts of him left; they'd even
eaten most of his clothes. The gulls flew him over the guardrail. They
dropped him into water with what barely qualified as a splash and
returned to Wayne's feet. The gulls eyed him puzzlingly.

*What's next, boss?* they asked. Killdeer's strong, cold hands had
deadened his excited heart.

More than a hundred black, drippy eyes stared into Wayne's soul.
He drowned in them.


Two years later, Wayne Pilsen finished out the day at Land
Lubber's Fish Market. He left Jerry Simmons, a part-time high
school runt, in charge of closing up shop. He'd proven himself to be
a good employee during the last few months, and Wayne intended
to bring him on full time.

"Have a good one, Jerry. And remember to scrape that skillet
clean and lock up. Can't have any drunk townies wandering in."

"I know, Mr. Pilsen. Have a nice night."

The evening air was dewy sweet as he walked across the small parking lot. It'd finished raining and a pink sun peeked through the thinning clouds.

Wayne reeked of fish and crab guts as he hopped into his truck, a hand-me-down from a certain Daddy who was now gull food. His coveralls were a plethora of squirts and chunks hopped up from some of the necessary chopping and fileting. Jerry was good with the stove and counting money, but he hadn't mastered the art of slicing bellies and scooping out insides. You really couldn't leave Land Lubber's without stinking, but the smell didn't bother him.

You got used to it. Even when it was rotten.

The truck sputtered onto Parrot Parkway as he plodded home, windows down, radio up. He knobbed through George Jones, Jimmy Buffett, and Alabama until the tuning needle disappeared somewhere to the left of 88.3 and a familiar dirge played up through the crackling speakers.

He rounded the north end of Killdeer Key, this time to the east. A gull stood on the shoulder—the same shoulder—eyeing him with great curiosity as it had that night a year ago. It flew off in the rearview. Wayne had an idea where it might be headed.

He turned onto Tortuga Lane, and Mary Gilespie Pilsen stood in the front window of their double-wide, smiling nervously, her hand resting on her bulging stomach. She was seven months along. They'd gotten to talking at Coconutz almost a year ago. Wayne exuded a new aura of confidence, and she was immediately drawn to it. She couldn't stop complimenting his big blue eyes, his taking over his awful daddy's shop and his manly *smell*. She was knocked up a few months later.

Wayne gave her a little smirk and grabbed the bag next to him, hopped down out of the cab, and went up the walk—the same walk Bevvy had stumbled up drunk as a skunk all those years ago.

Mary greeted him at the door, and he kissed her, putting his own hand on her tummy. "It's gonna be a boy. I can tell," he said, just as he had each day since she started showing. They both smiled, although hers seemed a bit strained.

Her kids, now legally Wayne's also, Sandy and George, sat on a new corduroy couch. "Hi, Daddy Wayne," they said in unison. It still sounded coached and a bit insincere, but he gave them a nod of approval and went into the kitchen.

Wayne set his work bag down on the kitchen table and went to the fridge for a Pabst. He sighed and took one of the remaining three. His fishy fingernail cracked the top with a satisfying *fssst,* and he downed half of it in three gulps. He belched, calmly walked over to Mary and belted her across the mouth.

"Three beers, you stupid whore? What the fuck am I gonna do with three beers? I told you to keep that fridge *stocked.*" He slapped her again, drawing blood.

"I'm sorry, Wayne." She held her reddened face, and her lips began to tremble. "I had so much to do today that I forgot…"

Sandy buried her head into the couch cushions, and George fled to his new room that once had held a world of books, but was now devoid of such things. They contained words of dissent and false hopes for young boys. Wayne wouldn't have them in his house.

Tears welled in Mary's eyes as she watched her boy run to his room and peek around the door, motioning her to follow. The boy would have to be dealt with soon enough, but his mother came first.

"You start cryin' and I'm gonna break your goddamn nose," he said, then belched.

An empty threat now, but give him a few more rounds and that pretty nose of hers might not be so pretty anymore. He reached into his pocket and tossed his keys at her. She fumbled them, and they clanged to the floor. She did her best to squat and grab them; with her pregnant stomach, she looked like a sumo wrestler assuming the position.

Shaking his head and smiling scornfully, he turned from his wife and took the bag off the kitchen table, strolling out the back door on to the old cement patio.

The night it all happened, Wayne went to Sheriff Sutton in a daze, soaked and shivering. He spilled—for lack of a better word—his guts. He'd expected the man to be taken aback, sickened. Sutton only nodded calmly. Wayne expected an urgent phone call to the state police after he'd finished. Sutton, fat and somewhat drunk already, moved to the liquor cabinet, poured two glasses of brandy, and brought one to Wayne. He plopped his large body down next to Wayne on his deer hide couch.

"Drink this," he said. "It'll warm you to the balls." They both drank deeply. "No use startin' a media circus, stirrin' up old feelings by pulling all those dead 'uns out from their graves. You and me have to keep the peace, just like me and your daddy used to." He put an arm around Wayne. His eyes had gone black. *Oozing.*

"Part of that peace is keeping the people *here*. On Killdeer. Spittin' out babies and greasin' the wheels of our little machine. Killy gets upset when the machine slows down…" he smiled with teeth as black and wet as his eyes.

"Some of our flock ferget what a great little place we've got here." He eyed Wayne cautiously. Fatherly, almost. "Your job is to remind 'em from time to time."

Wayne nodded, somehow understanding it all perfectly.

"'Sides, no use cleanin' up any of those cars when there's room for plenty more. You just remember: *nobody* leaves Wayne Pilsen."

In the days just after, Willy was rumored to have run off north to the mainland with a heavily tattooed hooker from Key West within a day of his fling with one upset optometrist. Disgusted with herself for associating with a pig and sexaholic—as she then believed Willy to be—she never visited Killdeer again. Her house was sold to a newly married couple with a pair of runts. Sheriff Sutton, Daddy's only friend who might know such things, told the island's residents as much.

None of the sheep believed it, but, in their passive way, they accepted it with few whispers. The sheriff had made that night disappear, and the memory Willy Pilsen faded into obscurity while his body rested in his own graveyard at the end of the world.

The world *is* flat.

Wayne stood on his cement stage. Farther into the yard was an old burn barrel for yard brush, garbage, and other things of past importance. Atop the growing level of ash in the rusted-out cylinder lay what once was a thing of wondrous humanity, poetic and brave, now reduced to a crispy spine and an unusually large piece of ash where you could just barely make out the words *Silver* and *Lightning*.

He opened the feed bag for his audience, pulling out the first strip of rancid meat his fingers touched. They stood in silence, as if waiting for a magician to perform his first trick of devilry. Heads flicked between the strip of rotting hogfish and Wayne's fading blue eyes.

"Who's hungry?" he asked playfully.

The gulls screamed.

⋊○⋉⋊○⋉ ⋊○⋉⋊○⋉ ⋊○⋉⋊○⋉ ⋊○⋉

# About the Author

Matt Meyer lives in the suburbs of Chicago with his partner, Dan, and their two galactic beasts of terror and destruction, Tucker the Treacherous and Chewbert, Hoarder of Souls (and chew toys). According to their paperwork, they're German shepherds…but he knows better. You can witness some of their antics on Instagram should you not believe him: @mattmeyer701.

# Cyan, Magenta, Yellow, and Key

Clay McLeod Chapman

*Inspired by* The Ten-Cent Plague: The Great Comic-Book Scare and How It Changed America *by David Hajdu*

The brave boys from Bear Scout Troop 237 were my crusaders against corruption. My defenders of decency. My righteous knights of the highest order. These scrupulous scouts had exceeded the highest of my expectations, gathering around a thousand comic books, all told, for our purification drive. Each uniformed boy shuffled up with a Radio Flyer filled to its hilt with comics confiscated from around town, dumping the smut into a heaping pile for all to see.

We had purged our pharmacies of their indecencies.

We had eradicated our newsstands of their filth.

Here was the cancer that had crept into our small town, insinuating its sinfulness within the minds of our youngest, most innocent citizens, stacked three feet high and rising.

Mount Pornography.

Their flimsy pages flittered in the wind as the heap kept growing. *Swelling*. Toppling over in an avalanche of sex and violence. Wanton lust. Repugnant busts. Nothing but pages upon pages of illustrated licentiousness.

"Keep 'em coming, boys," I called out. "Toss 'em all in! Every last comic…I want our pyre to reach as high as the heavens!"

L'il Lonnie Wilder couldn't even reach the peak anymore. When it was his turn to contribute his comics to the pile, that poor, pudgy boy had to lift himself up onto his tippy-toes, holding his shoe box over his head, and shake them all out, each filthy issue showering down.

*Tales of Terror.*

*Killer Comics.*

*Crime Pays and You're Buying.*

L'il Lonnie here didn't realize that I was well aware of the fact that this was his own *personal* stash. Believe you me, I knew he was a peruser of these prurient pamphlets. All through Sunday school, I'd find him flipping through the pages of one of his so-called horror comics. I'd confiscate it faster than you can say *sodomite*—but just like the head on a hydra, the very next Sunday, out sprouted another copy. I've got a whole file cabinet crammed full of comics commandeered from none other than our L'il Lonnie here. His poor saint of a mother had high hopes that the Bear Scouts would pull him out of his lecherous shell. Build up some character in him. Add a dash of moral fiber to flush out his objectionable habits once and for all.

Well, you better believe I put in a personal call to Mrs. Wilder first thing after kick-starting our comic campaign, suggesting she *might* look under L'il Lonnie's bed mattress to see if he *might* be squandering a copy or two that she *might* wish to contribute to our crusade.

And me oh my, what a treasure trove of atrocities did Mrs. Wilder find waiting for her…

*Bare-Knuckle Bulletin.*

*Fearsome Funnies.*

*Sci-Fi Sarcophagus.*

Poor L'il Lonnie had tears in his eyes. He'd been at the back of the line for quite some time, letting every other troop member step ahead of him. Seemed to me he was stalling. As if I'd decide at the last minute that we had enough kindling. That L'il Lonnie could keep his comics.

"What've we got here, scout?" I pinched Lonnie's copy of *Petrified Pages* from the back of his belt loop, as if I wouldn't have seen it poking out from his pants. As if I'd actually spare it.

"Were you hiding this from me, Lonnie?"

"No, sir…"

"Don't mumble now. Speak up."

"Yes, Pastor Nat, sir."

I flipped through, glancing over all the decapitations. The half-dressed harlots running from lumbering corpses. An endless parade of four-color fornication.

My eyes halted upon a particular story—if you could call it a story—some pornographic paean to a cloven-hoofed demon of some sort. Lord only knows what kind of debauchee comes up with this stuff. I was only half-reading it, to be honest, impatiently perusing the pictures as if to prove a point to our L'il Lonnie here that I would not tolerate harboring smut such as this.

Frankly, I wasn't sure what exactly I was looking at. Some negrotic abomination. It had the blackest skin. Red eyes sunk deep into its sockets. And if I wasn't mistaken, there, between its legs, dangled what I could only presume was a grinning python. My fingers *just so happened* to rub over the image. Its black-as-pitch visage smudged, cheap ink smearing across my skin.

"Do you find these types of stories entertaining, young man?" I held the foulness up to his face, practically pressing the page against his perspiring cheek. "Do you enjoy the objectification of the female form? The reverie of rape and murder? Do you, Lonnie? Do you?"

"No, Pastor Nat, sir…"

"Look at me when I'm speaking to you. Do you know what you're doing to your poor mother, reading this vulgar rubbish? Do you know what you're doing to yourself? To your own mind? I imagine it must look like Swiss cheese by now. Cramming it full of stories of this…deca—"

"*Decarabrian.*" He hissed its name with such venom. Lonnie snapped his head up at me, pinching his eyes into the thinnest slits, each crab-apple cheek turning a deep purple.

There was defiance in those beady eyes.

I saw rage.

"It's indecent is what it is, young man, and it has no place in our homes." I rolled up his copy of *Petrified Pages* into a tight tube, as tight as I could, a four-colored fagot for our comic book conflagration. "Which is why I want you to have the honors of lighting the fire, Lonnie…"

I had put in a call to the local newspaper to cover today's event. I'd given them the exact time and place—noon on Saturday in our church's parking lot. I even waited an additional twenty minutes after our designated start time just to be sure the photographer had arrived.

Showtime, folks…

"We have gathered here today to take a stand against the insidious rise of comic books within our community," I announced to our prepubescent audience. There had to be more than three dozen boys and girls circled around the mound by now. Our doe-eyed future. "It is our firm belief that this type of *literature* poses a morally objectionable threat to the mental and physical well-being of our children—which is why, today, before the watchful eyes of our lord and savior, and our parents, we pledge to commit these desecrations on the page to whence they came…"

It was utterly unnecessary of me, I know, but I went ahead and soused the pile with a hefty dose of lighter fluid, like dousing a dollop of holy water on the damned. I wanted to be sure we had ourselves one heck of a finale here. I wanted this fire to be seen as far as two counties over. Let everyone know our town will not stand for this type of pictorial pederasty.

"Gather 'round, children," I called out. "Don't be afraid. Circle in, nice and tight…"

I lit L'il Lonnie's comic with a match, letting the flames chew through that dirty devil *Decarabrian* and his dark ding-a-ling before handing it back to him.

"Do you, boys and girls, consider comic books to be the ruin of many a youthful mind?"

"We do," the cheerful crowd chanted back.

"Do you pledge to take a stand against this type of corruption from this day forward?"

"We do."

"Then let us purify our minds and bodies once and for all."

I nodded to Lonnie. The boy only stared back at me with his bovine eyes.

I gave a gentle cough. "Lonnie."

We all watched him toss his comic. Watched its flames coil in a comet's tail.

Watched it land on top of the pile.

An incendiary hiss filled the air. Smoke rose up from the smoldering heap, roasting for just a moment before combusting altogether. It all went up. And what a glorious fireball it was, people! Such diminutive kindling. The pages hastened a retreat, wilting within the intense heat before the inevitable singe swept over, *the Power and the Glory*, punctuated in a sizzle and pop.

The flames…the flames towered over our heads.

I saw such wondrous colors.

Cyan. Magenta. Yellow. And key—black, black key.

The four inks used in the color printing process were pirouetting throughout the blaze.

Dots. I realized the flames were made of dots. Hundreds upon thousands upon millions of tiny half-toned spots were clustering together to compose a single continuous image.

Of fire.

I had to look away. My eyes were watering. Too much smoke. I rubbed them with my knuckles then glanced back only to see Troop 237 dancing around the fire now. They were grabbing hold of each other's hands and circling about the flames. Their voices lifting. Singing something or other. We had talked about belting out "The Star-Spangled Banner" once the fire was up and burning, but this— this didn't sound patriotic to me. Or English, for that matter.

I couldn't make out the words. Couldn't understand what they were singing. But they all buzzed in some larval harmony, prancing and chanting as the flames reached higher. Higher.

One boy began ripping the merit badges from his uniform. Just tore them off, one after the other, eating them. Why was he eating them? When that hadn't sated him, he kept clawing. Tearing through his uniform now. His undershirt. His skin. He dug as deep as his fingernails would allow, clawing up chunks of his own flesh now. Eating his skin by the handful.

I watched as another boy plucked his eyes out from his own sockets. He perched them in the palm of his hand so I could see.

The reflection of the conflagration lit up in his eyes, burning with an intensity that dared not subside. He popped one in his mouth. Swallowed it with a smile. Then gulped the other.

I watched another boy force his hand into the mouth of his friend. His fingers disappeared. His whole fist. Lips wrapped around his wrist. When he pulled his glistening fist back out, painted red, he brought his fellow scout's uprooted tongue with him—and ate it.

They were eating each other. The whole troop. My Bear Scouts had their own intestines dangling in their hands, garlands weaving about the fire, as they continued to dance and sing.

An eternal ring. A snake devouring its own tail. Infinite. Boundless.

"You unleashed him, Pastor Nat…"

The voice had piped up from behind me. I wasn't sure if I'd even heard it at first, or if I'd just imagined it—but when I spun around, I found Lonnie, L'il Lonnie Wilder, staring back at me with empty eyes, blood dribbling out from his hollow sockets, running down his pudgy cheeks.

"Decarabrian," he said, rather matter-of-factly. "The sixty-ninth spirit. The darkest star on the pentacle. He's been imprisoned for years. But now he's free. *You* set him free, Pastor Nat."

Lonnie kept talking, but truth told, the rest of what he said was a bit garbled to my ear, considering he was now chewing on his tongue. I couldn't help myself from *tsk-tsk*ing the boy for talking with his mouth full, but this wasn't the time nor the place for a lesson in politeness.

A breeze blew through, whisking off with a few panels. The embers were so thin—the cinders instantly disintegrated as soon as they cooled, dissolving altogether in the afternoon air.

Sulfur lingered through the church parking lot, scorched and organic. The smell was unavoidable now. It crept into my nostrils. The odor of calcinated tissue wafting along.

Flesh. I smelled flesh on fire.

Our fire. Our victory against idolatry.

I glanced at my arms and discovered they were covered in colors. Colors that shouldn't be. Cyan, magenta, yellow, and key—the four inks of the apocalypse.

A countless amount of the tiniest dots came together along my flesh to form images.

Panels. Actual panels scabbing my skin.

I flipped through. Flipped through my leprous flesh. Each page revealed another image. Another layer on this endless comic. Down, down, all the way down to the bone.

One more sermon from me: as a boy, I had always been obsessed with the saints. During church services, I would stare up at the stained glass window of St. Giles. I would lose myself counting the scabs scaling his face. The sun would seep through his cheeks, lighting up his leprosy, the colors casting themselves across the aisle—and I'd place my hand underneath the beam. The redness of his sores soaked into my skin. I'd make believe I'd been afflicted with whatever sickness he had. At my most prideful, I'd imagine what it would be like to have my own stained glass window. What it would take to have my own image soldered along with all the apostles. Boys and girls for years to come would look upon my window and pray unto me.

St. Nathaniel—Patron Saint of the Pure. The Innocent. Protector against pornography. Crusader against comics.

Saints make sacrifices of themselves.

So I stepped across the scorched asphalt, through the ash pockmarking the pavement, over the burnt Bear Scouts, the heap of their blackened bodies, into the fire.

The purifying fire.

XOXOX XOXOX XOXOX X

# About the Author

Clay McLeod Chapman writes books, children's books, comic books and film. Visit him at www.claymcleodchapman.com.

# DECLARATIONS OF LOVE

Doug Russell

When Lorna opened the door, I wanted to both hold her close and punch her right in the face. It's not like I didn't expect to see her; it's just that I thought I was prepared for it and found I'd been wrong.

"Hello, Ray." The smooth sound of her voice made my heart begin to break all over again. Made me long for her to say my name once more, softly, with her lips lightly brushing my ear. Made me hate her again.

She stepped aside to let me into Kyle's house, the house where, until some months before, I had spent more time than at my own.

"It's good to see you," she lied. "Kyle thought you might not come."

I looked into her eyes. "But you knew I would." Of course she did. She was sure that no matter the pain, I wouldn't be able to resist seeing her. That, coupled with what Kyle had told me on the phone, had made it a certainty.

As if it were her house, she led the way down the hall and to the back, where the lab was.

When we entered, Kyle, handsome as always, looked up from his computer and smiled awkwardly. "I wasn't sure what I was going to say to you if you came," he said, "but now that you're here, I think I'll just say it's good to see you."

I smiled back but didn't reply. I still wanted to strangle him. Or worse. Something even slower, with more pain.

He motioned over to the left wall, and Lorna and I met him there. On the work table, much as it had been when I was last there, was the slab. It lay flat, extra table legs supporting its weight. Seven feet long, three feet wide, three inches thick. Hundreds of years ago it would have been thought of as an altar, and it would have been outdoors, perhaps in a secluded forest. Some would have thought it evil, others would have thought of it as a link to the gods.

The last time I saw it, the top surface had been smooth and polished. Now, chiseled neatly into its face, there were a series of runes, all familiar to me from the ancient manuscripts, folios, and *objets d'art* I had in my collection, or Kyle's, or had seen and studied in the collections of others.

Brushing my fingertips lightly over the carvings, I turned to see Kyle now grinning, the same grin he'd sported that day back in grad school, when we were so close we could almost finish each other's thoughts and sentences.

Although we had been completing advanced science degrees at the time, we were fascinated by the occult, as were many college students. Dark rites, nearly forgotten rituals, archaic beliefs and superstitions. Of them all, the ones that most occupied our nearly compulsive interest were the stories of other worlds and other gods.

"What if," I said that evening at a bar near campus, refilling Lorna and Kyle's glasses with beer from a pitcher the waitress had left, "what if all those horror stories were true—"

"But," Kyle broke in, picking up the thought, "not really horrors at all?"

"Right." I wiped beer foam from my mouth. "Hundreds of years ago, before the scientific principle, any sort of, well, outré phenomena—"

"Would be explained at the time in terms of a religion," Kyle finished.

"Right, right," I nearly yelled. I turned to Lorna—I clearly remember how a stray strand of blonde hair sort of circled around her brow, framing her right eye, and how much I was just loving that moment and loving her and even loving Kyle—and said to her, "You see what we're saying?" even though I was sure she did. She was usually the one of us who could crystallize a thought or an idea down to its essence.

She set her glass on the table. "You're suggesting that now, in the time of science, when bizarre concepts such as string theory, parallel universes, wormholes, things like that, are discussed seriously, interdimensional visitors—shambling and gooey or not—don't sound evil, but like serious possibilities?"

"Exactly." I was so animated I almost spilled my own beer. "Maybe, with some combination of chanting at the right frequencies, burning or mixing the right oils, finding the right time to utilize the proper gravitational forces of the moon . . . I don't know exactly, but a rite is very similar to a formula. If people discovered a sequence that worked, that achieved miraculous results, they'd continue the ritual as it was. Today, though, assuming the old stories have truths buried in them, we should be able to find the right combination and scientifically eliminate the unnecessary elements—the religious ones."

Lorna brought it to its essence. "We could open a doorway to the gods."

All of our eyes met and a profound feeling of purpose swept over the table. I kissed Lorna. Our road was set before us.

Now, more than six years later, I stood beside her and a stone slab in Kyle's home laboratory, rubbed my fingers across its now chiseled and grooved face, and heard Lorna say simply, "We've made great progress."

Kyle nodded. "She's the one who had the insight, the epiphany. She was going back over the Brickley manuscript, rereading fragments C and D."

Lorna moved up close to the slab. "If the manuscript were complete, I'm sure that not only would we have unlocked the secret earlier, we also could have made this perfectly." She brushed her hand across the runes, almost touching my fingers. "As it is, it's somewhat unpredictable."

"What is?" I knew what they were talking about, but I wanted one of them to say it, wanted to hear it aloud so it would feel real to me.

"Your main thesis was correct," Lorna said. "The runes aren't just a lost language. They're a formula. But what we were missing is that it isn't just the figures, it's also the spacing and depth of the grooves and the angle of the cuts. All of that matters."

"And you're telling me what?" They seemed reluctant to come out with it. Were they afraid of how angry I would be when I found out the breakthrough had come without me?

"Ray," Kyle said, gazing at the surface of the slab, "we've opened a portal."

I knew I'd be mad. I'd grown angrier and angrier in the car on the way over when I only suspected what they had to tell me. Yet I was unprepared for the amount of rage and hatred that rose up in me, nearly overwhelming me. I was furious, but I kept a lid on it as best I could. I was also surprised by the other emotions welling up. Sure, I was angry that the breakthrough had happened without me, but I was also satisfied that my ideas had proven to be correct, excited by the possibilities of what we might find, and fearful that whatever we *did* find might not at all be to our liking.

They both watched my face, trying to gauge my reaction and— knowing this—I kept every wild emotion subdued. I knew that somehow I would gain control of the whole project again. Kyle was a smart researcher; Lorna was a sharp problem solver; but they needed me, the creative thinker and manager.

Lorna took some steps to stand beside Kyle. "It opens and closes, but so far not all the times are predictable. We've started a spreadsheet to keep track, to look for patterns."

"Spreadsheet?" I said. "How often has it opened?"

They exchanged a look and Kyle, avoiding my eyes, said, "So far, twelve times."

The anger rose again. "And you're just now telling me?" I nearly screamed.

Lorna flinched. "We wanted to tell you sooner, but with everything that's happened between us all—well. It opens frequently, Ray. It's not like weeks have passed. It's only been a day and a half."

Kyle brought up the spreadsheet on his laptop. There were columns for the date, time, and duration. "So far, we haven't seen a pattern, but the portal has opened at least once every three hours. Sometimes just for a minute or two, other times for as long as nine minutes."

"And you're sure it's a portal?" I asked. "Maybe it's a vision of some kind, or a bizarre telescope with just a view of somewhere else or some other time."

Kyle shook his head. "No, no, it's an opening, all right. We sent something through."

He didn't catch the quick look that Lorna shot him, but I did.

"What did you send?"

"Just one of Lorna's origami cranes."

My stomach tightened and my mouth went sour. Of course: how goddamn fitting.

Early in our relationship, Lorna had become infatuated with origami. She spent hours folding little paper cranes, jumping paper frogs, intricate little paper boxes. The puzzle of folding a single sheet of paper into three-dimensional shapes fascinated her. In fact, that may have been why, of the three of us, she was the one who'd realized the shapes, spacing, and depth of the runes were crucial to turning the slab into a portal.

Once, in the midst of the origami fever coinciding with the period of our relationship when we couldn't keep our hands off each other, she had, after making love, removed my condom. Rather than just wadding it into a tissue, she'd instead deftly folded the Kleenex, making neat crisp flaps, and deposited the rubber into a paper cube, making a little X-rated package.

"Look," she'd said, holding up what otherwise might have made her pregnant. "A not-a-birthday present."

While maybe not a Groucho Marx level pun, we'd laughed and laughed at that. Over the next couple of years it became the usual way we ended our lovemaking, although she rarely said the line; she'd just fold the package, hold it up, and we'd both smile.

That all ended one day there in Kyle's house. I was in his bathroom and, having blown my nose, went to toss my tissue into the wastebasket beneath the wash basin, and saw one of those little not-a-birthday presents resting right on top.

That was the last time I'd seen Kyle. Lorna I saw twice more— both times, she did some crying and I did some yelling.

Kyle now brought me back to the present, still talking about the origami crane. "We tossed one in and that little bird went flying through, no problem. We saw it land on the sandy surface. You'll see. The portal always opens onto the same place. At least, so far. There's a rectangular object always at the same spot in the distance and the ground looks like dark black sand. The little white crane went through and landed about four feet away.

"We planned on trying to get it back the next time the portal opened, only it wasn't there. Same rectangular shape in the distance, same black sand, same *place*. So, where did the crane go? Did it blow away? Or did something take it?"

I flashed on the image of a little paper crane in some otherworld museum, giant alien eyes marveling at it. Why I pictured them with giant eyes, I don't know, but I wondered sourly what they would have made of the thing if Kyle had tossed over one of Lorna's other origami specialties.

Quite suddenly, Lorna spoke up. "Here we go."

I watched in complete amazement as the top surface of the slab began to change. Instead of the solid gray it had been, with the deep-cut runes, it quickly seemed to soften and take on a sort of misty or foggy form, the ancient symbols appearing to almost float on the surface.

I heard tapping behind me and saw Kyle bent over his computer, entering the time into his spreadsheet.

Turning back to the slab, I almost couldn't believe what I was seeing. The gray mist and the runes were gone, replaced with a bizarre view into, or *through*, the slab, like a wide-open but disorienting window. Looking down into the slab, I was looking at another world.

The ground did look sandy and black. The sky was the gray of an overcast day but with no hint of clouds or fog. A ways off, far enough away that I couldn't judge distance or size, was the rectangular object Kyle had mentioned. It too was gray, lighter than the black sand but darker than the sky.

Lorna went to a nearby table and came back with a homemade contraption—a yardstick with a small digital movie camera tied to it with duct tape. She smiled. "Only the finest equipment for us."

She started the video camera and, holding the opposite end of the yardstick, carefully lowered the camera through the portal. Once it was as far in as she could get it without putting her hand beneath the surface of the slab, she slowly turned and twisted the stick, pointing the camera in as many different directions as possible.

"Until now," she said, "we've only had one view: forward. We haven't wanted to risk putting any part of our bodies through the opening. Kyle thought of this idea while we waited for you."

As Lorna continued to maneuver the camera, Kyle came over carrying a small wire cage containing one sniffing and curious white mouse. Kyle unraveled a long cord tied to the top of the cage, wrapped a length of it around one hand, and held the cage above the open portal.

"Okay, Algernon," he said to the mouse, "let's see what you can tell us."

He tossed the cage down and we watched it bounce out and onto the sand until the cord pulled tight. The mouse got banged around some, but it didn't seem to be hurt. At first it squeaked in alarm, but then it settled down.

Lorna aimed the camera at it, I assumed to record whether the mouse had trouble breathing. From our distance—and exactly how far was that?—it seemed to be fine.

"Well," Kyle said, "he doesn't—"

And suddenly the slab was solid. No gradual hardening or fading out; a weird open doorway one moment and solid stone the next. Kyle was left holding the end of a now slack cord and Lorna was left with almost exactly seven inches of the yardstick. The rest—camera, cage, and mouse—gone.

Looking a bit stunned, Kyle entered the time into his spreadsheet. "Four minutes shorter than the previous opening." He studied the figures. "Since it's opened at least once every three hours so far, I assume you'd like to stick around."

I gave the surface of the rock a quick rap with my knuckles, confirming its solidity. "Of course I would."

⋊⋉⋊⋉

Over the next couple of hours we discussed what they did know and what they didn't. Or more accurately, what they had observed and what they hadn't.

The most obvious question was, where was *there*? They had never felt any breeze or suction, into or out of the portal, so if there was a difference in atmospheric pressure it was minimal. They had not smelled a scent of any kind, and the only sound they had heard so far was the startled squeak of the mouse when his cage had landed.

They had no idea how much time passed there as compared to here, but they speculated, with my prompting, that it moved at the same rate or, theoretically, we would have seen the mouse's actions speed up or slow down relative to us. They had observed, though, that no matter if it were day or night here, the portal always opened on the same gray scene over there, never brighter nor darker.

As we puzzled over it all, gathered in one corner of the lab, now and then Kyle or Lorna would run to the kitchen to refill our coffee mugs, and now and then one or all of us would glance over at the slab to see if it had changed.

I leaned back in my chair in what I consciously considered a professorial position—a leader's position. After all, the project was my baby. They may have temporarily kidnapped it, but it was back in my hands, and I would lead us from here. "So what is it we have here? A doorway to another planet? Another universe? Or is it just a shortcut to some weird location on Earth with lousy scenery?"

"That," Lorna pointed out, "would still be quite an amazing thing."

"We'd put the airlines out of business, that's for sure. But our thesis began with the old religions and their stories about, and sacrifices to, other gods. If it's just a transport to somewhere else on Earth, are we to believe our ancestors mistook an unknown bird or some bizarre lizard they'd never seen before as a god?"

They both shook their heads.

"No, I don't think so either. And all that gray and black, like an old movie—I've never seen any place like that in *National Geographic*."

I walked over to the slab and ran my hand along its side, feeling the smooth cold stone. "I think it goes somewhere *else*, and whether they're gods or aliens, I think there are beings there, and that they've come through before."

Kyle and Lorna nodded in agreement. I was reinstating myself as the leader of the group, and I decided right then, watching them both nod, that not only would I have the project back, I would have Lorna back, too.

As usual, it was Lorna who leapt ahead to the point I was making. "If something came through hundreds of years ago, now that we've reopened the doorway, it's only a matter of time before something comes crawling through again."

"Exactly," I said. "And if that happens, what are we prepared to do?"

They gave each other blank looks and turned back to me. Had they really not considered this? Apparently, they had been so caught up in their sudden success that they hadn't thought about the possible consequences.

Just then, a vague movement caught my eye and I stood to see the surface of the slab grow pale. Kyle entered the time on his spreadsheet as Lorna and I watched the rock grow insubstantial, then misty, then clear until the portal was open and we could once again see the black sandy view on the other side. In the distance, the tall gray obelisk still stood. It was the object nearer to us that made us gasp.

Little Algernon's metal cage was still there, but it had been ripped apart, the bars bent and broken, and the mouse was gone.

Before either of us could stop him, Kyle reached downward and through the slab, grabbed the cut end of the cord still attached to the broken cage, and hauled the mangled thing back through.

At that instant, just as Lorna began to scream at him for taking such a risk, the portal closed. Kyle went white and all of us considered what his fate would have been if part of him had still been on the other side.

Lorna was beside herself. "What in hell were you thinking?"

"I . . . I thought we should examine this. Maybe we can tell if a tool was used to tear it apart."

I briefly considered what kinds of germs and microbes he may have brought back with it, but decided if the portal had been opened centuries ago, it was far too late to worry about that. Still, if he'd had to grab something, I would rather have had the camera, but now I couldn't even remember if I'd seen it there or not

Shaking a little from his close call, he took the cage over to a workbench and began examining it under a bright lamp. Lorna gave me an exasperated look and that little secret exchange between us made me even more determined to get her back. Right then, instantly clear in my mind, I knew what I was going to do to make it happen.

I pointed to the cage. "What are we going to do when whatever did *that* comes over here? Think of those bent wires as your ribcage."

"Whatever our ancestors summoned didn't kill them," Lorna said.

It was lecture time again. "I'm not sure that's true. There are plenty of dark tales of nameless and dangerous things and the attempts to appease them. Even if you're right, we're not sure what we have here. We don't know that our slab opens to the same place theirs did. Kyle, you still have that gun? The one we used to shoot at Clayton Lake back in college?"

He was looking at the slab with a certain fear. He put the cage down. "Yes, and cartridges. I'll be right back."

I turned to Lorna. "Until we know more, I suggest we never leave the slab unattended. We'll take shifts and sit up with it through the nights." Again, she nodded in agreement. "Looks like I'm moving in for a while. The guest room still empty?"

"It is. I'll go put fresh sheets on the bed."

As she left, Kyle came back in, handing me his gun and a dusty box of ammunition. I loaded the weapon and then fate took over: the slab misted and opened.

Kyle was surprised. "Wow, it's even more erratic than it has been."

He turned to note the time on his spreadsheet and stopped short when he saw I had the gun pointed right at his head.

I motioned to the slab with my head. "Get in."

His brow furrowed, as if at first he didn't understand what I was saying.

"Get in." I held the gun steady. "I'm not going to screw around until it closes again. Get in or I'll shoot you right here."

He put it together quickly and tried puffing himself up some. "And explain it to Lorna how?"

I shrugged. "I'll think of something. I was a boy genius."

"I'll die over there."

"Maybe, maybe not. The mouse seemed okay. Here you die, there you have a chance." He didn't—I already knew I was going to shoot him as soon as he went through. "I'll fire on two. One . . ."

He hopped up on the table.

"Don't dally," I warned. "We don't want most of you over there and your head over here when it closes."

He took confirming glances at the barrel of the gun and the deadly serious look on my face, saw that he had no choice, and jumped through.

I stepped forward, peeked down into the opening, and saw Kyle looking back, his expression a mix of fear and—now that I think about it—awe. I leveled the gun, wondering if the transit through the portal would alter the trajectory of the bullet I planned on putting into his head, took my best aim . . . and the portal closed.

"Damn it."

I set the gun on the worktable and was trying to decide what to do next when Lorna came back in.

I slapped a look of shock onto my face.

"What? Where's Kyle?"

"I tried to stop him." At this point I was making it up as I went.

She frowned. "What are you saying?" But she knew what I was saying.

"It opened and he could see the camera." I kept my voice flat. A lie simply told is best. "It was out of reach. He thought he could get it, like the cage."

I watched her closely to see if she would take me at my word. With the gun over on the table and Kyle's earlier behavior of reaching through the portal, she had no reason to suspect anything.

She screamed, ran to the slab, and pounded her fists on its solid surface. "No. Kyle, no." She wiped at sudden tears and clung to the stone, crying and shaking.

I let her be. I was going to have her again, I had no doubt, but if I pushed it, touched her, or made any comment that could be interpreted as insincere, I'd tip my hand. So I waited, head down as if in respect, and waited until her crying lessened.

Eventually, she looked up at me, her eyes wet and red. "What are we going to do?"

Calmly, and with as much conviction as I could muster, I said, "One of us will continue to stay here at all times. When the portal opens again, we'll pull him back through."

"Can he live?"

She wanted me to tell her that he could. So I told her the same thing I had told Kyle, and it was the thing I now feared the most, because if Kyle came crawling back through the next time the portal opened, then all was lost. "He could. The mouse seemed to be able to breathe."

Taking what comfort she could from that, she considered the surface of the slab. "It's too erratic. God knows how long he'll have to make it before it opens again."

"Then we'll just wait and hope." Of course, we'd be hoping for different things.

I wanted her out of the room. It was getting late, so I had little trouble convincing her we should to take turns sleeping, so that one of us would always be there. While Lorna had been bent and crying over the slab, I had decided that I must, at the first opportunity, break the thing. I'd come up with some excuse to explain it. Then I could work on reestablishing my relationship with Lorna. I'd insist on more research before we began working on a new slab, long after Kyle would have certainly died of starvation. I wanted first watch.

"No, you sleep first." She ran fingers through her hair. "I'm too anxious to sleep—too keyed up."

I was afraid if I were overly insistent I might raise her suspicions, so I tried to be as pleasantly persuasive as I could, when once again the portal opened.

Lorna rushed to it, leaned over the opening, cupped her hands around her mouth, and desperately called Kyle's name.

Moving up beside her, I looked in and, reluctantly, also called for him. I was happy to see he wasn't there, but it would have been better to see him dead—considering how it all turned out, it would've been *much* better to have seen him dead—but not there was still something at that point.

Continuing to call his name, Lorna more frantically than myself, I noted the camera was nowhere to be seen either. Had Kyle moved it? Or had something else?

We were still calling his name when the portal shut. I don't think Lorna noticed, but she was leaning in close enough that a lock of her blonde hair was snipped off.

Tears streaked her face and her lips were chapped. She had a sudden idea. "I'll be right back." Minutes later she returned with an armful of food. Some fruit, a box of cereal, some bottled water. "The next time it opens, we'll send him something to eat."

"I'm sorry to say this, but if he were okay," I asked, "why would he have wandered away?"

Her eyes narrowed with angry determination. "I'm sending him food and water."

She picked up the gun and sat with it in her lap. "You go on and get some sleep. I'll take first watch."

For fear of making her angry, I relented and headed off to the spare bedroom, with no intention of actually sleeping. Somehow, I had to make sure Kyle was gone for good. I stretched out on the top of the guest bed as I considered my options. If I couldn't prove he was dead, then I'd have to break that slab when we switched watches. It was just too much of a risk.

As I thought about how to explain it, I must have nodded off without knowing, because the next thing I knew I was coming awake to the sound of a gunshot.

I leapt to my feet, heart racing, and it took me a moment to get a grip on where I was. A second shot rang out before I was to the bedroom door.

Running down the hall and wishing that I, too, were armed, I saw Lorna come rushing from the lab, screaming.

"What?" I shouted over her and over the shots still ringing in my ears. "What's happened?"

She thrust the gun at me and I had to reach around to take it by the grip to avoid the hot barrel and open muzzle.

She pointed down the hall. "Something came through. Crawled up out of the slab. Oh, God! All thick and . . . and . . . *ropey*. It came at me. Reached for me with its, with—tentacles."

I put an arm around her and peered down the hallway, waiting to see if something would come shambling forth.

She was shaking. "I shot it. I think it's dead. It might be dead."

She let me hold her while we waited there. Eventually, when nothing crawled through the doorway, I checked that there were still bullets in the gun, and took my arm from around her. "I guess I better go look."

Only stupid men have no fear. I inched down that hallway fighting a bizarre mixture of terror, hope, and curiosity, the gun held steady and ready all the way.

I entered the lab and immediately saw the thing wasn't dead after all. Later, I discovered one of Lorna's shots hadn't even hit it, the bullet lodged in the far wall. Still, the one that had found her target seemed to have done considerable damage.

The thing was thick and—as Lorna had said pretty accurately—ropey. It looked sort of a like a repugnant and impossible crossbreeding of a squid and an ape. It crouched in the center of the floor, heavy yellow fluid leaking from a gaping hole in what might have been its abdomen. One of its tentacles twitched against the floor.

As I moved cautiously toward it, Lorna called my name from the hallway.

"Stay there," I shouted.

I was close enough to see what the thing was doing with its twitching arm. It was clearly dying and had one last goal. The horror of it made me shudder and promise myself I would never speak of it to Lorna.

I put the gun flat against what had to be the horrid thing's head and pulled the trigger.

"Ray!" Lorna screamed.

The thing stopped moving.

"I'm okay," I yelled, running back out into the hallway.

Her eyes were wide with fright and worry. "Is it dead?"

"I think so, but stay here."

I hurried to the bathroom, grabbed some towels, and tore the plastic shower curtain from its rod.

Back in the lab, I got down on my knees to roll the thing onto the shower curtain. It felt like what I imagined a walrus might, sort of both rubbery and furry. It was heavy and it, or its gore, had an unpleasant and rusty metallic odor. Once I had it on the curtain, I rolled the creature up in it the best I could. With the towels, I wiped up as much of the fluid as possible.

I went back out to get Lorna. "When the portal opens next time, we're going to send it back. I'll need your help to lift it."

"You're sure it's dead?"

"Yes."

She shuddered. "I don't want to touch it."

"I've wrapped it up." I took her hand. "Come on. I can't do it alone."

She came and, grimacing, helped me drag the thing as close to the slab as possible. I tossed the soiled towels on top of it. Then we sat and waited. Both of us avoided looking at the heavy bundle.

After a while, Lorna looked up at me, tears streaming down her face. "Kyle's dead, isn't he?"

I let that go unanswered. We sat in silence.

Almost an hour passed before the portal opened again. Lorna had nodded off, chin tucked down. I wonder now what would've happened if I hadn't wakened her. Could I have managed by myself? Would I have everything I wanted?

I nudged her and she started awake, then frowned as reality came back to her. She stood and took a look down into the portal, surely checking to see if Kyle was there.

I tossed the soiled bath towels in and they landed softly on the alien black sand. Then Lorna and I knelt and hefted the creature up and onto the edge of the slab.

When I replay it in my mind—which I still do even after all this time—I'm still not sure exactly what happened. I know as we pushed it, to let it tumble in, some of the plastic curtain came undone and one blubbery tentacle flopped out as the thing rolled. Whether it was the momentum of the roll, or whether it wasn't dead after all and was reaching out for one of us, I can't say. Whichever it was, the tentacle wrapped around Lorna's right wrist and the weight began to pull her through. She screamed as her arm, shoulder, and head dipped beneath the surface of the slab. Her feet lifted from the floor and I grabbed her waist.

Then portal closed and I lost it all.

What was left of Lorna on this side, I lowered to the floor.

At first, I was too shocked to do anything. I didn't scream or cry or even turn away. I just stood, frozen and almost blind. Then slowly, as the minutes ticked by, a fury grew inside me; a storm of hatred formed and began to rage. Kyle. Kyle had stolen everything from me once again. Part of me wanted to explode, to let the anger roar loose. Another part of me just wanted to collapse into a ball and shut down. Yet I knew I could do neither. Before the portal opened again, I had worked out what had to be done. After all, no matter the losses and shattered dreams, self-preservation trumped all.

It took three more openings of the portal to take care of everything.

During the first, I deposited Lorna's severed body.

During the second, I deposited the bloody towels and rags I used to clean up her blood.

During the third opening, I threw in all the notes and drawings and records I could find, and finally, just before the portal closed for the last time, I hurled the computer through and watched it tumble across the strange black sand.

I took a deep breath and moved behind the large table, leveraged my back against the wall, and pushed the heavy stone slab, first against one end and then the next, until it teetered off the table and crashed to the floor, breaking in two.

A forensic team would have no trouble finding my fingerprints. They would easily discover there had been a lot of blood on the floor. They would surely even find traces of the yellow ichor, but good luck to them identifying it. Still, there were no bodies, and there never would be. My life might be hell for a while, but there was nothing anyone could prove.

Before I left the house, I stopped and looked into the bathroom, remembering that day I'd found Lorna's little not-a-birthday present in the wastebasket. *That was the day I'd lost everything*, I told myself, *not today*. No matter the horrible things I'd seen in the last few hours, the image that stayed with me was of the little origami bundle in Kyle's trash.

I had loved her most. Of that, I was certain. I would never have tortured her the way Kyle had tried to, and I'd had no intention of ever telling her what I'd seen in the lab after she had shot the creature. If she'd known, it would have driven her mad.

When I walked in there, gun ready, the dying thing, with one twitching tentacle, was using the dripping yellow fluid to *write*.

Before I wiped it away with a bath towel, the thing had managed to scrawl, *Lorna, I love y . . .*

XOXOX XOXOX XOXOX X

# About the Author

Douglas Russell's work has appeared in *Space and Time Magazine, Cover of Darkness, Weirdbook, Trysts of Fate,* and *Skeptic Magazine.* Two of his stories received honorable mention in *The Year's Best Fantasy and Horror.*

# SMOKE SIGNALS TO THE DEVIL

Kathleen Wolak

"I'm sorry, John. It's just the way the market is turning."

John Callan looked across the bleak, shining conference table at the man taking his livelihood away. John had never met him before—he had been sent in by a nameless corporate drone who had no idea how many lives were being destroyed. The man before him was younger than John by at least two decades and had mastered a look of pseudo-concern that made John think that he was maybe the twentieth person fired that day.

"The good news is you aren't leaving empty-handed. We know how hard you've worked for the company." The man reached into his jacket pocket and withdrew a thin envelope. He strode over to John as though he were handing him the Olympic torch. The man pressed the envelope into John's hand and gave him a good-natured smack on the back.

"Tha-thank you," John stammered. He suddenly felt very foggy, as though his body was operating completely on its own with no help from his mind as he hoisted himself out of the uncomfortable boardroom chair and walked out of his former office building.

John found himself crossing the street from his former office building, wandering toward a vacant bench. He walked slowly over, almost hoping for a car to collide with him en route. He sighed heavily as he made the step from the curb to the springy Kelly green grass. Folding into the bench, he withdrew a crumpled pack of smokes from his jacket pocket. John lit a slightly bent cigarette before tearing open the long envelope he'd received as a parting gift. Inside was a tri-folded letter containing only six lines of text:

*Dear Mr. Callan,*

*Context Global Marketing would like to heartily thank you for your years of service to the company.*

*Without the dedication of you and your peers, the innovation we deliver on a daily basis would not be possible. We welcome the chance for you to use us as a recommendation on your new career journey.*

*Kindest Regards,*

*CGM*

John blew a thick cloud at the letter before crumpling it into a tiny ball and sticking it in his pocket. He leaned forward and looked at the ground beneath his feet, wondering just who would hire a fifty-five-year-old man with more debt than he knew what to do with. John hadn't looked for a job in more than twenty years. He didn't even know where to start.

As he contemplated the unthinkable, John blew three tiny smoke circles into the grass. He watched as they expanded and vanished in dancing, mystical patterns.

"Can I trouble you for a cigarette?"

Startled, John jerked his head up to see a small man with silver hair smiling down at him. He wore a tailored, dark emerald suit with a black tie, and spoke with a clipped yet kindly transatlantic accent.

"Oh, I'm terribly sorry. I didn't mean to frighten you." The man sat down beside John. "It's just so rare to see anybody with a cigarette these days. Devil sticks, they call them." The man chuckled. "Personally, I don't think there's a statement further from the truth. In the right moment, I find them to be absolute life-savers."

For some reason, John couldn't take his eyes off the man. He kept his gaze fixated even as he dug into his jacket to retrieve a cigarette for his new companion.

"Dreadful, the way things are these days, wouldn't you say?" The man lit his cigarette with a gold lighter that seemed to appear out of thin air.

John nodded, and for the first time, looked away from the man.

"You're telling me, pal." John dug into his pocket and retrieved his balled up termination letter. He tried to smooth it out as much as possible before handing it over.

"I've been with this company for twenty years. Twenty years! And boom, one day, it's 'Well, sorry about all of your jobs, but we don't need you anymore because an app or computer can do your job now, and they don't need money to survive.' Never mind the people who got fired—who can't eat or live or even find a job now. No…we got *that*."

John pointed to the letter he had given the man, who was reading through it with great interest. Panting, John finally got a hold of himself.

"I-I'm sorry about that, mister. A bit of a delayed reaction, I guess. I don't mean to bother you with my troubles."

The man smiled gently. "Nonsense! I find man's atrocities toward man absolutely fascinating. And by the looks of this, my friend"— the man smacked the crinkled letter with the back of his hand—"a foul atrocity was committed, indeed."

John nodded into his chest. "A lousy recommendation. That's what I get for missing family dinners, staying up nights, stressing about *their* best interest ahead of…" Something caught in John's throat, and he felt the very unwelcome warmth of tears in the corners of his eyes.

"…the people I love," he finished with some effort.

The silver-haired man clucked his tongue as he neatly folded the letter and handed it back to John.

"It's unfortunate, isn't it?" The man took a long drag off his cigarette. John couldn't help but be impressed by the fast-appearing snake of ash that the man's cigarette was turning into. When he finally exhaled, the smoke encircled them like a thick, fluffy blanket. John swiveled his head, trying to make sense of the dense cloud now shielding them from view. The smoke hung completely still, suspended in the air.

"How the hell did you do that, pal? Are you some kind of magician?" John asked, eyeing the man's emerald suit.

The man let out another little chuckle. "No, John, I'm not what you would call a magician—but I would like to show you something, if I may?"

John's eyes narrowed at the man's smiling face. "Wait—how did you know my name? Is this a gag? Because I gotta be honest, pal, I'm not really in the mood." John tried to wave away the smoke, but it was useless. He couldn't even move the thick clouds; they were walled in.

"I know you, John. I know all mankind." The silver-haired man spoke calmly but with unavoidable purpose. Suddenly, the smoke pulsed and turned black. John sat frozen, unable to even see an opening to leave.

"The man who gave you that letter—did you know he has no peripheral vision? It was lost when he was a child and stared too long at the sun. Not the sharpest knife in the drawer, clearly."

He waved his hand, and up from the ground sprung the man who'd fired John. He stood there for a moment with a blank expression on his face.

"What the hell is this?" John demanded.

The silver-haired man ignored John's question and terrified expression. "His name is David Keillor. And poor David can't see the M11 bus…"

John yelped as a huge bus broke through the thick black smoke and flattened David Keillor against the front grate like a rag doll. John saw David's body only briefly, but he could make out that his head had been smashed into something resembling cherry pie filling.

John lurched forward, vomiting between his feet. When he looked back up, there was nothing there but the hanging black smoke.

"Or how about your former boss, Douglas Hall?" The stranger once again waved his hand, and a pudgy, pig-like man appeared out of the ground. "Did you know the reason you were let go was because ol' Dougie didn't want to take a pay cut?"

John wiped his mouth and looked weakly at the magician. "What's going on?"

The man didn't take his eyes off of Doug. "That's right, John. If Doug had just taken a ten percent decrease in his pay, dropping his annual income down to only five million dollars a year, you would still have your job—along with several other poor folks just like you."

The silver-haired man smiled at the blank-faced Doug. "His mistress ultimately made the call, mind you. It seems she just can't live without the finer things in life."

The man snapped his fingers and a small ember rose from the ground and landed on Doug's shoulder. Within moments, it burst into flames, consuming Doug. John watched in stunned horror as his old boss's face curdled and peeled into black and red fragments. The silver-haired man lazily waved his hand, and the burning Doug vanished.

"And then there's your ex-wife." The man rubbed his hands together as a blonde, petite woman sprang up.

"Holly." John stared at her expressionless doppelganger.

"All those long hours you worked to provide for her, and how did she thank you? Why, by running off with your neighbor, the lawyer."

An oily, tan man appeared next to Holly. John recognized her new husband and his former neighbor, Greg.

"How does someone do that to another person, I wonder? Ah! But that is one of life's little mysteries, I suppose. How should we punish these two, John? The money she took from you during the divorce paid for a little convertible…" The silver-haired man tapped on his cigarette, and an electric-blue Porsche appeared around Holly and Greg. "They drive all around those twisting, turning California mountain roads every Saturday, you know."

John watched Holly and Greg maneuver their car around a phantom road as though he were simply watching a movie screen.

A bright flash of light and a sharp crash rang out in the smoky cocoon. When John could finally see again, Holly and Greg lay in a mangled, bloody pile at his feet.

John looked down at his ex-wife, whose head was turned all the way around. Before he could get a good look at the wreckage, everything vanished. The black smoke encasing the two men was gone, and they were now surrounded by bustling traffic and frantic pedestrians.

John finally felt as though he could move. He jumped up from the bench as the man casually took one last pull on his cigarette before stubbing it out.

"Listen, mister, I really don't know what's going on here, but I…I've just gotta go."

"Relax, John." His companion got up as well. "These are merely visions, brought on by the desperation only a man in your position can feel."

"Who the hell *are* you?" John asked.

"Oh, I think you know." The silver-haired man pressed something cold into John's hand. "This is for you, should you require my services in the real world, but for now, let the shadows comfort you."

John opened his palm to see the gold lighter.

"Just light your cigarette with this, and I'll be back to discuss any deals you may be interested in making."

"Yeah, okay, pal." John turned the lighter over in his hand. "You know, I've met some disturbing people in this city, but—" John looked up to see the silver-haired man had vanished.

Dazed, and feeling incredibly weak, John slumped back onto the bench. He wanted to throw the lighter in the trash can a few feet away. That's what he would do—he would even quit smoking so he'd never be tempted to call on the man in the emerald suit. John tried to gather the energy to stand, but the visions played freshly in his mind, and he was so consumed by what he'd just seen he didn't notice David Keillor striding toward him, gym bag in hand.

"Hey there, Jim…you know those devil sticks are bad for you, right?" David pointed at the cigarette in John's hand before walking confidently toward his Mercedes SUV in the commuter lot on the other side of the small park. John's eyes narrowed on David as he slid easily into his shining, oversized chariot, which happened to have been blocking in John's battered Honda. The Honda that he still owed several months' worth of payments on.

John let his hot, red gaze follow David to the parking lot before he calmly stubbed out his cigarette.

As he watched David speed down the street, narrowly missing a city bus, John reached once more into his jacket pocket, withdrawing another crumpled cigarette.

)X(X()X( )X(X()X( )X(X()X( )X(

# About the Author

Kathleen Wolak is a writer from Hamden, Conneticut. Her short fiction has appeared in over twenty literary magazines, including *KZine, Hello Horror,* and *Danse Macabre.*

# GRAND ELECTRIC
# GESTURES OF LOVE

Mario E. Martinez

I

Abel Verduzco had been in love with Cleo Reilly since they were ten years old. She'd come into his elementary school classroom and bewitched him with her red hair and blue eyes. Throughout the years, he'd had to contend with these feelings daily, since the town of Four Creeks didn't have more than three thousand people in it. The constant desire to speak to her, to be near her, but unable to act on those desires, made him nervous and shy. Most of Four Creeks took this as a sign he was strange.

He watched her in high school, dating all the wrong kinds of boys and walking the halls without so much as glancing at Abel. But he always carried a bit of hope that went deeper than the awkward silence and acne. The boys she went out with weren't serious and, he thought, the town was so small, eventually Cleo would have to look at him in a new way. Abel clung to that hope until Cleo started going out with Ryan Wandmacher, a kid from San Casimiro, just fifteen miles down the highway.

With Ryan in the mix, Abel felt his hopes get torn to bits. He dropped out of school soon after and found a part-time job with the county in the Dead Animal Cleanup Department. Sure, he heard the whispers, the rumors. The town thought it was because he was quiet and weird and stupid. Not fit to be around people. In reality, he took the job to get lost in something that wasn't Cleo Reilly. He saw her in just about anything and everything. But whenever Abel had to pick up half an armadillo, sun baked to the density of a bowling ball, he didn't think of Cleo or her red hair or her blue eyes.

It wasn't the ideal life, but Abel could at least say he had money in his pocket and a job to go to every week. The routine, though reaching a new level of grotesque with every outing, helped ease his loss of hope, and for that the department earned Abel's fierce loyalty. After a while, things were almost pleasant.

Then, in 1950, the men were called to Korea, and Abel, along with a few folks from Four Creeks, had to take a bus down to Puentes to get a physical and his assignment.

The bus carrying Abel had stopped at neighboring towns like San Casimiro and Gaston as well. To Abel's dismay, Ryan Wandmacher was sitting in the front. Throughout the ride, Abel couldn't help but look up and see the smug shape of his head and inwardly snarl at how much it made him think of blue-eyed Cleo and her red hair all over Ryan.

At the base in Puentes, Abel was examined and turned away. Though he'd been able to do all of the physical exercises and thought he did all right on the written exam, the draft officer found the smell coming off him so repulsive, the man considered it his duty to declare Abel Verduzco unfit for service, sending him home with a document that said he had flat feet, which "rendered him unable to perform the duties of a member of the United States Army."

Abel and a few others rode back to Four Creeks that evening. Out of the four others that weren't selected, two were so elated they couldn't help but laugh the entire time.

Abel was quiet, because he was ashamed. Truthfully, he didn't want to go to war with anyone. He'd never heard much about the Koreans, and he was sure they were nice people—except for the ones they were fighting—but he had no desire to see their country or get shot in it. A part of him wanted to enjoy the feeling of relief, like the two laughing men. But another part that, until that day, had lain dormant, told him Ryan Wandmacher had gone to Puentes, had been looked at and examined same as him…except the U.S. of A. *wanted* Ryan Wandmacher when they needed brave men to fight. Men like Ryan, men who could go out with a woman like Cleo Reilly.

Like Cleo, the draft had looked at Abel and thought he wasn't fit for service.

## ‖

B y 1952, Abel had returned to his routine and the serenity it brought. The new highway to the Rio Grande Valley had opened, giving him a new stretch of road to clean. With it came more vitality to the town. A few new businesses, an extra filling station, and a few more families. That same year, Abel sat in the office across from Chuck Aaron, his boss. Abel was drinking his coffee while Chuck went over each of the country newspapers.

For a while, the only sound in the office was the rustling of those pages, but then Chuck sucked his tongue and shook his head. "Well, ain't that a shame," he said. "Local kid, Wandmacher, uh, Ryan— apparently he got killed. Over something called Hill 266. Shit, can you imagine? Dying for something that doesn't even have a proper name."

"Let me see that," Abel said, taking the paper.

"You know the guy?"

"Kind of, sort of," Abel said, reading the obituary. It was a list of awards and was heavy with words like *valor* and *brave* and *patriot*. Ryan was to be buried in Arlington National Cemetery alongside other Texans that had *given their lives to help those in a foreign land*. Abel kept staring at it, one part of him thinking that all this did was exalt Ryan to the status of local legend. But another part of him kept whispering a single phrase, one that disgusted and excited him all at once: *Cleo Reilly was single*.

Any thought of capitalizing on that fact was quickly tossed aside when Cleo and the Wandmachers returned from the capital. Cleo covered herself in black and rarely left the house Ryan had built for them. Usually a ray of light in the bleak town, now she dressed for mourning, never smiling the way she used to. This went on until the first Four Creeks Winter Festival.

The town managed to get a Ferris wheel, and some local vendors to bake pies and sell tacos. Along with them came the carnival men and their pit show. They set up a large tent that, for a nickel a person, served as a looking ground of oddities. Among them was a man with teeth filed to points, and tattoos from the top of his head down to his feet. Another was the fat lady, an enormous woman with ankles as thick as a cannon. Another still was the pinhead—a deformed thing who grunted at the crowds and occasionally bit the head off mice that had been provided in a bucket.

Abel, like most of the county, had been there that first night, enjoying a break from monotonous small town life. Inside the pit show tent, he spotted Cleo Reilly among a group of girls they'd gone to high school with. Two things about Cleo struck Abel as odd. The first was that she wore a blue brooch on her black dress, which he took as some cosmic sign that the shell of mourning Cleo had surrounded herself with was finally deteriorating.

The second—and most profound—was that she was laughing.

It was something she hid behind her gloved hand, but it was a genuine giggle, one that brought a smile with it.

Still, none of those omens gave him the courage to go up to that same display she'd stopped to see and exchange even the most innocent of pleasantries. She'd smell his true intentions, he thought. It would make her think he was somehow dirty. Instead, he waited in the crowd until she left whatever had gotten a giggle out of her. Wanting to see what it was, he made his way to it.

Abel was surprised. It was a rack with shelves, each with its own specimen in a jar of embalming fluid. In front of them, a young carnival worker pointed at each and told their histories. A two-headed piglet from South Hampton. A set of shrunken heads from Peru set in an empty jar like cookies. The one getting the most attention was in a tank, and took up a shelf all its own.

It was a mermaid. According to the announcer, the thing had washed up on the shores of Greece and had been preserved for decades to be shown around the world. Looking close, Abel shook his head. It wasn't anything more than a shaved monkey cut in half and stitched to the back end of a catfish. Abel scoffed, but the people around him stood in collective shock, and the air around him filled with whispers of astonishment.

He couldn't believe it. His boss Chuck dabbled in taxidermy and went on about it whenever they got called to pick up any animal that wasn't soup-splattered across the highway. Sometimes, Chuck even brought some of his pieces to work. The man preferred smaller animals and liked to make them stand in ridiculous poses.

Jack rabbits at a dinner table arguing over the bills, including a little beer can and tiny pink notices. Other times, it was field mice jumping rope with grass snakes. He'd even told Abel about the ways people used to make two-headed animals or little cryptids with hardly more than some sawdust, thread, and some animal parts. He'd even said that was why they were usually kept in jars and shown in dimly lit tents: so no one could see the stitching.

People paying good money and squawking about something Chuck Aaron could do over a long weekend was ridiculous. But… those things in the jars had somehow charmed Cleo.

Then and there, Abel's mind compiled and cemented something that smelled and sounded like a plan. If such things were enough to get Cleo to smile while in mourning, then he'd spend the next year of his life creating something so spectacular by comparison that she'd smile and blush and dance and wear so many colors, and she'd never forget it wasn't anyone but Abel Verduzco who did it for her.

# III

The project, the deadline, the thoughts of Cleo's happy expression at the sight of his finished work—all of it gave Abel an energy he hadn't felt in so long, it bordered on being a new experience. He woke up without the same aches and pains or the sour feeling in his stomach from the anxiety of a new day.

That first morning after Cleo smiled at the fair, Abel went to work early. In the gray dawn, he took the county truck and cruised the highways looking for animals on the road. His project painted every mundane part of his day in new and wondrous ways. He was hoping for fresh kills, their blood still wet on the road, not so when he scraped his shovel beneath them, the stink wouldn't be so bad—instead, he wanted the freshest because they'd make the best materials.

Those next months found him busy to the point of exhaustion. Mornings and evenings, he scanned the highways, pulling over to examine the roadkill before putting it in the truck. Abel knelt with a young spike whose back end had been smashed by a semi, holding the face in his hands to feel the bones beneath for any breaks. He massaged its ribs to see how far up the fractures went. Thinking at least the head was salvageable, he set to cutting it off with a shovel.

The whole process—the setting of the shovel blade and the stomping through muscle and bone—took a few minutes, which left him covered up to the thighs in clotted blood and gore. He placed the head delicately in a bag in the truck and threw the rest of the corpse in the bed. On the drive home, where he'd throw the bagged head in the ice box with some of his other materials, Abel's arms were heavy and trembled from the exertion of decapitation. He decided he needed more tools if he was going to make a proper oddity for Cleo.

Before long, a big knife and machete rode along with him.

During his working hours, Abel never let on that he had any designs to do anything but waste away at a cushy county job. Still, he didn't squander those eight hours a day. There was a project to complete. To pass the time, Abel asked Chuck questions about taxidermy. Normally, most people would've been suspicious of another asking them about such a morbid hobby, but Chuck seemed to genuinely enjoy the ancient practice.

For weeks, it was a ritual. Over coffee and donuts, Chuck rambled on about the proper solutions for skin preservation, which brand of twine held the surest and the longest. The best way to slice quickest and how a rotten liver could make a bobcat mount stink for decades past the day it was stuffed. And, as Chuck spoke, Abel took notes.

He wanted to keep the project a secret. Somehow, he felt telling anyone would give doubt a chance to seep in and mess up the works. Abel, despite his school records and profession, was not a fool. He knew that trying to get a woman like Cleo Reilly to look at him like he was a man was, frankly, a long shot. It didn't matter if he had a million trinkets: Abel would always be Abel, and Cleo would always be in a pantheon above him. But, in all the years he'd yearned for her, the decade of masturbation to her and her alone, he'd never had a better idea.

So he jotted down his notes, in the form of crossword puzzles that Abel filled in with taxidermy tips and methods. He'd just smile when Chuck called him an idiot for spending hours on the same crossword. Abel would fold the puzzle up, saying he'd work on it at home later. Abel suspected Chuck pictured him staring at a stupid puzzle that most of the biddies in town could complete in an afternoon.

Abel didn't care, though.

Let Chuck and the rest think he was just smelly, weird, and stupid. If they thought those things, sure, they'd spread their rumors—but they'd leave him alone. Leave him be with his freezer full of paws and torsos and heads, his tiny house filling with bones and twine and sawdust. The people outside weren't part of it. They weren't going to help. Only the parts would.

When it was too dark to go out looking for fresh supplies, Abel sat at his small table and tried to sketch something that would be enough to not only get Cleo to smile, but would have her clapping and giggling every time she thought of it. Before too long, he found he was even less talented with a sketchpad than he was with wooing women.

At the San Casimiro Library, he picked up books on art and drawing and found a few on native animals of the area. Those he copied and traced until the most beautiful examples were decorating his walls. He found their sketched eyes unsettling. They watched him look over his inventory, praying that going over his materials again and again would give him inspiration. After a few weeks, he felt those penciled eyes were judging him.

They reminded him that any idea he sketched would be too small, too insignificant to get the reaction he wanted. Even though some of his sketches made for stuffed creatures the size of feral hogs, most of them hardly rivaled the mermaid. No matter how he arranged the pieces in his mind, they were failures.

The frustration bled into his work: the scrapes of the shovel were messier and the hauling to the pit was in silence. Yet the change in mood hardly seemed to register with Chuck. One day at the pit—a hole in the ground on the county line where they threw the animal pieces—Chuck, leaning against the truck with a beer in hand, rambled on about taxidermy.

"But, as you can imagine, people don't really look at taxidermy as a noble art anymore," Chuck said. "Used to be that was the only way to see any animals from other places. Stories didn't work. Hell, you go to England—"

"You've never been out of Texas," Abel said with a sigh.

"Don't have to leave Texas to read a book," Chuck said. "But, if you were to ever go there, you'd see carvings on the cathedrals. These scaly things with a mane, but the rest looks like a dragon, you know? And why? Because when they were told to carve a lion, they didn't know what the shit one looked like. Taxidermists were goddamn pioneers of information—"

"Weren't you telling me they used to make up a ton of it?" Abel climbed down from the back of the truck. "Like that mermaid at the fair."

"That's what I'm saying," Chuck said, tipping his beer at Abel. "Purveyors of knowledge painted as conmen and morbid twits, all because of a few sons of bitches. Worst of them was this guy, Gio Aldani, 1800s and shit. This guy used to bring the dead back to life. Stuck copper wires up dead animal asses and, like, hanged criminals and shit. Jolt them and get them to dance. Used to tour all over Europe."

"He did what…" Abel said, trailing off. The mention of electricity seemed to float just out of reach, whimsical and entrancing while being infinitely frustrating.

Chuck scoffed. "Not only that, they knighted the bastard for it. Can you believe it? Having to call that ghoul 'sir' and bow and shit. All for what? Playing dolls with dead stuff."

Abel didn't say anything.

"Hey, don't get me wrong, a mount is preservation," Chuck mused. "A snapshot of life. But that shit—it's like going to a five-star steakhouse and playing with your food."

Abel nodded, but was unaware of what Chuck had actually said. The pieces were falling into place. All they'd needed was wire and a stage to dance.

# IV

Once the weather cooled, Abel started calling in sick. Half days. Full days. He went out in the mornings and evenings, scanning the roads. But unlike the first months of covert scouting, where Abel felt as though he were just seeing what could be made out of what he found, now Abel was hunting for something. The design was in his mind, burning there like an idol, and all he had to do was find the right materials.

He had to buy another ice box on credit, which meant a strict diet of bologna and canned beans, but all the stomach cramps and stringy shits would be forgotten at the sight of Cleo Reilly's smile.

A month before the Winter Festival, luck fell on Abel. It took the form of a semi plowing into a bunch of cows that had broken away from the San Casimiro cattle auction a few miles down the highway.

When they'd gotten the call, Chuck and Abel had expected a mess, but found a scene like neither had ever seen in their professional careers. The truck had struck five cows—a pair directly, while only clipping the other three—but the force was enough to pulverize them, scattering chunks and limbs all over the highway. A half a torso wedged in the tires. A cow's back end flung across the road and tangled on a barbed wire fence.

Chuck and Abel worked all day in sight of the highway travelers and the vultures. Even ripped apart, the pieces themselves were heavy and messy. Dragging the hind legs left a trail of guts and juices, and hefting a front quarter had the bones inside sliding out of the skin as if it were a sleeve. The heat and smell seemed to call every fly for a mile, and soon the men had to tie bandanas across their faces to keep from inhaling some of the living cloud.

The flies followed them all the way to the pit, where they spread out to the other bones and rot, mingling with the fat blue bottles congregating there. Chuck threw the pieces in a hurry, griping that it was evening already, and overtime wasn't enough to keep him away from his recliner and beer. Abel, too, acted drained; his choosing of the pieces and chunks was careful and each time he tossed them, it was near the lip of the pit.

"Looks like the day's got you too," Chuck said once they were in the truck. "At least it's over."

"Sure is," Abel said, though he was hardly paying attention. He was envisioning the legs of good cowhide and the sturdy hooves that would serve as a solid base.

It was all coming together, and it was going to be beautiful.

# V

The air finally turned cold and November came to a close. The nights froze and the days were blanketed by an iron gray sky. The festival was only three weeks away, so Abel called Chuck and told him he needed to take time off. Whatever his vacation days couldn't cover, Abel told him to dock his sick days too. When Chuck pressed him for a reason, Abel said he needed time.

"Time? Time for what?" Chuck asked that morning.

"Gestures of love," Abel told him and hung up. Usually, he'd have been a bit apprehensive about calling in like that, but it was all coming together. For the first time, Abel Verduzco had felt the hand of Fate and was convinced he was taking part in his destiny.

He'd been born into a little nothing town like Four Creeks so he could meet Cleo Reilly and never have her. Up to that point, Abel thought it was some cosmic joke, but realized now it had been for the best. If he'd had her in his youth, he would've been shy and awkward—his pimples or his smell or gangly frame would've made him a passing phase for her. Even when she went with Wandmacher, Abel still wasn't ready, didn't understand the commitment it would take to get a woman like Cleo Reilly.

On top of that was the highway itself.

There was no randomness to the festival, to the cabinets of curiosities, not even to Ryan Wandmacher's death. The universe had done it all. Gave him his job, Chuck's knowledge, and the tools to use it. It had sent those cows running right into that semi. Even made some old European revive corpses a century ago. The universe made a trillion things happen so Abel could do what he'd been put on the earth to do.

That first morning of his self-inflicted exile, Abel turned off the heat and opened all the windows until the entire place was the dry forty degrees of the outside. He dressed against it—thermals and sweaters and a thick coat—and then brought out all the things he'd need.

Abel set them anywhere there was space to accommodate the spools the thread and coils of wire and the collection of carcass parts. He stood among them for over an hour, never touching, only looking. Though he'd sketched his creation out, figured where the wires needed to connect for it to really move, Abel didn't look at them again.

In his mind's eye, the pieces arranged themselves before him, the parts rolling over to the table and stacking on top of one another, the wires snaking into the frozen meat and bones while the needle and thread danced over the seams like a busy bee. It was all there, looming in front of him. All he need do was make it.

For all the books he'd read, Abel found he wasn't very good with the needle, nor did the cold help with his hands' dexterity. The skins didn't obey the same way they had in the books and manuals. Chuck described a process that was quite simple given the knowledge and dedication. Yet for Abel, it nearly drove him mad.

While he made his creation, he slept only a few hours at a time. He ate enough to avoid starvation or whenever his body was so weak his hands shook. Withering beneath his clothes, Abel worked tirelessly, tinkering and perfecting. The only thing to keep him company was the radio, which only served to remind him that the Winter Festival was coming. And, for a while, those were the stories of his days. Toil. Sleep. Toil. Life by the jingles for the festival…for Cleo's heart.

Three days before the festival, as the trucks rolled in and the tents went up, Abel came out of his trance and was confronted with what days before had been a vision and was now a reality standing before him, motionless without electric life.

Abel looked upon his creation and wept.

# VI

The turnout was larger than expected. People from all over the county and as far as Puentes came into town to either buy or sell, clogging up the fairgrounds. Abel had begged a friend on the planning committee to give him a spot inside the pit show. After reminding his old classmate that he'd never told anyone what he'd seen transpire between his classmate and another altar boy twenty years before, Abel secured a spot in the back corner of the pit show tent.

The morning of the festival, Abel went in to set up his work and to see the competition. Another troupe came in, boasting a bearded woman and two aborigines, who didn't look too awe-inspiring before the crowds arrived—the bearded woman did laundry while the aborigines read a single copy of Dostoyevsky. The least impressive was the cabinet of curiosities. A two-faced cat. A hand with seven fingers. A frog with the fangs of a dog.

Abel smiled. Next to them, his creation would be like the breath of God. Yet to his dismay, once the people arrived, they fawned over the smelly jars and obvious needlework.

He'd built a little stage for his creation so it could be better viewed, and to hide the wires that ran up its back like ivies. Behind it, Abel set his switches and record player. His creation needed music to dance: otherwise it would just be dead animal parts jerking around on a stage. It would be beautiful, and it would get Cleo to smile those black clothes right into a trashcan. She'd see what he was capable of and would cherish him as he'd cherished her.

By the time Cleo showed up at the festival, Abel had kept the curtain he'd strung up closed for so long his fingers were cramped.

For hours, curious children and couples hovered just outside the curtain, pulling at it or trying to peek beneath. All they found was Abel hissing them away.

He spotted Cleo in the middle of a gaggle of former classmates. She wore a dark gray dress and coat. As if the gray—so much more inviting than black—weren't enough reason to get excited, she wore a bright red brooch the shape of a cardinal. Abel bit down on his lip at the sight of it. He knew what that color meant.

He waited for her to get closer to the curiosities before he opened the curtains to his hastily erected stage. At first, people could only see the general shape of it. The mystery drew them in, including Cleo and her friends, to see what new attraction the fair offered.

Abel turned on his record player, and the gentle notes of a guitar broke through the whispers and drunken barks as Bing Crosby crooned.

Abel hit the lights.

They gasped. Of course they would, Abel knew. It was the first time, he figured, that some of them had ever seen something made with pure love and devotion. But they'd only seen the shape, the form.

He connected the cable to a car battery. The stage lights surged, Bing skipped, and then the creation was dancing for the crowd, for Cleo. Its legs, which curtsied up and down like pistons, were composed of deer legs covered with bobcat fur and turkey feathers. They were sewn onto the upper half of a pig's torso, which wore a vest of skunk and possum skins buttoned shut with bird legs painted the color of Cleo's eyes. Each arm was a pair of cow legs positioned so that every jolt of electricity brought the hooves together like clapping cymbals.

The face was that of a javelina stretched over a horse skull and set to look like it smiled with a mouth full of flat cow teeth. What the javelina skin couldn't cover, Abel had filled in with jackrabbit ears and vulture feathers. To make it all come together, he'd set an old stovetop hat on its head, which he'd had to tack on since it fell off every time the thing danced.

Once it got moving, Abel's creation silenced the crowd. With a sort of hypnotic reverence, they watched it bob and sway, clapping a set of broken hooves together like a fool at play.

Abel left the battery and snuck around the stage to watch their reactions, one especially. The angst and aches drained away once he saw her face, her eyes wide and beautiful lips opened just a little in awe of what was meant for her and her alone.

He couldn't enjoy the moment long.

Bing's voice slowed to a palsied pace. He looked in time to see some of the lights burst in a shower of sparks. One of the legs glowed red before a tongue of flame erupted from his creation's thigh, catching some of the pelt vest, too.

Abel took the coat off his shoulders and ran to his construction. He swatted at the fire until it was only embers. It sent out a thick smoke that had most of the crowd scattering. Through it all, the creation danced its few lumbering steps, grinning and watching the crowd with marble eyes. Once Abel got the fire out, he turned to face the people gathered there. Of all that had seen the curtain open, all but one backed away from the stage, clutching their noses and coughing.

Cleo Reilly stood apart from the crowd. She stared at the dancing figure as if entranced by it and its song. Abel took a step toward her, imagining all the things he would say. Fantasizing about how she'd be amazed at his dedication, embarrassed at the thought of him loving her for years, and touched by his grand electric gesture of love.

The closer he got to her, the less he could trace any of the grief that he'd seen in her for over a year. *It's all for you*, he wanted to say, and she would listen. She'd think it was sweet, and would to fall into his arms in front of the whole county, even in front of the remaining Wandmachers and all the people who thought he was a nobody. She'd fall into his arms and tell him he was her man.

Within a few steps of Cleo Reilly, Abel Verduzco opened his arms to accept her embrace, and she violently vomited onto his boots.

✕◊✕◊✕ ✕◊✕◊✕ ✕◊✕◊✕ ✕

# About the Author

South Texas author Mario E. Martinez has been featured in *Reflections, DVINO, Antesalas, The Laredo Morning Times, Nothing. No One. Nowhere., Turbulence Magazine, Collective Exile: A Literary Magazine, Deadman's Tome*, and in the *Along the River Vol.3, Robbed of Sleep Vol. 5*, and *Pulp Modern Vol. 2*. His fantasy novel, *Twin Burials*, and first short story collection, *San Casimiro, Texas*, were published by Author House. He recently published his second collection of short stories, *A Pig Named Orrenius & Other Strange Tales*.

# AFTER KURT

Adam Michael Nicks

B efore I tried to blow my brains out, like Kurt Cobain, I left a letter behind in one of my journals that was word for word what he'd written when he'd succeeded. The part that really spoke to me was: *The fact is, I can't fool any one of you. It simply isn't fair to you or me. The worst crime I can think of would be to rip people off by faking it and pretending as if I'm having 100% fun.* I made sure to underline that a few times so my mom and stepdad, Marc, would really get it for once, that these might as well have been my words, too.

But it didn't matter. The note got ruined from all the blood when I ran around with my jaw hanging off. What was left of my right cheek slapped against my collarbone as I tried to put myself back together.

The note started with: *Speaking from the tongue of an experienced simpleton who obviously would rather be an emasculated infantile complain-ee. This note should be pretty easy to understand.* That's genius. That's me. That's what Kurt was so good at—thinking of stuff I couldn't and saying it when I wouldn't.

My older brother showed me Nirvana with the song "Paper Cuts." It was before *Nevermind* and everybody discovered them. That grinding guitar and guttural scream sounded like Kurt was ripping out his soul for me. Sometimes I think I'm the only one who gets what he was trying to say—that there's no point in anything. So why bother? If Kurt Cobain can't survive in this world, what chance do I have? Do you have? Does anyone have? I didn't get it until he died.

Doctors said if my mom had come down just ten seconds later, I would have bled out. Lucky me. We were oh-so-lucky she was washing Marc's bowling shirts upstairs and heard the noise of the hunting rifle he kept on the mantle. Someone must've been looking out for me, the neighbors told us, that we just happened to live right down the street from a hospital. It was a blessing in disguise, local pastors added, that I was too much of a stoned screw-up to even kill myself right. Thank God, relatives phoned in to say, that all the bullet did was sever my vocal cords and force the surgeons to reconstruct my face like it was made out of Silly Putty.

I'm so lucky to be alive. Everyone tells me so. But I'd rather be dead.

If I had moved the muzzle over two centimeters, I would've hit something more vital. It's something to keep in mind for next time—but I didn't know anything could be more vital than your face. Just a little while ago I celebrated my seventeenth birthday half-asleep and handcuffed, bedridden in bandages with a catheter in my cock. When I woke up again, they told me they'd found all of my journals, and had gone through each and every page. The police did too, and they weren't happy with what they found, especially the "concerning lists" I'd made. Kurt Cobain kept journals his whole life. Every thought I'd ever had, every drawing I ever did, every single thing I ever knew was in my journals, which is why I'm in here.

This place is much worse than the actual hospital. Before, I could just lie there and pretend I was dead. Tubes and surgeries and morphine. Here, they want me to live. Counseling and medications and memories. But they don't seem to get that I don't belong in here either. *It's better to burn out than fade away.* That was in the note, too.

Dr. Thomas's official title is probably something lame, like Specialist of Obsessive Celebrity Disorders. He runs the study out of the southern wing of the facility and was doing it long before I ever got here. I hate him, but when he told me this morning at breakfast that I have a surprise coming, it actually made me kind of excited. I know it means he's finally going to let me out. The perfect surprise.

And when he does, I'm going to kill myself again.

They still make me sit around the circle like any other day and listen to the guys in group therapy, even though I can't talk. They thought all this would help. It hasn't. It won't. I've already seen how hollow things are. I made sure they knew this, especially after they took away my cassettes, because it makes me sick to think about my copy of *Bleach* gathering dust in Dr. Thomas's desk. When I get my tapes back, the first song I'm going to listen to is "Something in The Way" off *MTV Unplugged in New York*.

The wide-ruled spiral notebook they gave me to write in—and that I know they check when they put me back in my room, even though they think I don't know—I fill with little sketches of Dr. Thomas screwing different animals. Pigs. Cows. Pandas. T-Rexes. It helps keep me busy. I hope Dr. Thomas puts everything I draw in the book he's writing on us.

"Terry, why don't you start us off today?" Dr. Thomas says.

Terry's this big, 250-pound, former college scholarship linebacker, bodybuilder, professional wrestling fanatic—the type of guy the jocks from my school would've had a wet dream over if they saw him in the gym. He's practically a cartoon caveman with a crew cut above his sloping brow, a square jawline above his undefined neck, and cannon-sized arms with pin thin legs.

I don't think they even make a size in our standard-issue white cotton sweatpants and T-shirt uniforms to fit Terry's barrel chest. Mine are itchy and loose and slightly stained brown from where my face drips. Terry requested his sleeves be cut off at the shoulder so his biceps could breathe, and for some reason they did it.

"Well I just wanted to say, Dr. Tom, that I feel like I'm getting a lot better. And I was just thinking that I think it's time, if you think, that you let me have my wrestling magazines again so I can see what's happening." He stares at his thick, bright horizontal lines of scarring on the insides of his wrists—the only spots on his body where the veins don't break out. "What do you think?"

"I don't think that would be a very good idea." Dr. Thomas picks lint off his stupid pink sweater vest.

"But I could handle it better now. It's really because of all the good lessons and stuff you've been teaching me. It doesn't bother me at all. I know it's fake now." Terry gives a gap-toothed grin, but Dr. Thomas isn't convinced. When Kurt Cobain was in junior high, his dad signed him up for the school's wrestling team, but when he had to compete in tournaments, he'd just sit on the mat with his arms folded. I'd love to see what Terry would've done then.

Terry tried to kill himself because Hulk Hogan became a bad guy. During one of his many breakdowns when snot flew from his nose and he was huffing like he'd run a marathon, Terry whined about how all of his life he'd trained, said his prayers, and took his vitamins just like the Hulkster had instructed. Now he didn't know what to believe in anymore. Hulkamania had run wild and left him with the most pathetic identity crisis imaginable. If only every high school bully could have something like this happen. The Trevor Davicks, Wes Dwyers, Mitch Pellons, and Niko Bartells of the world.

"You-don't-under-stand," Terry gasped out a month earlier, during a group therapy session he'd hijacked. "When Macho Man Randy Savage was lying in the ring at *Bash at the Beach*, and he needed help…" Terry sniffed, slurped that back, then started slapping his own ears with his palms. "Hulk Hogan was his best friend. His best friend. And then he just…leg dropped him like he was nothing. How could he do that to Macho Man?"

Terry lost television privileges last Monday when he tried to switch the station to watch wrestling. We're only allowed PBS— *Sesame Street, Mister Rogers' Neighborhood,* and *The Joy of Painting* reruns.

"I just think it would help me get better if I saw what was happening to him, so I could understand everything better. Don't you think? Dr. Tom? It's just a few magazines. Pictures. Not even the real thing." Terry's heels rise out of his slippers like he's ready to spring, and one of the white-scrubbed orderlies standing in front of the door moves closer.

"Terry, I think something like that might give you a little setback. That's all. Let's talk about this again later. Why don't you tell the group something about your—"

But before Dr. Thomas even knows what's happening, Terry grabs the pencil from my hand and lunges. It's kind of a weird coincidence, because when he goes to stab Dr. Thomas, I happen to be drawing a picture of Dr. Thomas getting impaled with a unicorn penis.

Unfortunately, the orderlies snatch Terry before he can do damage, and they sit on his head while he cries.

I pick up my pencil from the cold, gray ceramic floor and get back to my drawing. Nobody pays any attention to Terry, frothing and spitting out the pills they try to make him swallow as they drag him out. This happens. Just the other day, the old black guy who claims he used to jam with Stevie Wonder, Parliament-Funkadelic, and James Brown had to be taken away because he wouldn't stop shouting that Elvis was a racist who'd raped his mother. He hasn't been allowed out of his room since.

When they let me go home, I'm going to get that little bit of weed hidden under my mattress. Marc always threatened to turn my bedroom into a home gym, but that would require Marc to stop drinking and get up off the couch, so I'm not too concerned. First thing I'll do when I get back is smoke, then put on *In Utero,* then kill myself.

"Why don't you share with us today, Cameron?" Dr. Thomas nods at the two new strong orderlies who have stepped in.

"Like what?" Cameron asks.

"How about you start with something small? How're you feeling today?"

"How do I feel? I feel angry. I feel upset. I feel frustrated at the crippling amount of stupidity and neglect you people have for my safety, for your safety, for the safety of the entire world. That's how I feel. I don't want to talk anymore unless you let me say what I want to say."

"Go ahead, Cameron. The floor is yours." I see Dr. Thomas look over to make sure the camera is still filming everything behind the one-way mirror. It is. It always is.

"In the year 2003, popular action movie star Arnold Schwarzenegger will be sworn in as the Governor of California and begin to rise in power and influence. He'll pass laws that'll forever change America by amending the Constitution to allow foreign-born citizens to run for president. He will then succeed in his 2016 campaign and take over the Oval Office. Due to escalating tensions in the Middle East, he initiates a preemptive nuclear strike, killing most of the world's population. Of course, he's one of the few to survive it all, because he's actually a cybernetic organism. He then leads his army of machines to destroy the remainder of mankind."

Dr. Thomas lets out a sigh and rubs his bushy mustache.

"Listen. Just listen to me. I know how this sounds. I know it sounds like *The Terminator*. But he did that on purpose. Those movies were made to throw people off the truth. It's what he wants."

Cameron's face is red, and he's trembling, but he knows if he gets overexcited, Dr. Thomas will just have the orderlies sit on his head like they did to Terry. "I know all this because I'm from the future— one possible future, from your points of view. I was sent back to stop him by a small fringe group of rebels who are trying to prevent this from ever happening. I volunteered because of my background training."

"You mean your military service? You were a marine, Cameron. Do you remember? You fought in Kuwait." Dr. Thomas points at his own balding head, but what he's really pointing at is the metal plate inside Cameron's skull that they put in after a mortar blew him up.

"I am a soldier, but I wasn't in Kuwait. I was with the One Thirty-Second under Perry from 2021 to 2027, then I was assigned to Recon-Security the last two years under Connor." Cameron's fingertips graze the little ditches and holes that never closed up right above his eyebrows. I have similar skin, but a lumpier face. Nobody really likes to look at me.

"Last year, that cyborg was in two films that further solidified not only his diversity as an actor, but boosted his popularity amongst the general public. *Jingle All the Way* captured hearts by playing up his sensitive side with an emphasis on strong familial themes and a solid working-class mentality. His other film, *Eraser*, reminded everyone of his strength and power as a manly, take-no-prisoners action hero that always gets the bad guys. These are all things he'll capitalize on during the election."

The only one in the room in a straightjacket, Zack, lets his yellow greasy hair drop in front of his face as he cracks up. His glasses slide forward on his nose, and he cocks his head back to get them fixed, revealing shiny spots of braces in an otherwise darkened mouth. But it doesn't deter Cameron.

"He did bodybuilding to perfect his physical form and then ventured into motion pictures to achieve worldwide notoriety and fame. He married into a trusted political family, the Kennedys. Haven't you ever wondered how he's never been able to stop talking in that weird accent? Technology can only evolve so far so fast, people. His rising superstardom will grow into the nightmare of tomorrow."

I overheard an orderly talking once, and they said the reason Cameron was admitted was because he tried to carry out his *mission* of killing Schwarzenegger by sneaking onto the set of *Junior* with a gun. One of Danny DeVito's security guards saw him and got him arrested. Due to his decorated military background, lawyers were able to swing an insanity plea. His wife still visits every week and brings their infant daughter, but he doesn't ever look the kid in the eye. It reminds me of my own dad.

Zack mutters something about a robotic governor coming to theaters near you this summer: *The Governator.* "I'll be back." Zack does his best-worst impression of Arnold and goes into hysterics. No one else laughs.

"Thank you for sharing, Cameron." Dr. Thomas clears his throat and looks into the sunken eyes of Chip, the former-child-star-turned-drug-addict-turned-attempted-murderer of his Hollywood director father. He was all the rage for a few weeks in the tabloids and is obviously Dr. Thomas's favorite. Whenever his dad comes to visit, all of the staff get real excited and ask for autographs, and I know that pisses Chip off. He wanted to give me a cigarette once to see if I could blow smoke out of the hole in my chin, but I didn't try, even after he offered me a hundred bucks.

Chip doesn't look like he wants to talk today, as he avoids Dr. Thomas' glance and traces an imaginary connect-the-dots line over the track marks of his forearm. Everyone wants to avoid another one of those self-important rants punctuated with Chip screaming *don't you know who I am?*

"Well, Zack." Dr. Thomas raises his stupid caterpillar eyebrows. He folds his hands on his lap and smiles like he's practicing for his

Barbara Walters interview. "Since you seem so eager to contribute to our discussion today, why don't you share how you're feeling?"

Zack rocks back and forth in his seat and twists at his hips with his shoulders arched high, making it look like he's giving himself the hug he never got as a child. Zack was arrested for stalking Tiffani Amber-Thiessen, star of *Saved by the Bell* and *Beverly Hills, 90210*. Rumor has it he actually broke into her house once and tied her up. They keep him in a straightjacket because if his hands are free, he strips naked and touches himself. At night he moans her name.

"Today, I don't know what it was that made me think of this one time, but I remembered that there was this one time, this time after the first restraining order, when I was following her in a store where she was trying on dresses, and I saw her adjust her bra strap after she came out of the dressing room and that just…" Zack extends his slippered feet all the way out in front of him and tries to rip his arms free.

Dr. Thomas is probably thinking that this is where the money is. This is why he takes notes and tapes us, so one day Oprah will have him on her show to cry over us poor troubled individuals with severe psychological disorders stemming from a nation where our culture is poisoned by the media. This is the crap Dr. Thomas dreams about spewing during the eventual press tours so everyone thinks he's so smart, and that his job is so thankless.

One time, during a private counseling session, he told me he understood where I was coming from with Kurt Cobain's death. He said he'd felt similar despair when John Lennon was assassinated because of how much Lennon meant to him. But it's not the same. Not even close.

Somebody killed John Lennon. Kurt Cobain killed himself. What does that mean? What does that say about the rest of the world, that the guy who had it all and was the voice of our Generation X, the guy who was supposed to lead all of us disenfranchised, depressed youth to salvation, took the first ticket out he could find? He must've known things would never get better, that they'd only get worse. Kurt's message was that we should kill ourselves. It was all over his music, deep in each and every song. He was talking directly to me, telling me to do it, to wake up and join him. Did John Lennon ever do that?

That day, I drew a picture of Dr. Thomas blowing John Lennon. Yoko Ono watched.

After Zack doesn't stop cackling like an asthmatic hyena for a solid minute, Dr. Thomas ends his stupid group therapy and lets us leave. Which is fine by me. Every second brings me closer to my surprise, where my mom can pick me up, and I can go home. I think what I'll actually do is lock myself up in my bedroom and listen to every single Nirvana song before I kill myself. A final sendoff. They probably won't leave Marc's hunting rifle out on the mantle again, so I'll have to get creative. Can a headphone cable hold my weight? Probably not, but that would be so perfect.

After a lukewarm liquid lunch blended just for me, we have art therapy. It's my favorite part of the day. I keep waiting for Dr. Thomas to give me my surprise. To tell me I'm free. To have me sign a stack of papers that'll throw away any privacy and confidentiality of my time spent here. I can hardly wait to give him the finger when I see this whole place fade into the distance.

With all of the money the hospital has in every other department, you can tell the funding for Dr. Thomas's little project got the shaft. Since we don't have much space in this side of the building, we stay cramped in the mess hall and wait for them to hand out supplies at the foldout tables. Orderlies pass out sheets of multicolored construction paper and boxes of broken and missing crayons like we're in kindergarten. I never use any of it; I just stick with my pencil and notebook.

I'm pretty good at drawing Kurt from memory. I always used to draw him during class at school, too. The journals they found in my room were filled with sketches. But in here, if there's one silver lining to take away from all this wasted time, I've really perfected my skills. I can draw Kurt's portrait doing just about anything.

Today, for my last day, I'm wondering what things would've been like if Kurt didn't kill himself. What would he look like in twenty years? So, I start to draw it. And it's kind of weird, adding wrinkles that weren't there to his face and some gray to his hair. Imagining what could've been. I even try to draw Courtney Love and Frances, his daughter.

"Is that your family?" Zack asks as he walks around the room. I scoot my chair away and keep going.

Where would they all be with Kurt alive? What will his daughter grow up to be with Kurt in the picture? I think they'd be in front of a big house or something, not a mansion; I don't think Kurt would be into that sort of thing. He'd do something reasonable. Grounded. Normal.

"Don't you usually draw Kurt Cobain?" Zack's too-loud nasally voice comes in over my shoulder again. I thought he'd gone across the room to bother Cameron, but he's actually listening this time when they said to leave him alone.

I hunch over and write on a blank page of the notebook that this *is* Kurt Cobain, and Courtney, and Frances. But Zack just scrunches up his nose and shakes his head. "No, that doesn't look anything like him." And with that he walks away.

Normally I don't care what any of the freaks here think about me or what I do, and maybe it's because I'm finally leaving today, but something about Zack's words stick with me. Every second I stare at my drawing, the more I think he's right. Something is definitely off. I can't put my finger on it. I did the usual shading and cross-hatching, like I'd learned to do in art class. My teachers always said drawing was the one thing I was good at, probably because it was the only thing I ever tried in.

Courtney looks good, and I'm taking a total guess with Frances since she's just a baby, but something about Kurt isn't right. His chin? His eyes? His nose? The lines on his face don't even look that out of place. He would've looked good as an older guy.

Across the room, Chip works with an intense, vacant focus on the yellow paper he covered with a blue and purple spiral by holding the two colors together. Cameron is at the same table, whispering and nodding with vigor. He's making a map, tracing a route. An orderly tries to stop Zack from eating a gold crayon he's chewing. I still can't figure out what's wrong with this picture, and it's driving me crazy, and I want to grab my notebook and rip it to shreds and crumble the bits in my hands and start it over from scratch, but there isn't much time left in art, and I have to figure out what's wrong so I don't make the same mistake again, but I can't.

I think about what Zack said first, asking me if this was my family, and that's when it hits me that I didn't draw something that looks like Kurt, I drew something that looks like me. Or what I used to look like. This is what I'd look like if I didn't kill myself. And this could've been my future wife and daughter. This is what we'd all look like together. If Kurt didn't kill himself, maybe I wouldn't have tried. Maybe things would've been different.

The thing that doesn't make this Kurt is the smile. I can see that now. It's wrong because he never smiled. Every photo I've ever seen of him has been with an uninterested grimace and spaced-out stare. Out of all of the drawings I've ever done, this is the only one I rip out and tear up when we're finished. I don't want Dr. Thomas to see this. I don't want anyone to see it.


In the same room as art therapy, they hand out the multicolored medications—vitamins, they tell us—and we're allowed to sit at the tables playing cards and listening to classical music.

I think a lot about how I'm going to die. I always have. When Kurt was a kid, he loved to mess around with a Super 8 video camera and do home movies. One of them showed him pretending to commit suicide. I look at the dull tip of my pencil and dream about how much force it'd take to really stab myself with it, somewhere like the heart.

A nurse puts down a cup of electric blue liquid next to me. I can't take pills or chew solids anymore; everything needs to be a soup or paste. I shake my head and hold up my hand, but it doesn't work, she doesn't get that I'm leaving, so I drink it anyway. It won't matter, and I guess it's the last time I have to do it before my surprise, and I go home. It still hurts to swallow.

Zack runs up to a heavyset nurse wearing rubber gloves who puts his pills right into his mouth. He licks her fingers as she takes them away, then sits at one of the tables on the other side of the room and tries to grind against one of the legs.

Chip takes his cup full of goodies over to one of the barred windows. He looks out, not at the busy street but directly into the sun. He doesn't blink. The nurse makes sure he's taken them all, and he tells her he's never skipped out on taking a pill a day in his life. She makes him stick out his tongue just to be sure. He's not lying.

When I listened to Chip, that time he tried to give me a cigarette, he told me he didn't see what the big deal was about his dad. He ran his fingers through his hair, and I thought about how on the show he used to be on as a kid, his hair was really big—tall on top. That was his thing. Now it's shorter, thinner, but I guess it was a long time ago.

Chip talked for hours about how his dad forced him into show business, wanted him to grow up and be a big star like him, and win awards. I remember his show had a crossover episode with *The Monkees.* My mom let me stay up to watch the rerun one night after Marc held me down and put his cigarette out on my forehead. It was after my brother had left the house for good, so he wasn't there to protect me.

I like to sit at my own table. I don't like other people to talk to me. After the medication, most just shuffle around and mutter to themselves or to everybody all at once.

"Soldier," Cameron says, standing over me with stiff posture, hands linked behind his back. "I know you're not like the others. You're like me." But I'm not like him. I'm not like anybody else in here. That's why I'm going home. My surprise is probably the worst kept secret in here by now; I'm sure everyone knows.

He sits down. "That's why I'm coming to you to let you know of my plan. We both don't belong in here with these crazies, right? We can trick Dr. Thomas, we can fool all of them, and we can get out of here and complete the mission."

But his mission is different from mine. Cameron wants to put a bullet in Arnold's brain, and I only want to put one in my own. The only thing we have in common is that we'd do anything to get it done.

"We've been here long enough. We know what they want to hear. It doesn't matter if it's true. Just don't be like Terry and drop the act. I went to him first, but he's never getting out. No self-control."

I don't look up from my drawing of Dr. Thomas getting anally probed by Martians. A nurse taps Cameron on his shoulder and makes him back up. I add a little speech bubble to Dr. Thomas's stupid mouth, saying: "I love ABBA!" He probably does.

Cameron waits until the nurse walks away before he speaks. "Hey, that's pretty good, actually. Is that supposed to be Dr. Thomas?" He laughs and refocuses. "I'm going to escape when they least expect it. Do you know how?" I don't stop drawing or listening. "My intel"—his wife who can only get him to talk to her if she feeds him information about Schwarzenegger— "told me that you-know-who is filming a new movie right now. *Batman & Robin*. He's playing a villain: Mr. Freeze. Bold choice for him at this stage of his career; he must be getting overconfident in his public perception if he's willing to paint himself in a negative way. Shows range and vulnerability. Not good. Not good at all."

The nurse comes back, and Cameron covers his lips. "I'll sneak to your room and say the secret phrase: *come with me if you want to live*. That's how you'll know it's me." The speaker in the corner of the ceiling lets out a static squawk paging someone on another floor. "The machines are listening," Cameron says, bolting across the room to a table with a deck of cards. In an attempt to not seem suspicious, he picks up twelve at random and holds them over his face like a mask. His eyes peek over the top, locked on me.

I write a message for him on a new sheet of paper, outlining my words so he can see it perfectly clear from far away: *I'm getting out today*. His shoulders droop in defeat. I hate being locked up with these psychos, but I hate being out in the world with all the other ones even more. I can't wait to get my surprise, so I can go home and meet Kurt.

Just as everybody starts to get quiet and sleepy, they move us to our beds. The vitamins are kicking in. When Kurt was a kid, they made him get on a Ritalin prescription because of his inability to pay attention in school. A nurse tells me Dr. Thomas wants to speak with me. It's about my surprise. This is it. I'm finally getting out. I'm finally going home. I'm finally going to be dead. Finally.

I wonder if my mom's here yet. She's never come to this hospital. She used to come to the other one, especially right after she brought me in, but Marc doesn't let her see me. She said she doesn't like the way I am now. It upsets her.

I thought my brother would get word of what happened and visit, but he's probably just really busy in Seattle trying to hit it big. Trying to be the next Kurt Cobain. I have him to thank for showing me Nirvana, for changing everything, for showing me a way out. My Walkman and all of my cassette tapes are actually his. I wonder if he'll take them back when I'm dead.

Dr. Thomas has that stupid smile on his face, the one that makes me want to just flip everything off his cluttered desk. All of the papers and folders and files and plants and Beanie Babies and everything else he thinks make up his stupid, hollow, plastic life. "How are you feeling?" he asks.

I get the urge to take my whole notebook and shove it down his throat until the orderlies have to come into the tiny office and shoot me. But instead, I write down: *good.*

"And you're not having any pain?" He motions with a hairy knuckle to his cheek, his jaw, his throat, all of the places I don't really have anymore. "What with the…?"

I shake my head. Inside, I'm imagining how I'd pick up his mug of coffee and smash it over his face. Slit my wrists with the steaming shards that say *World's Best Therapist* and slice my jugular for good measure. Put that in your book. I could probably move fast enough to find my cassettes in the drawers before I bleed out. I'm guessing I could listen to two songs before the orderlies break in through the barricaded, locked door. But which songs do I pick?

"Good." He rearranges some papers, glancing down at a cardboard box sitting on his lap. "So you've been here for a long time, and I think with our one-on-one consultations we've been making some real progress." I look around to see if my mom's hiding in a corner or something, but they probably don't let people come back this far into the building. "That's why I called you in: to discuss your future here. I've got a surprise for you."

*I don't have a future here.* I start to write this down but then remember what Cameron said. I don't want anyone to think I'm being overdramatic and ruin my chances of getting out. The mission. So I scratch that out and jot down instead: *Where's my mom?*

"Your mother?" He looks out the window for a second, turns back to face me. Over his shoulder, on the street, I don't see her purple-brown Dodge Caravan with the wood paneling siding splitting it in two. It's the one I stained the inside of when I was a kid and threw up in the back of after eating McDonald's. It's the one that I stained the inside of when she picked me up and threw me in the back to take me to the hospital with my face hanging off. "I imagine she's at home, or uh, we could always contact her to make arrangements for her to visit you? I didn't know you wanted to see her. That's good, though."

My brother must be the one coming to get me. He probably wants his Nirvana tapes back. I can stay with him in Seattle, far away. I write his name in the notebook.

"You want us to contact your brother, too?"

Oh God, it must be Marc.

"Marc, your stepfather? I can fill out the forms today to have your family come and visit. I'll get right on it."

My surprise. Today is the day I'm supposed to leave. I'm supposed to get my tapes back and listen to every song. I'm supposed to go home and kill myself. I'm supposed to meet Kurt.

Dr. Thomas looks at the box he's hiding under the desk. "Well, I was thinking things could be easier for everybody around here, for you especially, if we got you something…" he fumbles with opening it and packaging peanuts spill out under the desk. I'm still waiting for my brother to jump out and reveal the joke is over. My surprise. Nothing makes any sense. Surprise. It never has.

"This"—with the gusto of a game show host, he pulls out what looks like a microphone—"is an electrolarynx, or a mechanical larynx. It's like a digital voice box; you just hold it up to your, uh, your chin, I guess, and you move your, uh"—he demonstrates—

"*your mouth to make words and it speaks them for you.*" That stupid smile comes back at hearing the voice. My new voice. My surprise.

"Cool, huh? Top of the line. I thought you'd enjoy being able to talk again. This way you can communicate with some of the other patients, make friends, contribute to our group sessions, and not have to write everything down in that notebook all the time."

I write in my notebook: *I'm better. I can go home now. The bad thoughts have stopped. I don't need that thing. I don't have anything to say.*

He gets up from his chair and puts the thing under the little ledge of my jaw that's left, and he tells me to move my mouth. He says he's not sure if it'll work, but it's worth a try. It hurts to open my mouth, but I feel like I have to so I can scream. The voice box makes a clunky, unnatural stretch of noise while I cry.

"I'm just trying to help you," Dr. Thomas says.

Before they drag me back to my room, Dr. Thomas confiscates my notebook and pencil. "You don't need this anymore. And after today's incident with Terry, this is really for the safety of everyone."

I let my mouth flap like a fish gasping on land and ask for my cassettes back. It's the first sentence I've said in I don't know how long. My voice is that of a throat cancer survivor, of an alien invader, of Dr. Thomas and his stupid smile. It makes me feel like my skin is being stripped off.

"Oh, I don't think that would be a good idea. Something like that might give you a little setback. Let's talk about that later."

It's almost exactly what he said to Terry when he asked for his wrestling magazines earlier in the day. But I'm not like him. I should be going home. Someone like Terry is never getting out.

"I think Terry has something he'd like to say." Dr. Thomas folds his arms over his stupid purple sweater vest.

Terry shifts in his seat and the shackles around his ankles that are connected to the handcuffs over his massive scarred wrists clink. "I'm sorry for my actions yesterday. It was wrong to try and attack Dr. Thomas. I'm sorry I interrupted everything and acted selfish. I realize now that a lot of what I do is selfish, and I'm going to try and work on that in the future." He looks in my general direction. "And I'm sorry I took your pencil."

"Thank you." Dr. Thomas nods. "Now I'm sure some of you have noticed that someone here is looking a little different, and I think it would be very special for us if he shared for the first time today." Everyone looks at me. But they don't look at me; they look at the microphone-shaped device in my palm and avert their eyes when I bring it up to my throat. Zack shudders.

It takes me a long time to think of something to say, but no one will talk again until I do. I remember what Cameron said about getting out. Fooling them. Telling them what they want to hear. Then we can escape and complete our missions. I try to wink at him, but since I only have one eye, it doesn't work. He doesn't notice. He cowers in fear. I guess in his mind I've become assimilated with the machines, a lost ally.

"*I have it good, very good, and I'm grateful, but since the age of seven, I've become hateful towards all humans in general. Only because it seems so easy for people to get along and have empathy. Only because I love and feel sorry for people too much, I guess.*" Everyone is looking at me now. Really looking at me.

"*I must be one of those narcissists who only appreciates things when they're gone. I'm too sensitive,*" my robotic voice drones. "*I need to be slightly numb in order to regain the enthusiasms I once had as a child.*"

Everyone is quiet. They watch like they want more, but I lower the electrolarynx and start crying pus tears. Dr. Thomas seems impressed, like this is a breakthrough. He smiles his stupid smile.

That was all just another part from Kurt's suicide note.

From my suicide note.


## About the Author

Adam Michael Nicks is a Pushcart Prize nominated writer and the recipient of the 2017 Leonard Trawick Award. He is currently finishing his MFA and his work has appeared in *Typehouse-Ink, Crack the Spine, Five on the Fifth, Dual Coast Magazine,* and *ReCap.*

# THE BEE FARMER

Todd Zack

"Mornin', Blood Bag," the Bee Farmer said, swinging open the big barn doors and stepping through. It was an early Indiana morning, midsummer, and the sunlight falling through the barn's disheveled interior colored all the haphazard piles of hay a rosily tinted tangerine. "Gotcher breakfast."

Blood Bag rolled over on his hay bed and wiped sleep from his eyes with one thickly knuckled hand. Warily, he watched the man approach holding his bucket full of breakfast. Blood Bag's stomach clenched. The sight of the bucket, as always, quickly made him hungry.

The Bee Farmer sauntered across the barn with a slight limp and took a seat facing Blood Bag's bed. He placed the bucket between his knees, reached into its depths, and dug out the food as Blood Bag scrambled forward through the hay. The Bee Farmer placed the goodies, one at a time, on the floor between them: cold chicken leg, raw honeycomb, a mason jar filled with milk. The breakfast on display, the Bee Farmer leaned back in his dark mahogany rocking chair and began to rock.

He was a tall man, long shinned and armed, naturally stooped in his upper body. His physique was such that when he sat, his knees came way up, mid chest, almost to the buttons of his overalls. With such an awkward display of limbs, the Bee Farmer appeared halfway transformed into a praying mantis when he took to rocking in his chair.

Blood Bag carefully looked over his breakfast, then turned his eyes up quizzically; something was amiss. There wasn't enough food. His favorite food was there, yes, but it wasn't *all* there.

The Bee Farmer returned Blood Bag's stare. "What? Yer chicken? Det's what ya git today. Et it up, or I'll et it up m'self." The Bee Farmer feigned toward the chicken leg, and Blood Bag nearly jumped out of his overalls to take possession of the leg for himself. Falling back upon his hay bed, Blood Bag gnashed through the prize with his crooked, rotted teeth, stripping the meat from the bone.

The Bee Farmer chuckled.

Blood Bag continued on to the honeycomb, eating it more carefully than the chicken; the comb could prove messy if he went too fast. He could lose some it into the hay, and if that happened, the hay would stick to him at night and wake him up, itching. So he ate in measured fashion, crushing waxy sections of the comb into his mouth, then expertly sealing the remnants with his tongue. In this way he consumed the syrupy honeycomb, chunk by delectable chunk, without waste. Chicken was the best, but honeycomb was almost as good, and then milk, that was always very good too—almost as good as the honeycomb.

"We can't have yer belly get too full," the Bee Farmer said. He pulled at one earlobe, stretching it thoughtfully, like a piece of putty. "T'day's the day." He pursed his lips, studying the boy. "Yer eight-teen t'day, Blood Bag. All grown up, yep?" The Bee Farmer slapped his own knees like a pair of bongos. "T'day's the day we been waitin' fer. T'day's the day."

Blood Bag had finished his milk with a contented smile, a thin milk mustache atop the rim of his thick upper lip.

The Bee Farmer rose and collected the empty milk jar and chicken bone, placing them in the bucket they'd arrived in. He walked toward the open doors, bucket held down by his knee. "Happy birthday to ya, Blood Bag," the Bee Farmer said. "I'll be back in a li'l bit." He swept the barn doors shut behind him, dropping the heavy lock in place.

Inside, the barn darkened.

Blood Bag stood. From one side of the barn, the morning light fell through a pair of cracks in the wood. He traveled clumsily to the cracks. One was larger than the other; Blood Bag chose this one to look through. He placed his forehead against the wall, focused one eye into the brightness, and, piece by piece, the world outside took form.

The Bee Farmer walked out into a field, holding his food bucket, the air stirring about him. Eventually he stopped, stooping before a wooden box about half his own height. The Bee Farmer lifted the lid, and a strange cloud gathered around him, shifting shape relentlessly as he reached down into the box. Blood Bag was delighted—the Bee Farmer was collecting more of his second favorite food! He licked his lips, watching attentively as the tall man placed a chunk of the sweet tasty stuff into the bucket, closed the lid, and began walking back toward the barn. Behind the Bee Farmer, the dark swirling air quieted. Blood Bag remembered his breakfast: his favorite food had been very small today. Maybe the Bee Farmer would make it up to him?

The farmer stepped out of the field and into the barnyard dirt, holding his freshly filled bucket, and continued walking by the barn; in a moment, he had disappeared from sight.

Blood Bag moaned softly, pulling his head away from the wall. Slowly, he shuffled across the barn floor and returned to bed.

Later that same day, the Bee Farmer returned.

He pushed open the barn doors, making quite a clamor. He was encumbered with important, homemade-looking medical equipment atop a makeshift gurney. Carefully, he pushed the wheeled equipment off the dirt path and up a notch, onto the cement floor of the barn.

Blood Bag looked up curiously as the man propelled the strange instruments across the hay-strewn floor. The Bee Farmer rolled his fancy equipment up next to Blood Bag's bed and, setting it there, wandered off crookedly to a far corner of the barn. Blood Bag sat on his haunches and watched the tall man rummage around in the shadows.

The Bee Farmer returned, noisily dragging a potato crate he set between the rocking chair and the hay bed. For some time he maneuvered the medical equipment, turning it this way and that, stopping for a moment to appraise its position, then turning it around some more. Finally satisfied with the equipment's location, he reached beneath the gurney and procured an electrical cord. Forked end in hand, he carried the long black cord across the barn floor and plugged it into a small generator atop a tool shelf blackened with oil stains and coated with a fine fur of hay dust. The Bee Farmer gave a satisfied nod and returned to the operating stage, Blood Bag's bed. He folded himself, like origami, down into his rocking chair, and with his sharp bony knees pulled up to his chest, began rocking slowly, rhythmically. The Bee Farmer tugged at one loose fleshy earlobe and set a serious eye on Blood Bag, at last addressing his prisoner with a sharp tongue. "You maht be a feckin' tart, but yer a healthy sum bitch."

Blood Bag stared.

The Bee Farmer, smiling, continued. "I got dis disease, Blood Bag, long time now. Blood disease, feckin' doctors say it's gonna kill me." The Bee Farmer tapped a tattoo upon the floor with his long skinny foot. "But I been lookin' into it, gitdimmit, and I find out what ta do. See, I'ma gonna take yer blood"—the Bee Farmer pointed at the plugged-in machinery, shining in the afternoon light—"and I'ma gonna give ya mine."

Blood Bag stared at the ominous machinery and rustled his legs in the hay.

The Bee Farmer nodded at Blood Bag's apprehension. "It aint gon hurt much. Yer a tough sum bitch, aintcha?"

Blood Bag sneezed. He scratched at his nostrils with a swollen finger, looking absently down at the hay-strewn floor.

"When it's over…Blood Bag, look at me…'n when it's over, I'ma gon git choo a whole big chicken, boy." The Bee Farmer held up his hands and mimed, in the air between them, a shape the size of a fat bird. "A whole big 'un!"

Blood Bag looked up. His eyes brightened. He knew that word: chicken. The man was talking about his favorite food!

"That's raht, a whole git dang chicken, Blood Bag, heh! You hear me?"

Blood Bag climbed to his feet and stood watching the tall man expectantly.

"That's raht. Now you set yerself down here on this crate." The Bee Farmer gestured toward the potato crate. "Set down here if you went yer chicken."

Blood Bag hesitated, then took a step forward.

"Set down, Blood Bag. Raht here." The Bee Farmer grabbed a fistful of Blood Bag's jeans and turned the boy around, backing him into the crate. As the crate caught the back of Blood Bag's knees, a sharp tug pulled him down. Blood Bag sat. The potato crate creaked. The tall man smiled.

The Bee Farmer stood up from his rocking chair, approached his machinery, and got to work. He took up a hypodermic needle, eight inches long, a tiny eye enshrined within its daggered point, the silver needle gleaming bright as a lure in the dusty tangerine sunlight. "N' this goes inna this," the Bee Farmer said, half to Blood Bag, half to himself, as he procured a clear length of tubing and delicately affixed one end to the bottom of the needle. "Then we git this thing." He dragged forward a metal pole, not unlike a coat rack, from which a large plastic bag hung suspended. Here, Blood Bag noticed the same clear tube attached to the needle also ran up into the big plastic bag. More equipment came forth, selected one item at a time from the shelved center of the mobile gurney—a tiny TV set, a radio, a miniature bicycle pump—curious things. The Bee Farmer fiddled earnestly with each object, building a kind of crude Lego tower on the floor by Blood Bag's feet. The man dropped to his knees and went about plugging things in and flicking little switches back and forth. He looked over his shoulder, his mouth lopsided in concentration. "I know what I'm doin', Blood Bag; don't git impatient."

Blood Bag sighed. His chicken was nowhere to be seen.

At last, The Bee Farmer stood. He took a step back, hands on hips, and admired his work. "That oughta do it!"

The Bee Farmer turned his attention to the boy, holding the hypodermic needle in one hand, like a conductor's baton. "Hold out yer arm, Blood Bag. It ain't gonna hurt much, but ya gotta stay still. Wir gonna take turns. It's gonna take some time." As the Bee Farmer pushed the needle into the crook of Blood Bag's arm, the boy sniffled. The man bent down and, somewhere, flicked a switch. An effortful whirling sound, like a carpet vacuum, commenced. The needle in Blood Bag's arm began vibrating softly. Blood Bag watched as the clean translucent tube stretched beside his arm jumped once and flooded red. Above his head, the plastic bag rumbled to life and began to fill, slow and deliberate as a thermometer on a warming day.

"Workin' fer yer chicken," the Bee Farmer said, dreamily. "Workin' fer yer chicken, ain't ya now, Blood Bag?"

Blood Bag woke to the distant twittering of morning birds and a dim blue light leaking through the walls of the barn. He rolled over in his hay bed and suddenly his left arm pained him. Placing the arm close to his eyes, he studied it. His arm had turned a funny color, like one big bruise, and this was odd, but already the pain was receding, and it wasn't very difficult for Blood Bag to put the issue out of mind. As he sat up, his foot crunched something; a maze of chicken bones spread before him on the floor. Now Blood Bag felt sick to his stomach. His head hurt too. His head hurt *badly*. There was a strange stink in the air, unlike anything he'd smelled before.

Something was wrong.

Blood Bag tried to stand; his body went numb from the legs up. It was like a body part falling asleep, but Blood Bag's *entire body* was falling asleep. Abruptly his vision blurred, dimmed, then erupted in a bright white blaze. Feeling suddenly light as a feather, Blood Bag swooned and fell backward into his hay bed, collapsing in an unconscious heap.

When Blood Bag again awoke, the barn was brighter. He sat up carefully this time, and gradually made his way to his feet. Again, his head hurt, but the knot of pain loosened as he stood there quietly breathing. Blood Bag's mouth was dry, his stomach sour. His legs, however, remained safely set beneath him. Blood Bag was thirsty; very thirsty. He desperately wanted a jar of cold milk.

When would the Bee Farmer bring breakfast?

Blood Bag made his way across the barn floor, toward the two cracks in the wall, reaching them after a few queasy pauses. He placed his forehead upon the wall, lined up an eye, and peered out into the world.

The Bee Farmer, bucket in hand, moved across the morning field in the direction of the barn. The air swirled wildly about him, and he waved one long arm above his head, moving through the tall tan grass quicker than Blood Bag had ever seen before.

Blood Bag smiled, returning to his hay bed, anticipating his cold jar of milk.

Breakfast was coming!

The barn doors opened and the Bee Farmer hurried inside, still waving distractedly at the air. "Git dang bees 'er all o'er me today! What's wrong with doz bastards?"

It was almost as if they could *smell* something on him.

He saw Blood Bag. "Ya still alive, boy? Git dang, ya are a tough sum bitch, aintcha?" He found his rocking chair, sat, and began pulling Blood Bag's breakfast out of the bucket. "Figured ya had 'bout 'nuff chicken last night, so I got'cha extra honey from dem feckin' bees. Extra milk too."

Blood Bag pulled himself through the hay and went for the milk first.

"Thirsty, huh? Yep. I was too. Got a headache, I bet." The Bee Farmer looked around at yesterday's operating area; there was a tremendous amount of blood splashed across the floor. "What a git dang mess!" The Bee Farmer complained. "Blood all o'er the feckin' place!"

Blood Bag finished his first jar of milk, placed it down in the hay, and immediately began the second, drinking it down with both hands.

The Bee Farmer came out of his rocking chair, a flurry of angular limbs. "Looks like murder, git dangit! Where'd I put dat silvent?"

Blood Bag watched over the rim of his upturned milk jar as the farmer moved limply across the barn, looking for something. He turned in a circle, started one way then another, a contemplative hand to his chin. Finally, he appeared to figure out which way to go. Chin up, he began walking forward—then suddenly stopped.

The Bee Farmer felt his breath leaving him as his lungs shrank like two salted slugs within his chest. Looking down at his long white arms with perplexity, he saw they were covered in red welts, the size and shape of dimes. The welts continued to rise like tiny balloons from the skin as he watched. Suddenly his face and neck itched something terrible. Putting one and two together, the Bee Farmer concluded he must be covered with these crazy welts from head to foot! As soon as this thought occurred to him, his feet began to itch. What was this? Was he having an allergic reaction? To what? Bee stings? That was impossible! He'd been stung a thousand times before! The Bee Farmer tried to shout, to draw attention. His throat, however, had sealed on him. All he managed was a pathetic squeak, like a mouse in a trap. Already his vision dimmed as he suffocated.

Blood Bag set his second empty milk jar down in the hay between his feet. Looking up he saw the Bee Farmer approaching with long deliberate steps, like a signaling bug, and tapping his chest with one nervous hand. His eyes were big and glassy and his face was covered with red marks, like a terrible rash. He moved his lips in the manner of making words, but no words came out. Blood Bag watched as the tapping hand came off the chest and reached up to his neck, squeezing and pulling at his own throat. Blood Bag wondered what he was trying to say.

The Bee Farmer collapsed like a tower, face-first onto the floor. A grainy cloud of yellow dust and straw popped up in the air around him, a few stray pieces of hay landing atop his back. A foot twitched awkwardly for a few moments, then an elbow. And then the Bee Farmer was silent, motionless.

Blood Bag sat on his hay bed and stared at the man for a long time.

Eventually Blood Bag made his way out of the barn—something the Bee Farmer had told him never to do—but the farmer was now... what? Blood Bag thought about it. He realized the tall man wasn't going to punish him anymore for anything, so he stepped outside into the sunlight.

The sun was good, warm, and the air smelled different out here. The air smelled pretty. Blood Bag looked up at the sky and the clouds. *Clouds.* He remembered that word now. It was a happy word. Everything was so bright out here, outside of the barn. Blood Bag turned slow circles in the dirt, face lifted to the sky, taking everything in, the bright sights and the pretty smells. He felt very good inside himself.

In time, Blood Bag began walking slowly away from the barn, following a dirt pathway along and up a little hill. As he moved along the path, he saw grass appear along its sides: green grass, and flowers, too. The flowers were all different colors. He remembered flowers, how pretty they were, how nice they smelled. Many things were coming back to Blood Bag now, words like *clouds* and *flowers*, familiar sights and smells, the feel of raw sunlight on his skin, and more.

That house up ahead. Blood Bag remembered the word, *house* and what it meant to him. He remembered *that* house right there, up at the end of the path.

Blood Bag quickened his pace, ignoring his still aching head.

When he reached the house, the door was open just a crack. He entered and lumbered up a familiar staircase. Reaching the first door, he looked in.

Blood Bag's mother sat in her wheelchair beside the window. She wore a loose gray gown and slippers, and had a book spread open in her lap. Slowly, she looked up from her book to see her son, for the first time in five years, standing there in the doorframe like a living dream. Her eyes filled with tears and her mouth quivered. For a long time mother and son stared at each other. Then the woman whispered, "Alex?" and opened her arms.

The spell of disbelief was broken, and the boy went to her. He fell to his knees before the wheelchair and gathered his mother, more frail than he remembered, into his arms. Together they cried.

Alex's mother spoke to him, her precious voice found beside his ear. "They told me you'd drowned, baby. They told me you was dead. I knew you was alive, baby. I knew you'd come home."

Alex ran his mother's hair through his hands like fine silk. He smelled her mommy smell, drawing it into him like a perfect medicine. His mother's tiny hands stroked his back, delicately brushing the sides of his face. They cuddled like this for a long time, without speaking. Eventually Alex leaned back and gazed into his mother's eyes, smiling.

Mother wiped the tears from her eyes, then from her son's, scooping them out from the furrows that had appeared in his now prematurely aged visage. "Baby, baby, what happened to you? God, if you could only tell me." Alex's mother peered curiously over her son's shoulder. "Where's your daddy, baby?" she asked him carefully. "Have you seen your daddy yet? Has he seen you?"

XXXX XXXX XXXX X

# About the Author

Todd Zack is a delivery driver, writer and musician living in southwest Florida. His alternative rock band, Tape Recorder 3, composes soundtracks for independent films and documentaries—most recently, the skateboard documentary *No Hope Kids* (2016). His journalism and fiction pieces have been published in *Thrasher Magazine*, *The Bad Times Newsletter*, *Jersey Devil Press* and *Crimson Streets*.

# LISTEN HARD

## Lynden Wade

"She won't listen," Daniel scoffed.

William, his brother, looked up from buttoning his waistcoat. "What do you mean?"

"Look at you, William! Proper scarecrow, you are. Shirt untucked and your shoelaces trailing."

"I have to try," his brother said, attempting to wave his arms around and shove his shirttails into his trousers at the same time. "I've thought about it for months now. It's spring, and the blackbird says it's time for wooing."

Daniel curled his lip. "What will a country girl like Annie want with fine words? She wants a provider, not a poet. Someone who can plow a field or build a cottage."

William laughed and bounded out the door of their tumbledown, two-room home, narrowly missing being hit by a passing donkey cart. He reached the pond where the workhorses drank and took a moment to look anxiously at his reflection. Raking with his fingers did nothing to flatten his straw-blond hair: nineteen years of experience told him that it would always stick out. All he could do was straighten his jacket and brush some dust off his necktie. His clothes were worn but clean—not bad for two brothers who had barely reached manhood with no living relatives to wash and mend for them.

Annie was in her mother's little garden, hanging out the washing. She looked up as William waved to her across the pond.

"Have you no work to do, William?" She frowned as if to scold, but it only charmed him more. Annie, with her pale skin, straight hair, and sandy eyelashes, was not generally considered the village beauty. To William, however, everything about her was enticing, and one of her rare smiles made his day.

"Soon, soon," William assured her. "Growing season is here. Farmer Prentice will be wanting help on the land very soon. What you mean is, why do I pass here every day?"

"Why do either of you pass here every day? It's either you or Daniel."

William paused, surprised. Daniel had never mentioned that he visited Annie or her mother. Still, it was a free country, wasn't it? "I want you to walk out with me. Will you, Annie? Will you? You're the prettiest girl in the village!"

Annie tilted her head. "You're the only one who thinks that. My mother says all men are liars."

"All!"

"My father certainly was; he said he'd never leave us, and he did."

"Come on, Annie. You've known me all my life. I'm not a liar." He felt his hope running aground.

"The washing needs hanging first," she said. "It will be faster if you give me a hand—seeing as you have nothing better to do." Her tone was tart, but she hadn't said no.

William took this as assent, and felt his hope set out to sea again, sails unfurling, flags flying. He grabbed a handful of pegs and a wet sheet, then set to the task with more enthusiasm than skill. She tutted and re-pegged most of his efforts while he darted between the flapping sheets and tried to steal a kiss. Somehow, without ever looking, she would step aside just as he made a fresh attempt, then slip him a sidelong look with a glimmer of a smile. Then they strolled out on the common. It was not private, but it was less busy than the village streets. A child watched over a grazing cow here, while a tethered pony cropped the clumpy grass.

"The roses will be out when we next come," he said, gesturing at the briars.

"What makes you so sure we will be walking out again?" she demanded.

"A little bird told me."

"Tush!"

"It's true! Look, he's flying over there right now. A linnet. Listen and he'll sing again."

She laughed. "You understand birds?"

"And the grass. And the wind. When they have a message for me."

She tilted her head and lifted an eyebrow. "And what does the cow say?"

"She says the flies are troubling her."

Annie snorted and leaned her cheek on his arm. He gazed down at the dear head, then very lightly brushed it with his lips.

⁓ ⁓ ** ⁓ ⁓

The next day Annie was surprised to see not William but Daniel looking over her fence.

"Annie," he said, "I know my brother asked you to walk out with him. But I adore you! Won't you give me a chance?"

Annie frowned. She had been considering what the linnet had said, that she would walk out with William again, but Daniel's eyes pleaded.

"Just one walk," he said. "How will you know if William is the one for you if you don't try me out? I swear to heaven I adore you as much as he does, if not more!"

His intensity disturbed her. She thought that William wore his love on his sleeve, but Daniel's was packed, like gunpowder, into the chamber of his heart, just behind his eyes. She agreed she would come out with him as soon as she had put out the latest batch of washing. Daniel pegged out sheets beside her. He was so much tidier than his brother that she didn't need to rehang anything, and the job was done twice as fast. She stole a look at him several times as they took the path round the back of the houses. Daniel's dark hair was smooth as a gentleman's. He talked not of birds and wind but of what he wanted to do. He wished he could buy a cottage for the two of them, with land for a cow and some pigs, and money for a new gown for her for Sundays. He was good with words in his own way but he did not make her laugh.

When they got back to her mother's cottage, she said, "Daniel, you have fine dreams, and you speak very well, but I don't think I will make you happy. I'm sorry."

His shoulders slumped. She was glad she'd not named the man she preferred.

The bird was right. Annie did walk out with William again. The next time they met was on a Sunday, for work had begun again on the land. William and Daniel were silently relieved that the hunger days were over for another few months. The winter had been got through with poaching and tightening of belts. But by the summer, they were working from the first glimmer of light to the last, and William had enough money to ask Annie another question as they walked on the common.

"I'll never be a rich man, Annie," he said, stopping under an old oak tree. "But with you, I'll be a very happy man, and I'll do all I can to make you happy too."

"You do make me happy," Annie said, "and I will marry you."

He threw his arms around her and spun her, then kissed her 'til she couldn't breathe.

"Ah, the oaks told me today was a good day!"

Annie laughed. "And what about that crow there on that tussock? What does he say?"

The crow flapped away with a harsh caw. William leaned and whispered in her ear with an impish smile. Her cheeks went pink, and she pulled back, giving him a harmless slap on the arm. "He does not, you wicked man!"

But they fell to kissing again. In a while, they nudged each other to the edge of the common, where they pulled apart, took hands, and disappeared into the woods. The girl guarding the cow gave them barely a glance; that was where most courting couples went, sooner or later.

The common was disappearing, the last of many up and down the country; the land where the villagers could graze their animals and collect firewood had been claimed by the landowners and shared out between them. At least this made work for laborers like the two brothers, digging ditches and putting up fences, turning the grazing land into a field for crops. William lingered as the others picked up their shovels and trudged home; Daniel, eager for a drink and a rest, wondered why his brother was delaying.

"There's going to be a change soon," William started. "Another change, I mean."

Daniel glanced up from wiping his blade clean. "What's that?"

"To me. To my state. I mean to marry. I asked Annie yesterday, and she said yes. We mean to marry just after Christmas."

Daniel stared at him.

"I know it seems strange—a scarecrow like me. But she'll have me, and—it's wonderful!"

Wonderful was not the word Daniel would use. "Congratulations," he said, forcing his voice to hide his true reaction. "She's an uncommon girl."

William let out a long breath. "For a minute there, I thought you were angry with me. Furious."

"Angry? Me? Why would I be angry?"

"Oh, I don't know. We'd best be getting home."

William slung his spade over his shoulder, jumped over the ditch, and started for home. Daniel picked up his spade too, made to copy the movement—then the fury he'd not quite hidden burst out, and he swung the tool hard at his brother's head. William crumpled to the ground.

Daniel dropped the spade, knelt, and scanned the lifeless face carefully. He felt the pulse and the heart. He leaned his cheek against William's lips, but there was no breath.

He looked round. Darkness had fallen, and everyone else was home at supper. Quickly Daniel picked up his spade again, walked a few paces away, and began to dig. The newly created field was already churned from the uprooting of shrubs and thistles; no one would notice.

Daniel made some excuse to Farmer Prentice for William's absence. Three days later, Annie came over to ask after him.

"He's been coming every evening after work," she said. "And now, nothing."

"I've not seen him myself," said Daniel. "I don't know what he thinks he's up to."

"Would he have gone off to the city for something, maybe?"

"London? Can't see why. Unless he thought to get work up there."

"Work? In London? We—we were going to get married."

"Married!" Daniel raised his eyebrows. "He never said anything to me."

Annie flinched. "Has he taken his things? Is his best coat gone?"

Daniel ducked back into the room he'd shared with William, leaving Annie on the doorstep. He came back shaking his head. "Coat's gone. And his spare shirt."

"Not his spare shirt," Annie said. "That's still with me. I was working on a stain."

Annie trudged back home, where she pulled out William's shirt and tried a third remedy. It got out the stain at last, and she hung the shirt on the line. A *whup-whup* sound reached her ears later. Looking out the window for the source, she started. For a second, she'd thought a scarecrow was pegged to the line. No, it was William's shirt, fat with wind, flapping wildly, a form without a body.

Daniel left it three months before he made his move. Meanwhile, he began to guess that Annie's haggard looks and gray face were not just signs of heartache. Word was whispered that she was sick every morning. His eyes skimmed her figure, and he saw her waist was not as trim as before. For a minute, rage filled him: his straw-headed brother had got there before him yet again, won her body as well as her heart and made a child with her. Then, as he smoldered, he saw the advantage this gave him.

William heard Annie's voice but could not see her. Why was it so dark? And so cold? He loved summer and its warmth and light, although he also liked the berries and the spangled spider webs of autumn, the frost and the pale sun of winter; but this was darker than any season he knew. He tried to get up but could not make his limbs move at all. So he lay back and listened.

He had to listen hard, because the messages were not for him. They were not messages at all. Beetles muttered about how hard the rocks were and worms whined about the quality of the soil. The worms were worryingly close; they seemed to be getting closer.

He concentrated on Annie again. Her voice sounded dreary, and she repeated something over and over. Another voice talked with her.

Daniel! He was trying to persuade her to do something. "Come on, Annie." What was he after?

All at once, the voices were clearer; they came from right over his head. He surmised they'd moved and were standing on the earth that separated him from them.

"He left you, remember, Annie? There's no point staying true to him. But I won't leave you. I'll care for both of you."

Panic surged into William. What was happening? Why did Daniel say he had left Annie? Why was his brother attempting to take Annie away? With every ounce of strength, he tried to push himself up, straining toward that dear, sad voice. He pushed and pushed, and nothing moved, not him nor the earth around him.

A memory came back—talking with Daniel in the field, William turning, a sudden pain in his head, the world going black…and now he was underground. He was dead! Buried under the soil, powerless to find Annie.

All that long winter, he lay despairing and cold. A voice or two reached him but never the one he wanted to hear. He barely noticed the earth warming, thawing. There was no thawing for him until the day he heard her voice again—with Daniel's.

"I'm not ready yet."

"You can't put it off much longer, Annie. People are talking. You're lucky they think it's mine, 'cause of the attention I'm paying you. I think Parson'll be speaking to you about getting wed."

"Baby's not due for another month." Her voice was weak, as if hope were leaking away.

"That's crazy talk, and you know it. It could come any day."

"Just one more week," she begged.

"He won't be back."

"I know."

The thought that she was giving in to Daniel made William throw all his strength against the weight of earth above him. He pushed and he strained and he raged to break out.

When he had burned up all his strength, he lay back and just listened—listened hard—and focused on her voice alone. Weaker than he'd known it, it tugged on his heart strings, tugged on his body, pulled his fingers until they stretched like tendrils and grew and twisted their way upward. It was not so cold at the end of his fingertips. There were glimpses of light cracking between clumps of earth. If he reached a little more…

The heat of the sun! The gentle warm air of spring! Something jabbed at his fingers; a croak told him it was a crow.

"Annie!" he shouted. "I'm here! I never left you!"

But she was already on the road, her back to him, Daniel following protectively behind.

The summer that followed was a long, hot one. More and more of William flowed up the shoots that had begun as his fingers, reaching for the sun. Shoots turned to sheaves and whispered in the breeze. Peter, the old dairyman, trudged past the field once or twice, muttering about talking wheat, but most of the villagers were too worn out from their hand-to-mouth existence to have time for such mad talk. William swung between hope that someone new would come by and listen and despair at Annie's misery.

One sweltering day, William looked up from his meditations to find the field surrounded by villagers, the women with their heads hooded in big bonnets, the men grasping wicked, curved sickles. Was this his last chance?

"No! Stop! Listen! Murder!"

Each man stepped forward. One of them waded into William's corner. A red, sweaty face blocked out the sun, something flashed, and—blank.

A long silence. Voices as if from afar, getting clearer. Children's voices, saying something about a scarecrow.

"That's Farmer Prentice's jacket, ent it?"

"Not his blouse, surely?"

Sniggers followed that. "Nah, his wife's. Reckon the breeches are from Sammy Prentice?"

William struggled to focus. He could see and hear again. He looked down. Those must be the breeches the children were talking about, straw poking out of the legs where feet should be, and a pole between them driven into the soil. *My hair won't be much different from when I was alive,* he thought.

Looking up, he saw a gaggle of dirty children staring at him, familiar faces from before his death. He tried out his new voice. It was hoarse, unpracticed. He could just manage a word or two: "bones" and "never leave."

Their eyes popped, and the three biggest fled. The little ones ran after, crying for them to wait.

Autumn flowed on. Mushrooms and toadstools sprang up in damp places, and the nights drew in. He wondered where Annie was these days and if she had she married his brother in the end. He hoped the baby had been born safely.

The sun was making a farewell appearance when a much-loved figure appeared from the houses. Annie! Did she have a child with her? His child?

She drew closer. Yes, she had a baby tied to her back, a cloth holding the child's head so William could not see its face. Annie's head was bowed and eyes were dull. She walked past William the scarecrow without giving him a glance and, under the oak tree, bent to gather acorns to put in a basket. Was it hunger that dulled her eyes? Had she continued to refuse his brother after all? Then she would be destitute, driven to scavenge for acorns to eat. He would rather she were married to Daniel than starving.

The baby started to wail. Annie sighed, put down the basket, and swung the baby off her back. "Hush, now," she said, walking up and down the edge of the field. "Hush now! We need acorns for the pig. How can I gather them if you are always crying?" But her voice was weary and agitated and seemed only to fret the child more.

No, not hunger, thought William—exhaustion and despair. He caught a glimpse of gold sticking out from the little cap, and wondered if its hair would be like his.

"Surely you can't want feeding again?" said Annie to the baby. She sat herself under the oak and pulled her gown down to offer the baby a breast. The child thrust its head this way and that, latching on for a moment only to pull off and whimper once more.

Annie gave a little cry of frustration. "He's right; he's right! I'm useless. Can't even manage a baby. I bet Daniel wishes he'd left us to the parish now."

With a weary sigh, she straightened her bodice and got up, turning for the first time so the baby faced the field. William looked into the big, wide eyes of a little girl—his daughter.

She stopped crying. She twisted as Annie made ready to leave, staring straight back into William's cloth eyes. Did she like his daft face, or was she fascinated by his flapping arms? Hope surged anew in William's straw-filled breast. He flapped his arms harder and forced a thin breath out of his cloth throat.

"It's me! William! I never left you!"

But Annie's head was sunk too low on her chest, and the circling crows cawed too loudly above. She didn't see his flapping or hear his whisper. The baby blinked, and her eyelids drooped. Annie trudged back along the edge of the field, disappearing again among the houses.

William sagged. The crows fluttered around, one by one settling into the field. One particularly glossy fellow sat on William's arm in a lordly way and peered round at his face.

"Look at you!" the bird said. "Proper scarecrow you are." He laughed at his own wit. "You're the fellow that got murdered, aren't you?"

"Yes, yes—that's me!" said William eagerly. "How do you know?"

"You've been telling us for months," said the crow, snapping his beak. "Haven't got a minute's peace here. All we wanted was a bit of grain, and there you were, flapping and whispering day and night. We only kept trying because the pickings are so good in a new field."

"You must help me," cried the scarecrow. "Annie thinks I abandoned her and our child, and my brother's treating her vilely."

"Ah—you want me to peck his eyes out." The crow perked up as if pleased at the thought.

"No, no. I want you to go and talk to Annie. Tell her I didn't leave her, that I'm still here."

"I'm not sure how that will help her," said the crow. "It's not like you can pull yourself up out of the ground and go be her man."

"It might make her heart lighter," said the scarecrow.

"And what do I get out of it?"

"Seed. If you go, I'll stop flapping and let you eat as much of the seed as you want."

"Farmer won't like it," said the crow. "He'll dock your wages!" And he laughed until he fell off William's arm and caught himself in a swoop.

William's heart lifted. The crow might be acerbic, but he was loud, too, and maybe Annie would listen to him. The crow flew off and William waited.

The sun went behind a cloud. When it came out again, it was low in the sky. It had sunk behind the village cottages by the time the crow swooped back.

"Did she listen? Did she understand?" burst out William.

"No," said the crow. "She flapped her apron at me and said I was keeping the baby awake."

"You must have tried more than once! You've been gone all day."

"Oh. That's right. Her man came in and shouted at your girl for not having supper ready. Said she'd been lazing around all day and cared more for the brat than for him. So I flew to the rooftop of the next cottage and shouted filthy names at him. When I tired of that, I told the whole village how he murdered you."

"And did anyone listen?"

The crow tilted his head. "One man did. He said, 'That's quite a story!' I told him it was a true tale. I said I saw he was a sensible man, as he dressed just like me, so I trusted him to see justice done."

"The vicar, maybe. Or the curate. Did he go and talk to Annie?"

"Talk to Annie! I'd rather he talked to the magistrate. No, I followed him to see where he went next, and all he did was go home and write something. Now, about that corn…"

It wasn't hard for William to stop flapping so the crow could eat the seed the farmer had planted. The scarecrow's worry for his lover and child dragged on his arms, and he drooped. The shreds of his hopeful spirit waited for news, but when it came, it was bad news.

The crow told him the cottage Daniel had taken Annie home to stood empty now. When Annie had taken the little girl into the bed she shared with Daniel, the child wet it. Daniel lost his temper and struck the child. The next morning, when Daniel went to work, she tied the child to her back and caught a lift east, with a cart bound for London.

Two months later, the crow brought news that Daniel had drunk himself to death and the brothers' cottage now lay empty. Hope died in William's straw breast. The weeks rolled into months. Winter crept in, and rain hammered down on the scarecrow's head, and he began to rot. After every rain, his form sagged a little more.

The wheat was sparse the next year. Farmer Prentice looked at the scraggly field and declared William the scarecrow to be useless. He pulled the straw man up and threw him down at the edge of the field, just next to where his body had been hidden. His spirit trickled down to join his bones. Without Annie's voice to yearn after, he had nothing to pull him back.


The century rolled out and a new one began. Country ways and country superstitions were forgotten, and people sought a different type of spirituality, with visions of angels and attempts to talk to the dead.

Ruth Gregson, journalist and skeptic, saw a story there that might be a way, at long last, to prove to the editor she could do more than report on society gossip and charity dinners. Ruth and her mother shared a tiny terraced house in a shabby corner of east London, and their neighbor was always enthusing about the séances she attended. Ruth had a pang of conscience about using the woman to further her career and confessed what she planned to do.

"Oh, you won't be a skeptic for long," said Mrs. Brown. "Not when you've heard the things we hear and seen the things we see. Then you can spread the word through your paper."

Ruth wasn't convinced at all by the séance. The knocking was clearly controlled by Mrs. Nash, otherwise known as Astarte, and the gaslight was going down because one of the servants had turned up a light in another room. After the performance, Ruth was sipping her tea and letting the chatter wash over her when a name caught her ear. It was the name of the village her mother came from, the village Ruth had been born in. Miss Foster, a keen séance attender, had a side interest in mysterious graves and strange sightings around them. She was particularly interested in a grave in the village where her father had been curate, of an unknown man whose bones were discovered when a large farming estate was sold and dug up for housing. Miss Foster intended to make a weekend of it and visit the grave at midnight to observe any mysterious sights and sounds for herself. Was anyone else interested?

"The local inn is said to have reasonable rates," she added.

"How delicious!" said Mrs. Watson. "Count me in."

"I'll come," said Ruth, "if I can find someone to look after Mother. She's very frail these days."

"I'll stop over and watch her," said Mrs. Brown, "if you're happy to trust me."

Mrs. Gregson was waiting up at home, ready for an amusing account of the séance. On finding out where her daughter was going, a cloud passed over her face. "I didn't think I'd ever hear of the place again," she said. "But go if you want. Satisfy your curiosity."


It was good to get out of London and breathe some clear country air. The train dropped off Miss Foster's party in the quaint fishing village with the inn they had booked; they rested in their rooms for the early evening, then took the last bus up the hill to the farming village with the mysterious grave.

Ruth thought they would attract lots of stares, three unaccompanied ladies walking into the graveyard of an ancient church. She was mistaken; her mother had described the village of her youth, but it had since grown into a town, its streets studded with shops and small businesses. The shop assistant walking home late and the drunkard looking for another pub did not give them a second glance. The three women slipped between the gravestones until they found the one they were looking for: a stone simply marked *Unknown Man* and the words *The Lord seeth all*.

They stood round it silently, waiting in the chilly night air. A taxi chuttered by; a door slammed farther up the street. Human noise fell away, and the whispers of night came into focus—the stirring of leaves, a bird adjusting itself in the bushes, a rat scuttling along the edge of the graveyard. To Ruth, nothing more mysterious happened than the rising of the moon, which rinsed the graveyard blue-gray, but a quick glance at her companions suggested they thought otherwise.

At one in the morning, the little group of women walked back down the hill to their inn absorbed in thought. Ruth thought longingly of those Londoners who earned enough to move out into the countryside and take the train into work. They bade one another goodnight and slipped into their rooms.

Over breakfast, Ruth found her suspicions about her companions were right. Miss Foster and Mrs. Watson compared notes excitedly.

"And the shiver that went over me as the clock struck midnight. Did you feel that too?" murmured Miss Foster.

"Oh, yes," agreed Mrs. Watson, eyes wide. "But I would call it more of a thrill."

"A thrill—yes—how well you put it. A presentiment of woe. And I'm certain I felt a hand on my arm. Miss Gregson, how about you?"

"I am a very prosaic character," said Ruth. "I saw and felt nothing."

The other two were momentarily disappointed but soon went back to comparing their experiences. This continued on the return train, and Ruth, who already had a headache from lack of sleep, asked to borrow Miss Foster's father's book to read so she didn't have to listen to any more ravings.

Her mother had been well looked after by Mrs. Brown, who was, after all, a kindly soul, even if she believed nonsense. Mrs. Gregson listened with interest, but no regret, to Ruth's description of the village they had left so long ago. She even showed one of her rare smiles at her daughter's account of the two ladies and their imaginary thrills at the graveside.

But then Ruth started to tell her about the story of the grave—of murder, of whispering wheat and a weeping scarecrow, and a girl who didn't listen.

Mrs. Gregson half rose from her chair, her smile wiped from her face, her eyes staring, almost glaring. "I need to go and see the grave."

Ruth jumped up from her stool, knocking it over in her haste. "Are you feeling all right, Mother? Shall I get your medicine?"

"Medicine? What do I want with medicine? We must go back— no." She subsided into the chair again. "You are tired, poor girl, and you need to go to work tomorrow."

But something had evidently upset Mrs. Gregson to her core. She would pull herself up from her chair and wander round the room, hanging onto the furniture to support her frail weight, then sink back against her cushions and stare at the wall, hardly breathing. Ruth put her to bed, but she moaned in her sleep, calling out "William, William!"

*Who is William?* Ruth wondered. Ruth was so frightened by the morning that she called her editor.

Her employer grumbled about old women who took an age to die and reluctantly agreed she could take the day off. Ruth went into her mother's bedroom to say she would stay at home today and fetch the doctor.

"Not a doctor," gasped Mrs. Gregson, "a train. I want to go and see the grave. We can make it there and back in one day."

"A day on the train? In your condition, Mother? You can't mean it."

"Never mind my condition. What does that matter now? Where's my purse? Look, I have enough to get us both there and back. And for a taxi too; I won't be able to take the bus."

"I can't allow it, Mother," cried Ruth, trying to exert some authority. "That's all your savings."

"Exactly," said Mrs. Gregson. "Now I know what I was saving up for. I'm sorry to put you to this trouble, but I won't be doing it again, I promise you."

An hour later, they were headed for the station, Mrs. Gregson bundled in rugs and clutching her shawl round her thin shoulders. On the half-empty train, she sank back into the seat, but as the houses thinned out and green slopes appeared, she leaned forward and her eyes grew clearer and brighter.

Ruth ventured a question.

"Mother, I never knew you believed in séances."

Mrs. Gregson turned to her daughter with a little frown. "I don't."

"Then why—"

"Silly hysterical old women," sniffed Mrs. Gregson. "Sitting in the dark and talking to tables. Listen to the world around, William said. Listen hard. The birds, the grass, the wind." She leaned back, smiling into space.

Ruth, already frightened for her mother's health, was further concerned at these shifting moods. She waited for Mrs. Gregson to continue, but when she did not, said, "Who is William, Mother?"

"William?" Mrs. Gregson turned to her again, her face lit up in a way Ruth had never seen before.

"He was your father."

*I thought my father was called Daniel?* But Ruth could guess the story.

When the taxi drove them away from the station and up the high street of their old home, Mrs. Gregson shook her head at the bustle of shops and screech of cars, and she looked quite bewildered at the stretch of houses covering the fields she once knew. But when the taxi dropped them at the crossroad, Mrs. Gregson stepped onto the pavement purposefully, looking up at the old Norman church with a nod of recognition.

Visiting the grave again, Ruth was alerted to how little peace there was by day. The unknown grave, however, was tucked in an obscure corner farthest from the road. A low branch of a nearby bush brushed over its wording.

Mrs. Gregson nodded. "Moss and leaves, that's good. He should be able to hear the birds and the wind here. Ruth, I need an hour or two. Find yourself some lunch, my dear, and come back for me at two o'clock. No, not for me; I won't be needing anything to eat."

Ruth didn't like leaving her alone and without food, but she'd never been able to argue with her mother. She seated the old woman on a nearby bench and walked away from the church, up the little high street. A cyclist wobbled past her. A woman wheeling a wide baby carriage around the potholes nodded a good afternoon to her.

Ruth felt too anxious to eat, so kept walking until she found the estate built on the field. It was hard enough to imagine it as a green field, and as for the rest of the tale—her father a scarecrow? This wasn't a story her editor would print!

A lace curtain twitched in a window. She realized she'd been staring at that house, absorbed in thought. It was time to go back to the churchyard.

Ruth hurried back from the estate. As she passed through the gate, her heart lurched; her mother lay back with her eyes gazing into the middle distance, completely still. But as Ruth leaned over her, Mrs. Gregson swiveled her gaze and snorted.

"Thought I was dead, didn't you? Draped across my dead lover's grave like Isolde and Tristan. No, I'm still here, and ready for a nice cup of tea. Shall we find a little tea shop?"

There was a pretty tea garden back on the high street, built so close to the bend that its latticed woodwork obscured the view for traffic. A woman with the slow ways of the country took their order, and they settled back, knowing the wait would be much longer than in London.

"You want to know what I saw and heard, don't you?" said Mrs. Gregson with a chuckle.

Ruth drew a breath, then decided for silence. They loved each other and dealt with each other very well for two single women living hand-to-mouth in one little terrace, but Ruth had a romantic streak, embarrassing at her age, that her mother sometimes liked to scoff at.

Mrs. Gregson leaned back and watched a taxi overtake a horse and cab. The tea tray arrived.

"He said he'd never left us," said Mrs. Gregson suddenly. "He hadn't run away. He was always there." She leaned back and closed her eyes.

The tea tray was placed on the table, the cups and saucers laid out. Ruth poured the milk, helped the two of them to sugar, and pondered as the tea brewed. Then she poured her mother a cup and held it out it to her.

Mrs. Gregson had gone to sleep. She often did that these days. Ruth shook her arm gently, then with more vigor, murmuring in her ear, then calling more loudly. She knocked over a teacup and called in a panicky voice for a doctor.

The tea shop owner was very calm about having a death in her shop, and the doctor was kind and helped Ruth with the calls needed to report the death. It was harder to persuade the rector to bury Mrs. Gregson in the grave of the unknown man, but Ruth persevered, absolutely certain he was not unknown, and that her mother needed to be by his side.

When at last her mother was laid next to her father and the earth was raked back over the wound, Ruth waited for the sexton and rector to go, then tried to listen, to listen hard.

She heard some women stopping to talk in the street. She heard the whine of traffic. She honed in on the noises close at hand: a nut falling out of the tree behind her, the patter of a squirrel darting up a tree, the rustle of a bird in the undergrowth, the slight breeze in the trees.

She heard no voices. But maybe that was because there was nothing she needed to hear that day. It had all been said.

✝✝✝ ✝✝✝ ✝✝✝ ✝

# About the Author

Lynden Wade spends as much time as possible in other worlds to avoid the dirty dishes piling up in her home. She enjoys writing stories inspired by history, legends, and fairy tales. She has had pieces published in the *JL Anthologies* and in *The Forgotten and the Fantastical* series. She is still hoping for a house elf. You can find her on lyndenwadeauthor.weebly.com and on Facebook.

# I Dream in
# Black and White

Ted Myers

# I

It's eleven in the morning, and I still don't want to wake up. I don't want to tear myself away from the dream, but already it's beginning to recede. My shoulders hurt the way they always do when I try to stay in bed too long. But why get up? What is there to look forward to? The earlier I get up, the longer the day, and I want it to be night. It's the same thing every day since I retired from the ad agency. I'd been working as a copywriter, but I was sick of writing the pap demanded by my clients. I wanted to pen real literature. So I retired. But I haven't had one solid idea, either for a book or even a short story in two years.

I get the spam out of my email box, do a few floor exercises: stretches for my bad back, my bum knees, my torn rotator cuffs, the aches and pains that come with age. I do my truncated ten-minute yoga-breathing, mantra-saying meditation. I eat the same cereal with blueberries for breakfast. Then, the high point of my day: the bike ride. The same six-mile circuit every day, as long as the weather is nice—and, in Santa Monica, California, the weather is almost always nice. Thaw something for dinner, maybe do a little reading. Is it late enough to start drinking? At first it was five, then four, now 3:45 is acceptable for drink one: brandy and soda. Then make dinner, eat, a few more drinks—straight brandy this time—and try to zombie myself to sleep with TV. Old movies, especially the black and white ones, are my favorites. But it seems like I've seen them all. At last, after five drinks, a ten-milligram Valium, and a melatonin, I start to get drowsy. I can't wait to see what happens tonight…

XOXOX

It's always the same dream, or, more precisely, a continuation of the same movie. It's more movielike than dreamlike. There are none of the symbolic images, the non-sequiturs, the people from my past who really represent someone else, the maze-like houses, trains, landscapes, and roads that used to populate my dreams. This is a completely linear movie, with a plot and characters who remain consistently themselves throughout. And it's in black and white. It's not like any dream I've ever had.

I'm driving my brand new 1941 Plymouth coupe fast through rainy streets. I think it's L.A. I'm running away from someone. The cops? People who want to kill me? I can't remember. The answers are in last night's dream, and the night before. But I can't remember. All I know is, I've been dreaming one long film noir for—I don't know—weeks? Months?

The car skids on the slick pavement as I round a turn. I take a quick right onto La Brea, up past Hollywood Boulevard, another quick right onto Franklin. In my rearview, I see a set of lights that have been following me since I left the house. I go two blocks and make a quick left onto Outpost. I'm headed up Outpost, and those lights are still behind me. They disappear around a curve, and I take a quick right onto a little side street, Senalda Road, and turn my lights off. The big Packard speeds past. I think I've lost them. Am I supposed to meet someone? Yes, I think that's it. A rendezvous of some kind. Now it starts to come back to me…

I had been contacted by a beautiful blonde, Adeline Keys (played by a very young Lana Turner), to turn over some film I had taken of her wearing a certain necklace. I'm a freelance photographer, and I usually sell my stuff to the *L.A. Star,* a local gossip rag. She was offering me two years' income not to give the shots to the *Star*—or anyone else.

It was a family heirloom, she said. It had belonged to her mother, who had died when she was quite young. Adeline's father, Montgomery Keys, had been a politically influential financier, a man who, while he never held office, controlled the men in city hall and even the state capital in his prime. He was already old when Adeline was born. He often wondered if she was really his. Now he was a reclusive invalid—never saw or spoke to anyone, except his daughter and Jerome, his trusted manservant. He didn't leave his inner sanctum, a huge, cluttered, chaotic mess of a room that composed most of the second floor of the east wing of the Keys mansion. He spent his days drinking and mumbling to himself. Adeline was beginning to worry she might have to have the old man put away.

Jerome had occupied a little room next to Keys's for thirty years. He was a small, black Jamaican man of about sixty—although he looked much older—who spoke the King's English and had a weakness for Jamaican rum and opium. Keys (played by John Barrymore) was an alcoholic himself and, as long as Jerome brought him his gin and lime, and an occasional meal, Keys was satisfied. More than satisfied. He had a genuine affection for Jerome, enjoyed his witty conversation. It was hardly your typical master-servant relationship. The two would spend hours telling wild stories and cackling like a pair of lunatics. Jerome even got Keys to smoke opium with him. Keys liked that it made his legs stop hurting, but then it put him to sleep, and he didn't like that. "I'll sleep when I'm dead," he said and refused the stuff after that. In point of fact, aside from Adeline, Jerome was Keys's closest friend and confidant.

Albert, Keys's son by his first wife, occupied the west wing, along with the cook, butler, and a couple of maids. Although Keys had disowned him, Adeline had let him move back into the family estate out of pity. He was broke, having gone through all the money he'd embezzled from his father, and devoid of any employable skills. If the old man found out he was living there, he would surely have Albert thrown out of the house. But the old man never left his lair, so Adeline swore everyone to secrecy and let Albert stay. She didn't like him and didn't trust him, but he was, after all, her half brother. Albert knew Keys had written him out of his will: that, when the old man kicked, everything would go to Adeline—if Adeline was alive.

The necklace, twelve inches of flawless emeralds set in antique twenty-four karat gold, was kept locked in a wall safe, hidden behind a painting in the old man's bedroom. There was also a big, ostentatious safe in plain view. But it was a decoy, filled with a lot of worthless papers. Adeline had been expressly forbidden by her father to ever wear the necklace, show it to anyone, or even mention its existence. The only reason she knew about it was that she was the only one entrusted with the safe's location and combination, in case anything happened to Keys. His will was in there too. Adeline knew the dark secret surrounding the necklace, but she was young and wild and couldn't resist wearing it to the Governor's Ball, just this once. It had all happened so long ago, surely no one would remember. So, late the night before the ball, when her father was heavily drugged and snoring his head off, she sneaked into his room and opened the safe. Each time she saw it, the necklace took her breath away. The next evening, she stashed it in her gold mesh reticule.

Her date, Reggie Storrow, a rich, self-absorbed fop, arrived in his limo, right on time as always. Adeline cared nothing about him. Reggie was equally devoid of feeling, but was always happy to be seen in all the right places with Adeline. Reggie and Adeline shared another dark secret, one that I knew nothing about until much later.

Once in the back seat of the limo, she put on the necklace.

"Wow, that's some sparkler," remarked Reggie.

"Just paste," said Adeline casually.

She hadn't thought about the gaggle of photographers who'd be waiting as the limos pulled up in front of the Wadsworth mansion, one of those pretentious behemoths in Hancock Park. As soon as Reggie's chauffeur opened her door and Adeline stepped out, I was Johnny-on-the-spot. I snapped a beautiful shot of her and the mysterious necklace. *What a dish*, I thought. She was dazzling in her floor-length silver satin gown that clung to her curves like a second skin. She immediately retreated back into the car as the other paparazzi snapped away, removed the necklace, stashed it in her purse, hastily scribbled a note, and entered the party on Reggie's arm, smiling as though nothing had happened. I was the only one with a shot of the necklace. As she and Reggie entered the ball, Reggie's chauffeur, a massive black man, silent and expressionless, walked up to me and handed me the note:

*Urgent you call me. Regent 5-096. Do not print that photo. I'll make it worth your while.* It was simply signed *A.* The chauffeur eyed my press badge as I read the note.

I snapped a few other celebrities that night, then packed up and went home. Out of the corner of my eye, I spotted a guy in the crowd who didn't quite fit the picture. He wore a long coat and a gray fedora. He wasn't snapping pictures, and he didn't look like a celebrity hound; he looked like a thug, and he was certainly eyeing me. I got in my car and beat it out of there.

My phone was ringing as I walked in the door.

"Mr. Holden?"

In the dream my name is Larry Holden. I'm twenty-six, six-feet, one-inch tall; I have wavy brown hair and a good face. I'm strong and healthy. I'm the only one in the dream not played by a recognizable actor. I'm me, the Dreamer. Only my name and physical appearance are different.

"Yes?"

"No need to call me," she said. "I found you."

"Miss Keys?"

"Yes. Are you the only person that got a picture of me wearing that necklace?"

"Yes, I think so."

"Did you get my note?"

"Yes."

"I'll give you $5,000 for the undeveloped roll of film." A moment of stunned silence on my end. "Do we have a deal?"

"Am I in some kind of danger?"

"Not if you follow my instructions. Do we have a deal?"

"Five grand, cash?"

"Yes."

"All right."

"Now listen carefully. Meet me in an hour at Mulholland and Pacific View Drive. Can you find that?"

"Yeah."

"Bring the film from tonight. I'll need to see that no prints were made of that photo."

"Okay."

"And I'll bring the cash. One hour from now makes it one a.m. Be there."

She hung up. I lingered with the phone to my ear a moment longer. I heard a second click. Somebody else had been listening.

I wound my way up Outpost slowly, wanting to put as much distance between me and the Packard that had been tailing me as possible. I took a left on Mulholland when I reached the top. It was about 1,800 feet to Pacific View Drive, which zig-zagged off to the right. The rain had stopped, and the landscape was illuminated by a bright full moon. I turned off my lights and parked on Mulholland, a hundred feet from Pacific View. I decided to walk from there. If that Packard and whoever was in it were lying in wait for me, I wanted to see them before they saw me. I had the exposed roll of film hidden in the trunk of my car. After hearing that second click over the phone, I knew someone else was in on this, someone up to no good. Hence, the Packard. In my pocket was a roll of blank film. I kept my car keys in my hand in case I had to turn tail and make a run for it.

When I got to the intersection of Mulholland and Pacific View, I saw her, seated in the driver's seat of a convertible. The steering wheel was on the right, like an English car. It was the most spectacular car I had ever seen. If this dream were in color, it would be the color of dark, ripe cherries. But these days, I only dream in black and white.

Her light blonde hair shone in the moonlight. I couldn't decide which was more luminous: her or the car. I decided it was her. I approached, proffering the roll of blank film. I guess it was right then I decided I had to make her mine.

At the same moment, the big black Packard came screeching up from the steep hill Pacific View took downward toward the Valley. I was momentarily blinded by the headlights. Adeline fired up the V-12.

"Get in," she yelled. I jumped in beside her. "Hold onto your hat!"

It wasn't just a figure of speech. That machine took off like a bat out of hell and my hat nearly went flying.

She took a hard right, and we headed west on Mulholland, the Packard in hot pursuit.

"Jeez, what kind of car is this, anyway?" I asked.

"A '39 Delahaye type 165 Cabriolet. It's French; one of six ever made," she said. "I took one look, and I just had to have it. Hang on . . ."

We took a sharp left and barreled through a maze of narrow streets winding through the Hollywood Hills. I couldn't see the lights behind us anymore. She suddenly turned off onto a dirt trail and stopped in front of a garage about 200 yards up the road.

"Would you open the garage door, please?" she asked, cool as a cucumber.

I got out, opened the garage, and she pulled the car in. She got out, and I closed it up. Next to the garage was a cute little cottage.

"Nobody knows about this place. I come here sometimes when I want to be alone. You're the first person I've ever brought here." She gave me a little smile. I went all gooey inside. But there was light inside the house.

"Why is there a light on?" she said. "There must be somebody in there."

"Maybe we should get out of here."

"No. I've got to see who's in my house."

She took out her keys, but I just turned the knob and the door swung open.

"Hiya, Adie!" It was Albert, a sleazily cheerful young man with slicked-back blond hair (played by Dan Duryea). He was stretched out on her couch.

"What are you doing here, Albert?" Adeline was clearly not pleased to see him.

"Now, is that any way to talk to your dear ol' big brother?"

"How the hell did you know about this place?"

"I'm a very resourceful person, Adie. You should give me more credit."

"What do you want?"

"Aren't you gonna introduce me to your friend?"

"Albert, this is Larry Holden. Mr. Holden, this is Albert Keys, my half brother. He was banished from the family after he embezzled $25,000 from Father's bank."

"A fine way to introduce me to a stranger. Listen, bud, there's a lot more to the story than that."

"Nobody cares, Albert. You got away with it; let's leave it at that. Now, get out!"

"Not just yet, Adie. I have it on very good account that you are in possession of a roll of film that people are willing to pay a great deal of money for. Even kill for."

"How could you know that?"

"Never mind that." Albert drew a .38 snub nose revolver from his belt. "Just give me the film."

"Why, you ungrateful bastard!" cried Adeline. "After I gave you a roof over your head!" I looked at Adeline. "Give it to him," she said.

I tossed Albert the blank roll; he put it in his pocket. "A pleasure doin' business with ya." And off he went.

"You better be packed and gone by the time I get home," she shouted after him.

We heard his car start up and pull away. There were tears in her eyes. I wanted to take her in my arms and hold her so bad I could taste it. Instead I just looked deep into those eyes. The tears made them deeper and greener than those emeralds. How I knew this in my black and white world, I don't know, but I did.

"Suppose you tell me what's going on," I said, barely maintaining my composure.

"Like a drink?"

"Yeah, I could use one."

She poured us both a few fingers of straight scotch. She downed hers in a single gulp and poured herself another.

"I think he's going to use the necklace to blackmail my father," she said tearfully.

"I don't understand."

"Of course you don't. You're not supposed to. It's a secret, see?"

"Before you tell me your secret, I think I'd better tell you mine: that roll of film I gave Albert was blank. The real one is stashed in the trunk of my car—up on Mulholland." I gestured in the general direction of where I thought Mulholland was, but after all those twists and turns, who could tell? Her face brightened, and she gave me a smile that positively gave me goosebumps.

"Why, you darling! You absolute, brilliant darling!" And she kissed me.

It was a kiss that started soft—a gratitude kiss—but then increased in intensity. We kissed long and passionately. I hoped she was feeling what I was feeling, because my heart was being taken by storm.

"Now, how can I ever repay you?" she asked with an impish grin. She took me by the hand. "Let me show you the bedroom."

The bedroom was beautifully decked out in bamboo and Japanese paper lanterns. The bed had a polished bamboo headboard that twisted like a pretzel. The bedspread and pillows were also adorned with Japanese motifs: cherry blossoms and lotus leaves. I started to grab her.

"Wait!" she said, holding up her hand. "Just stand right there." She backed up a few paces until she was standing right by the bed. Then she ever-so-slowly peeled off that silver satin gown. It dropped to the floor around her ankles. She had nothing on underneath. As a young art student in the '30s, I had been to Paris, had seen all the great works in the Louvre, but she was the most beautiful thing I had ever laid eyes on. Then she started to fade. Oh no! *Not now; please, not now!* I became conscious of my shoulder hurting. *Damn!* As I regained consciousness, the dream began to fade from my memory, like always. This time I wasn't going to let it go. I grabbed a pencil and a pad of paper. But by the time I was ready to write it down, all I could remember was Lana Turner standing before me, naked. I tried like hell to hang onto that image, but soon it was only words on paper.

## II

I had read some stuff about hypnotherapy. I got the idea that, if a hypno-shrink put me under, perhaps they could get me to remember the dream. I looked for one near me on Yelp. Most were women, and many of them were pretty damn hot-looking. But, since I knew there would be sexual content in my dream, I was a bit self-conscious about going to a woman. Besides, most of the therapists listed were not even real doctors—they had credentials after their names like CHt. What was that? I looked a little further afield and found a guy in Beverly Hills by the name of Bryan Schrock, MD. Besides having the MD after his name, instead of the usual lose weight and stop smoking promises they all touted, his services included *life regression hypnosis*. Being an old hippie, I knew what that meant: he took you back into past lives. I was impressed that any MD would even believe in past lives, let alone take you back into them. No one specifically advertised that they could cure amnesia or help you remember forgotten dreams, so I called Dr. Schrock's office and made an appointment. Luckily, I was able to get in the next day. That meant I only missed one night of the dream. But what a night!

The next morning I awoke with a vague recollection of being beaten up by two thugs. I arrived at Dr. Schrock's office on time and was ushered into his inner sanctum about ten minutes later. I had brought my little Zoom digital recorder, an artifact left over from the last of my songwriting days. I wanted to record what I said in these sessions and listen to it at home.

Schrock was a tall man in his mid-forties, handsome, with receding brown hair combed straight back, and a commanding presence. We shook hands and introduced ourselves.

"Do you do 'Schrock therapy'?" I quipped, in an effort to lighten the mood.

He looked at me and gave me a condescending half smile.

"You've heard that one before."

"Only about a hundred times. But I compliment you on your intelligence. You know what Alfred Hitchcock said?"

"No, what?"

"'Puns are the highest form of literature.'"

Alfred Hitchcock! I knew this was the guy for me.

"Well, that gives me the perfect segue into why I've come to you."

He said nothing, just gave me a look that said *I'm listening.*

I told him about the dream, how it was all one movie, in black and white, 1940s film noir, how every night I got a new installment of the same ongoing story, and how I could never remember the dream upon waking. Just slivers, fragments.

"If you hypnotize me, do you think you can get me to remember the dreams—the dream?"

"It's possible. You say you dream a continuation of the same story every night?"

"Yes. I want you to take me back to the beginning of the story, and I want to record it into this." I showed him the Zoom.

"What do you do during the day?"

"I wait for night."

He laid me out on an extremely comfortable leather recliner. I started recording.

"I'm going to tell every muscle in your body to relax." And then he went through the laundry list, starting with my feet and working his way up.

"Relax your feet, relax your ankles, your calves, your thighs," and so on. "Now, drop your shoulders and relax your arms. Your arms are very, very heavy. Too heavy for you to lift." When he got to my head, he did the back of my neck, my forehead, my temples, and then my eyes. "Your eyelids are very heavy, too heavy for you to open them. Keep them closed. You are more deeply relaxed than you have ever been. Picture a blue sky with ten white clouds. Each cloud has a number on it. Now picture each cloud blowing away. As you blow away each cloud, say its number. As you blow away each cloud you become more and more tired." I started with one and got up to five. Then I was too tired to count clouds anymore. I was way under. The next thing I knew, I was awake and feeling fine.

"Did I remember the dream?"

"You did."

"Why can't I remember anything about this session?"

"Because I told you not to. For some reason you never remember anything about the dream in waking life, and vice versa. I didn't want to tamper with your natural predilections. It's all on there." He indicated the Zoom recorder.

"When can I come back and record more?"

"Come again same time next Wednesday, and we'll record a week's worth of your dream."

It seemed a long time to wait, but I agreed. What follows is what was on the recording I took home:

Dr. Schrock: When did you first have the dream?

Me: Wednesday, May eleventh.

Dr. Schrock: A month ago today.

Me: Yes.

Dr. Schrock: Now you're going back to the beginning. To the first night you had it. Tell me the dream.

The next voice that came out of the recorder was not my own. It was Larry Holden's, a younger, deeper voice than mine. He sounded very authentic, like one of those actors who play the private eye in the '40s movies.

"I'm in my shabby Hollywood apartment. I've converted a laundry room into a darkroom. Prints hang from clips on lines strung up between two walls. It's a tiny room, so I need three lines to accommodate enough prints for a roll of film.

"I get a call from Fritzy Johnson, the editor of the *L.A. Star*. That's a crummy tabloid I work for sometimes. He wants me to go to an address in Hancock Park that night, the Wadsworth mansion, to photograph everyone who emerges from the fancy cars and limos as they pull up for the Governor's Ball. 'It starts at nine. Get there early,' he says…"

As I listened, I could visualize everything perfectly.

The rest, although all of this was completely new to me in my waking life, I have already recounted—right up to Lana Turner playing Adeline standing before me naked, so I'll just skip ahead to that scene…

Adeline reached out and took my hand, gently pulling me down onto the bed. She started unbuttoning my shirt, then undid my belt. I shed the rest of my clothes in record time. She was the wildest, least-inhibited girl I had ever known. Thank God there was no Hollywood Production Code to censor my dream movie. We did things that night I had only read about in dirty magazines, things they only have words for in France. It was, in short, the fuck of my life. If I was hooked before, now I was completely landed, flopping around on the pier, helpless and gasping for breath. I was hers, hook, line, and sinker.

Afterward, we laid around, smoking.

"Where did you learn tricks like that?"

"Nowhere," she said emphatically. I gave her a skeptical look. "No, really. I just did what came naturally. Okay, I'm not a virgin. I did it once before—and it was terrible: five seconds of feverish pumping then, 'night-night.' But I swear, Larry, I've never experienced anything like this before…I think I might love you."

"So what are we gonna do about it?"

"Nothing. This is terribly inconvenient."

"That's one word for it."

"I could never marry anyone poor."

"Of course not. And who could blame you? I couldn't support even a regular girl, let alone someone like you."

"So don't propose, okay?"

"Don't worry."

"'Cause I might say yes. And then we'd both be in a lot of trouble."

I turned her to face me. "We already are, baby."

We kissed. If either of us thought this wasn't the real thing, we were kidding ourselves. Still, I had lingering doubts about her story of *doing what came naturally*. This girl had experience, but, at that point, I didn't care.

There was a long silence. "Well," I said, "What d'ya say we get up to Mulholland and get the real film before my car gets towed…and make me $5,000 closer to being rich."

We put our clothes on, then she locked up the house.

The sun was just coming up as we drove back through the winding deserted streets.

"So now you tell me: What is it about this necklace that makes everybody want to get that film? How could your brother use it to blackmail your father?"

"I—I don't know."

I gave her a look that said *Aw, c'mon*.

"No, really. I just know there's some secret surrounding that necklace, and my father doesn't want it to get out. I should never have put it on. He forbade me to ever wear it or even speak of it. It's not supposed to exist. That's all I know."

"Well, a whole lot of other people sure seem to know it exists. Who was following us in that Packard?"

"I have no idea. I think that's your car up there…"

She made a U-turn and pulled up behind my car. I got out and opened the trunk.

"What made you take a blank roll and hide the real film in your trunk?"

"When you called me, there was a second click after you hung up. Someone was listening in, so I knew there was gonna be trouble."

"Probably Albert," she said.

I leaned into the trunk to fish out the film, and suddenly the Packard appeared out of nowhere and screeched to a halt beside us. Two men got out and pulled guns. One was big and looked like an over-the-hill boxer who had taken one too many shots to the head. The other was the guy I had seen at the Wadsworth mansion, the one who was clocking me. He was smaller, with cruel eyes and a crooked smile. This one had enough brains to be really dangerous. I could see there was someone in the back seat of the Packard, a man in a hat, but I couldn't get a good look at him.

"Hand over the film, smart guy," said the small mean one.

The back door of the car opened and out stepped the man in the hat. He was a short, stocky guy with thick lips. He chewed on a big cigar and wore an expensive topcoat. He had the look of the streets, but the edges were smoothed out a bit. In my dream, he was played by Edward G. Robinson (of course. I must've seen *Double Indemnity* fifteen times). "Take it easy, Rollo. I'm sure Mr. Holden will cooperate." He reached into his pocket and flashed some kind of badge. It wasn't an L.A.P.D. badge. "Vincent Schiaparelli, Allied Insurance Company."

"Insurance? What d'ya want with me?" I asked.

"The necklace."

"What necklace?" Adeline and I asked as one.

"Don't bullshit me. Excuse the French, miss, but Rollo here saw you wearing it." He turned to me. "And he saw you take the picture." Adeline and I continued to play dumb. "They're known as the Burdell emeralds."

Burdell was Adeline's mother's maiden name.

"Let me refresh your memories. You were both kids at the time, but in 1929, this necklace was supposedly stolen from the Keys Mansion. Your father was wiped out in the crash, so he had a good motive to commit insurance fraud, and I think that's exactly what he did. He had city hall in his pocket at the time, so the cops handled the investigation with kid gloves. Intentionally sloppy. The United Insurance Company ended up paying out a million dollars to your pop after no one could come up with any clues whatsoever. This, and the depression, caused United to go bankrupt. Keys thought he was home free, but my company, Allied, bought United out of bankruptcy, and I've decided to reopen the case. We're offering a $100,000 reward to whoever turns in the emeralds. Of course, we'd have to prosecute your father—unless he paid back the million United gave him. With interest, of course."

Adeline and I just looked at each other and kept silent.

"The film, Mack," said Rollo.

I reached into the trunk and got the roll of film. I handed it to Rollo, but kept hold of the tag of film I always leave sticking out, so I can easily extract it for development. When he grabbed the canister, I pulled on the end of the film, and the whole roll came spilling out all over Mulholland Drive, exposing and ruining all the negatives.

"Why, you…"

The little guy slugged me behind my left ear with the butt of his gun. I saw stars. Reflexively, I took a swing at him. He caught it in his left eye and went down. I immediately felt that familiar queasiness in my stomach. It happens every time I hit somebody.

I was born in New York City. Hell's Kitchen. Both my parents died in the flu epidemic of 1918. I was three. They put me and my two brothers in an orphanage. It was—harsh, to say the least. Both my brothers died there. I ran away when I was ten. I had to fight a lot to survive on the streets of New York. But, ever since I fought my best friend on a rooftop over something stupid, and I slugged him, and he fell off and died, violence has made me physically ill.

Then the big guy stepped in and started pounding away on my face. I was too sick to fight back. The last thing I heard before everything went black was Adeline screaming:

"Leave him alone!"

The pain went from my head to my left shoulder, and I woke up, lying on my left side, in my dreary, full-color bedroom.

# III

Life dragged on at its petty pace until Wednesday rolled around. I felt like a kid at Christmas as I took my little recorder and headed over to Dr. Schrock's office. Here's what was on the Zoom when I got it home.

I came to in the driver's seat of my car. My hat was pulled down over my eyes. Something hard was poking me in the shoulder. I lifted the brim to see a cop poking me with his nightstick. There was a patrol car with another cop in it parked behind me.

"Wake up, buddy. You can't sleep here…say, what happened to you?"

My head seemed to be enlarging and shrinking in rhythmic waves of pain, accompanied by a humming sound that got louder when my head expanded and softer when it contracted. How long had I been out? No way to tell. The Packard was gone, and so was Adeline's car. I had to come up with a credible story fast, and my brain was really in no condition.

"Well, let me see…"

"Hey, what's this?" asked cop number two, picking up the mangled roll of film from the pavement behind my car.

"I'm a photographer," I said. It seemed like a good idea to start off with something true. "I sell a lot of shots to the *Star*." Then a story just magically materialized. It's amazing what the brain is capable of when one's ass is on the line. "I crashed a party last night around here somewhere, and there were some celebrities and movie stars there, and I snapped some pictures. They didn't like it and had a couple of bouncers throw me out and work me over."

"Where's your camera?" asked cop number one.

"I don't know. They probably took it or smashed it up. That film is what I shot last night. I guess they exposed the whole roll."

"Let's see some I.D.," said cop number one. I reached into my inside pocket for my wallet and felt an envelope that wasn't there before. I showed him my press card from the *Star*.

"Okay, get outta here"—he looked at the card—"Larry. And stop pokin' your nose where it don't belong."

I could barely see straight, but I had to find Adeline. I decided to drive over to the Keys mansion. On the way, I pulled the envelope out of my pocket. In it were fifty 100-dollar bills. On the envelope, she had scribbled an address on Broad Beach Road, way out in Malibu. Then I noticed a crumpled up brown paper bag on the floor of my car. I pulled over and picked it up. In it were the Burdell emeralds.

I headed for Malibu.


The address Adeline had written was for a large bungalow perched about thirty feet above the beach. It was way above Malibu, at Trancas, and this was the only house within 200 yards. I didn't see Adeline's car. I took the brown paper bag and locked it in my trunk, then rang the doorbell. No answer. I waited a few minutes, then rang again.

I faintly heard a woman's voice from deep inside the house. "I'm comin', I'm comin'. Hold yer horses!" Then the shuffling of old-woman feet.

After another minute, the door was opened by an elderly housekeeper. "Well?" she asked irritably.

"My name is Holden. Is Adeline Keys here?"

Without responding, the old woman turned and walked through the foyer. "This way." She led me into a comfortably appointed living room. "Wait in here," she said. "Don't bother trying to get a drink. She keeps the liquor locked up."

"You'll have to excuse Hattie. She's not known for her social graces." It was an elderly, aristocratic lady (played by Ethel Barrymore) with kind, sharp eyes that scrutinized me carefully. "Are you Mr. Holden?"

"Yes, ma'am."

She turned to the housekeeper. "That'll be all, Hattie. You can go to bed." Hattie shuffled upstairs. "Sit down, won't you? Adeline said to expect you. I'm Clara Leighton, Adeline's aunt—her father's sister. Adeline should be here in a while. I got a call from her earlier. She used her father's private line. We don't think it's tapped. She's bringing her father. They're going into hiding."

"Here?"

"No. This is just the first stop."

I took off my hat and stepped into the light.

"My God, what did they do to you? Lie down on the couch. I'll get some ice." I did as I was told. She went off to the kitchen and came back with a makeshift ice pack, made with a hot water bottle and some ice cubes. "Here, put this on that lump behind your ear." Then she got a washcloth and cleaned my face up a bit. I'd been on my own since I was ten, and it felt good to be mothered. She gave me some aspirin and water. Then offered me a tall scotch, which I accepted eagerly.

"Those guys that worked me over. They're insurance investigators."

"So she told me."

"I'm pretty certain they'll follow her."

"She knows that. She was expecting them to knock on the door at any moment when she called. She expects they'll want to search the house. While they're busy searching, her plan is to spirit her father out through a secret passageway that leads from his inner sanctum to the garage and get a head start on them."

"Her brother, Albert. He's got it in for Adeline and your brother. I think he's in with the thugs. There's a big reward for that necklace."

"Yes. I know the whole story. Albert's always been a bad kid. Oh my god! I just realized—Adeline and Albert used to come out here when they were children in the summertime. Albert knows about this place!"

"Then he'll probably lead the insurance thugs right to us."

"Adeline told me she gave you the necklace. Do you have it?"

I hesitated, but I trusted her, so answered honestly. "Yeah."

"Where is it?"

"In the trunk of my car."

"Can you get it?"

I went outside and opened the trunk. Then I heard footsteps.

"Hiya, Larry ol' pal." It was Albert. I turned to see him with his .38 pointed right at me. "Don't tell me she gave *you* the bauble. This is even better than I planned!" He came closer. "You don't pack iron, do ya?"

"No." I opened my coat and showed him.

"Then just hand it over, pal."

As he reached for the bag, I accidentally-on-purpose let the necklace fall to the ground. In that split second, as he watched it drop, I caught him with a hard right on the chin. He dropped like a stone. I grabbed the gun.

And that's where the recording ended.

# IV

The next day I resolved to do something that involved other people.

Since I had retired two years ago, I'd lived on a very modest fixed income in the rent-controlled apartment I had occupied for twenty years. There was little room in my budget for social activities. I almost never saw anyone. I spoke on the phone with a few old friends, but they all lived very far away. I wouldn't say I was lonely exactly, but I did feel a certain sense of isolation.

My last relationship with a woman had ended six years ago, when I was still working and earning what most would consider a middle class income. But not Margot. Margot had been married to a cartoonist who stumbled into the video game business in its infancy, in the early '80s. He'd designed a war game that made him millions. When they divorced, Margot walked away with three million dollars. In addition, she was an executive at a travel firm and pulled down a salary of $80,000 a year. But, for some reason, she loved me. Or said she loved me. She was beautiful and sexy and had a great house, so what could be bad? I fell for her like an avalanche. Then, after almost exactly a year of unwedded bliss, she sent me an email. We used to trade funny little rhymes. I had started it. I liked making them up for people's birthday cards, and this bled over to my relationship with Margot. But this email wasn't funny. It was entitled "A Sad Poem." What it lacked in literary merit, it made up for in emotional impact: it knocked my guts out.

I'm sorry to say this, my dear, but it is true,
I love you so, but I am blue.
I need more in life, that only money can buy

This is how we are different, oh why, oh why?
I can't carry us both, financially speaking,
This entire poem is leaving me weeping.

There was more, not in verse: she said she was miserable and admitted to being a chicken. I had never asked her to carry me financially, but I had made the fatal error of accepting a couple of loans from her. They were her idea, but I never should have gone along. When I was finally able to get through to her on the phone, she explained that she was never unhappy with me, but she needed to find someone with *financial parity* to her. It didn't have to be someone rich, just equal.

I remained in a state of shock and grief for several years. After that, I made no attempt to get back into the dating game. And, every time I looked in the mirror, the old man I saw there confirmed I had made the right decision.

But today I decided to attend a meeting of a neighborhood association whose main mission was to restrict the unbridled development taking place in my beloved town of Santa Monica. I had been getting emailed announcements for these meetings for maybe a year. I always marked them in my calendar, intending to go, but never went. I decided I would go tonight. The Montana Branch of the Santa Monica Public Library, where the meeting was being held, was a walk of maybe five blocks.

I got there before the meeting actually began, during the pre-meeting schmooze. Most of the attendees were elderly, like me. People in their fifties and older. These were my fellow long-time Santa Monica residents who didn't want the neighborhood to change, didn't want the rental laws protecting them to change, and didn't want to be forced out of their homes at this stage in life. I didn't know anyone there, but I did notice one attractive woman. She could have been in her fifties, although she looked much younger. The only thing that betrayed her age was her graying hair, which, had she chosen to dye it, would have made me conclude she was way too young for me. I admired that she didn't dye it. A lot of people in my neighborhood are physical fitness fanatics, organic eaters, yoga practitioners, especially the women. I pegged her for one of these.

To my surprise, she turned to me, looked me straight in the eye, and smiled. It was a lovely smile, and clearly an invitation.

"Hi," she said.

I introduced myself.

"Sharon Johnson. You live around here?"

"Yeah. 16th and California. You?"

"Idaho and 17th."

"So we live three blocks from each other."

"And I don't even know the people who live next door," she said.

"Must be serendipity," I said.

She had beautiful blue eyes. My last girlfriend had blue eyes, but she lived in Ventura County. Very inconvenient. But we'd managed to get together two or three nights a week, taking turns driving to each other's houses. After that, I resolved that I would only consider a serious romance with someone within walking—or at least biking—distance. Sharon rose to the standard admirably.

We sat next to each other at the meeting. I mostly listened. The speaker was a woman on the City Council, someone whom we had elected on her professed platform of opposition to the big development projects and changes in zoning laws now being considered by the Santa Monica City government.

At the Q&A, Sharon raised her hand.

"What I want to know is this: Why did I, and all the others here, who voted for you, vote for you? You ran on an 'anti-development' platform, and then you stabbed us in the back and voted to approve that giant mixed-use structure at Arizona and 5th Street. What's up with that?"

"That development will contain public park land and affordable housing," said the councilwoman.

"That is a half truth," said Sharon. "The 'public park land' you speak of would be mostly on the roof and patios of a gargantuan office building, and there would only be four or five affordable apartment units—out of fifty. Mainly, it would contain offices to which nine thousand commuters would drive and park their nine thousand cars every day."

Sharon was smart and well-informed. She impressed me enormously.

"Can I walk you home?" I asked after the meeting.

"Sure."

We talked about our interests—some of them mutual. We were both into classic rock and a few old new-wave groups. It turned out she was the widow of the lead guitarist of a famous British band who had died of a drug overdose back in 1981. The band, which will remain nameless here, was one of my all-time favorites. She was also heavy into yoga and Buddhist philosophy, something else we shared. I told her a little about my career as an almost-rock star—I had been leader and songwriter for several bands in the '60s, '70s and '80s, some of which were signed to major record companies—then as an A&R guy for a couple of record companies. In the early 2000s the record business imploded, and I developed my skills as a writer, editor, and proofreader. I had a brief career as a copywriter for several ad agencies before I'd decided to retire.

"So, way too much about me. What's your story?"

"I'm a film editor. Mostly documentaries and a few minor features so far. But I feel fortunate to be making a living at the thing I love."

We were both fans of the black-and-white movies of old. When we got to her building, we exchanged phone numbers and emails and agreed to keep in touch.

Walking home, I mused about the possibilities. I knew I liked her and was attracted to her, and I suspected she felt the same. This could represent a major life change for me. I had been a virtual recluse for several years. Another thing making it ideal was that we each had our own apartment, close enough to see each other at any time, but also a place to which we could each escape if we needed to. After three marriages and a few brief cohabitations, I knew, beyond any doubt, that I could never actually live with anyone ever again. For me, Sharon had all the makings of a perfect companion.

I waited a day or two, then called and asked her out to dinner. We went to Thai Dishes, the best Thai restaurant in all of L.A., and it was within walking distance of both our places. Sitting across from her at the table, I was able to gaze into those clear blue eyes, and I liked the way she was looking at me.

After dinner, we walked home. The June moon was bright and nearly full.

"Hey, you wanna see my place?" I said. "It's right on the way to yours."

I have good apartment karma. I got into this place twenty-two years ago, just before rent control became a thing of the past. It's on the ground floor of a rear, two-unit building. It's just a one bedroom, but it's nice. There's plenty of space for me and my cat, who comes in and out as he pleases. Outside, there's a patio with a table and chairs and a metal roof supported by filigreed wrought iron posts. Then there's a little lawn. My yard is sheltered from the property next door by a row of Cyprus trees that form a solid wall of green. There are potted plants all around. It's very quiet and private, sort of like a little guest house.

"My god, this is so charming," she said.

"It's perfect for me. C'mon in."

I put on a CD by a little-known female artist I really like called Joy Askew.

I was happy to learn Sharon was a fellow drinker. I made myself a brandy and soda, and she had white wine.

"Put on that vanity album you told me about," she said.

I was somewhat reticent to follow Joy, whose singing and songwriting is magnificent, but I played her the album I had made at my own expense several years ago. I hadn't promoted it, except to my friends on Facebook, and it sold about four copies. I didn't like my singing on it, but the songs were solid, if not current-sounding.

"I love it," said Sharon. "Especially that song 'Overboard.'"

I could see she wasn't bullshitting me. We ended up kissing and making out—something I hadn't done for six years.

At last she sighed. "I really have to go. I have to get up in the morning."

I was glad it hadn't gone any further. Over long years of experience in these matters, I've learned that rushing into bed with someone you hardly know is never a good idea. I walked her the three blocks to her place. I got a brief tour of her apartment, which had two floors and was much larger than mine. I was really impressed with her taste in décor. She had some embroidered Tibetan thangkas that must have cost a fortune, as well as a Buddha on an altar of sorts with incense, and some impressive Western art as well.

We kissed goodnight, and I walked home under the bright moon, enervated and dazed.


That night I slept soundly and dreamed I was part of a hippie tribe in Northern California. The dream was in full color, and I remembered a lot of it. It was the first time in months I hadn't dreamed a continuation of the film noir story of Larry and Adeline. I was alarmed and dismayed. I had grown very attached to my black-and-white adventure, and I wanted to know how it came out in the end. I wondered if it was gone forever. I wondered if it had anything to do with my growing feelings for Sharon.

Monday morning, I put in a call to Dr. Schrock, left a message with his assistant asking him to call me. A few hours later, he called back. I told him what had happened and about Sharon. I wondered if he could hypnotize me into going back to the black-and-white dream. He said he didn't know. I decided to keep my regular Wednesday appointment.

Meanwhile, I kept thinking about Sharon. I wanted to see her again. I didn't want her to think I wasn't interested. I saw that the Aero, our local Santa Monica art cinema, was showing a revival of two Fellini films: *La Dolce Vita* and *8½*. I had seen both of them multiple times but not in a theater in a long time. I called Sharon and asked if she wanted to go, maybe one night during the week, as I hated to go to movies on weekend nights. She said Wednesday would be good.

The rest of the week, I dreamed every night—in color, of insignificant things. It became clear I'd reverted to the standard dreaming I had always done before the advent of Adeline and Larry.

I saw Dr. Schrock Wednesday afternoon. He put me under and suggested I resume the dream of Adeline and Larry. He said that was all he could think of to do, and if I truly wanted to go back to that dream, I probably would. He agreed with me that the arrival of Sharon had probably triggered the change. He encouraged me to live my life while I was awake. "You'll be a long time dead," he concluded cheerfully.

"When we're dead, do you think we go to the place of our dreams?"

He shrugged. "That's as good a theory as any."

That evening, I met Sharon at a popular eatery on Montana, not far from the Aero. We had a bite to eat, and Sharon told me about her wild life as the wife of a rock star in England. This was at the beginning of the punk revolution, which happened almost exactly a decade after the Beatles revolution, the time of my first foray into rock 'n' roll. Sharon's husband's band was neither pure punk nor pure new wave, but rather a hybrid that bridged both worlds, which made them unique and, I dare say, immortal. After her husband's death, Sharon moved to New York City (my home town), where she studied film at NYU. She married a prominent architect and had a daughter, who became a successful model. I was shocked to learn she was fifty-eight years old. She looked much younger, but this fact gave me hope, even though I was still more than a decade older.

After dinner we walked to the theater. It was good seeing those old Fellini films again on the big screen. I especially loved *La Dolce Vita*, which was in black and white. Walking back toward my place, we discussed the films. She was a really astute viewer, being a professional editor. I remarked that, in all the fiction-writing classes I had taken—both as a college undergraduate and later as an adult—they had always stressed the importance of a story arc: a beginning, a middle, and an end, raising and dropping the tension until it built to a crescendo, a denouement of some kind, then a resolution. I remarked that *La Dolce Vita* had none of that. It was just a series of scenes from a guy's life, in which he gets increasingly decadent and emotionally lost. And it worked beautifully.

"You know, I've been flailing about, looking for a story idea and I think I might have just gotten one."

"Tell me," she said.

"Well, when I was thirteen I had this friend from 'the other side of the tracks.' His name was Richie, and he was a true juvenile delinquent. He was always dreaming up crazy stunts. Dangerous and destructive stunts. And I became his partner in crime. His enabler, you might say. No one actually got hurt or killed, but the potential was always there."

"Sounds intriguing," she said.

"But here's the thing: I could write this like *La Dolce Vita*; just a series of scenes in the life of these two boys. No story arc."

"I say go for it," she said.

"Thank you, muse," I said, only half-joking.

When we got to my house, I invited her in. We had drinks, we made out, and we wound up in bed together. Her body was, as Michael Caine said in *Alfie*, in beautiful condition. She looked a lot better than I did, that's for sure. I was nervous. I hadn't done this in six years, and I wasn't sure I still could. Maybe I was too old; maybe I had lost it. But she was incredibly open and affectionate and put me at my ease, and everything worked out pretty well for a first time.

Dr. Schrock's hypnotic suggestion didn't work. That night I dreamed I had a job driving an eighteen-wheel trailer truck. The cab was a bright blue, making it look more like a toy than a real truck. I knew I was doing a lousy job. I felt really bad about myself. My boss was very kind and understanding, but he just shook his head sadly. He knew I was hopeless as a truck driver, and he very gently fired me. It was just like a job I once had as a proofreader. The copy was of a highly technical nature, and there was an array of different legal language that had to be adhered to exactly for each of various different subsidiaries. I knew I was out of my depth, but I hung on as long as I could, because the money was really good. After a few gentle warnings that I wasn't cutting it, my boss sadly told me this would be my last day. My coworkers were very nice about it. "This isn't for everyone," they said. But the feeling of failure haunted me for quite a while—until I got a new job as a copywriter. Much less challenging and much more fun.

It looked like my black-and-white world of Adeline and Larry was gone forever. In spite of my happiness at finding Sharon, there was a pervasive sadness in my heart that surfaced every time I thought about Adeline. And I wondered what would become of her in that parallel universe.

Sharon and I continued to see each other and have sex a couple of times a week. She had just started work on a major Hollywood picture. It was a plum job, and she was anxious to make good. She worked long hours and on weekends, and I didn't get to see her as often. Although I called her almost every night, it was rare that I actually got to speak with her and, before long, weeks had passed, and we hadn't spoken. Finally, she called me back.

"I'm so sorry. It's been a strange time for me." Her voice was filled with trepidation.

"What's wrong, Sharon?"

"I-I hardly know how to begin. I've been seeing someone else."

"Ouch!" I said.

"Yeah, ouch."

"Anybody I know?"

"It's Jason Corelli, the director on the picture I've been editing."

Jason Corelli was a big name in Hollywood. He was younger than both me and her, and vastly richer and more powerful.

"I understand completely. No hard feelings. I wish you nothing but good things," I said, concealing my jealousy of the other man's clear superiority. This was, after all, Hollywood.

I felt an odd mix of emotions: pain and wounded pride at being rebuffed (In my youth, I was the one who left; now, it seemed, I was the one who *got* left) and, at the same time, a certain relief and a kind of hopefulness that perhaps my black-and-white dream world would now return. I now realized that, at some level, I resented Sharon for taking Adeline away from me.

# V

I started working on my short story. I decided to call it "J.D." and, true to *La Dolce Vita*, there was no story arc. After a few rewrites, I was pretty pleased with the way it read. I found a long online list of literary magazines that accepted submissions, and I began submitting "J.D." to all the ones that looked like they might go for something like this. It was an arduous process, but it kept me busy and kept my mind off the loss of my black-and-white dream world and the rejection I had suffered from Sharon.

Then the rejection letters started arriving. They were mostly form letters that basically said, in the gentlest terms possible, the same thing: that they had read it with interest, but it just wasn't right for their publication. All but one, which actually gave me personalized feedback: no story arc. In all, 149 publications rejected my piece. Then, one rainy day, I found in my mailbox an envelope that I recognized as one of my self-addressed, stamped envelopes, which had accompanied one of the few hard copy submissions I had made. *Another rejection*, I thought. But when I opened the soggy envelope, in it was a small slip of paper, about two inches by three inches. There was a letterhead from a magazine called *Manifesto*. There was a note sloppily scribbled in blue ink. Here is what it said:

*Dear Mr.*—and then my last name,

*OK* (then something crossed out) *On "J.D." (These "slice of life" stories are killing me). You'll receive two copies and a penny a word for the first North American serial rights.*

*Thank you.*

*Happy New Year!*

*Jonathan Blum*

This seemed to be an acceptance letter. I had never received one, so I wasn't sure. I showed it to a neighbor, and she confirmed: it *was* an acceptance letter! I immediately retraced my submission steps and went to the website of *Manifesto*. All it said was "Website Expired." All I had was a street address for Mr. Blum, so I wrote him a short note that had a photocopy of his acceptance letter at the bottom. I thanked him for accepting my story. Told him I couldn't wait to see it in print. Then I mentioned I had tried to go to his website and found it expired. I asked if he could please shoot me a quick email to the address on my letterhead and let me know what was going on. Had *Manifesto* gone belly-up? (Those were not my exact words.) I went back to the master list of literary magazines I had used as a resource, and *Manifesto* was no longer listed.

I never received a reply.

Every night, I would knock myself out in the customary manner and hope that my black-and-white dream would return. But no such luck. I decided to give Dr. Schrock another try. I called and made an appointment for the following Wednesday.

Dr. Schrock put me under again and suggested I continue my black-and-white dream, but to no avail. That night, I dreamed about some Irish guys in 1936 sending weapons to Generalissimo Franco in the Spanish Civil War.

The days and nights dragged on. I thought about trying to write my dream as a story, but it would just come out sounding like a cliché film noir plot—like one of those movies they made by the dozen in the '40s, or—if I was lucky—like a Raymond Chandler novel.

I went to another community meeting at the library. I didn't contribute, just listened. I wasn't that well informed about local politics, but I knew it was on the local level one could really make an impact on one's daily existence. I spotted Sharon seated a few rows in front of me. She didn't see me.

After the meeting, I just got up and walked out. I didn't feel like mingling. Then I heard her footsteps coming up fast behind me. She caught up with me and said, "Hi."

"Hi," I said. "How're things going?"

"Oh, busy." Her voice had a forlorn quality.

"How's the new relationship working out?"

"It didn't. The guy's an asshole. Big surprise. A major Hollywood director. What did I expect?"

"Sorry," I said.

"I made a big mistake to leave you. You're a great guy. You didn't deserve that…I don't suppose you'd be interested in us seeing each other again?"

This came as a complete surprise to me. In fact, I don't think anyone had ever come crawling back to me. I thought about it for a long moment. I hadn't really missed Sharon all that much—not as much as I missed Adeline. And it was because of Sharon that I lost Adeline. "I don't think it would work, Sharon. I wouldn't want to leave myself open for another blindside, and I don't think I could ever really trust you again."

Her eyes teared up. She looked really pretty that way. "Okay, sure. I understand. You take care." And she walked off fast.

I'm a little ashamed to admit it, but it gave me a rush to turn her down, to see her walk away with tears in her eyes. It made me feel powerful, attractive. Things I hadn't felt about myself in a very long time.

And, that night, Adeline came back to me.

# VI

As soon as I fell asleep, the dream picked up right where it had left off. When I awoke, I knew it had returned and immediately called Dr. Schrock and made an appointment. When I played back the recording, I heard me, speaking in Larry's voice…

I shoved the necklace back in the crumpled paper bag and took it inside, leaving Albert temporarily sprawled in the driveway. I put the bag on the table in front of Mrs. Leighton.

"What are you planning to do with this?" I asked.

"When Adeline gets here, we're going to deep-six it."

"Deep-six?"

"Literally. You and she are going to take the motorboat that's tied to the end of the dock behind my house, sail out a-ways, and toss this geegaw into the briny deep."

I excused myself, went in the bathroom, and threw up.

"What's wrong, Larry? You look green."

"I always throw up after I hit someone. It's a long story, Aunt Clara—is it okay if I call you that?"

"Delighted."

"Do you have some rope?"

"Rope?"

"Yeah. Enough to tie a guy up."

"I think so. Why?"

"Because your nephew, Albert, is passed out in your driveway, and I have to tie him up." I showed her the gun. "He pulled this on me and tried to take the necklace, so I had to knock him out."

"Well, bravo! A few feet of rope, coming up. Will you need any help getting him into the house?"

"Nope. I think I can manage." She got the rope. I went back outside and bound Albert's legs together at the ankles. I grabbed an arm and managed to sling him over my shoulder, fireman-style. I carried him into the house, and we sat him in a wooden chair. I tied his hands behind his back and him to the chair.

"Larry," said Aunt Clara. "Do you want to tell me why you were sick?"

"Let's just say it's something that happens to me every time I slug a guy and leave it at that. Looks like Sleeping Beauty is coming to…"

Albert shook his head, noticed he was bound hand and foot. "What the hell…?"

"Uh, uh, uh. Ladies present," I said.

"Ow. I think you busted my jaw, you…dirty rat!"

"If it were busted, you wouldn't be talking so much."

"We were kind of expecting you, Albert," Aunt Clara chimed in. "I realized—a bit late—that you and Adeline used to visit here when you were kids."

"Oh, hi, Aunt Clara. Nice to see you again," said Albert.

"Did you lead the insurance boys here?" I asked.

"They have the address. I expect they'll be along directly."

"How did they get my address, Albert?" said Aunt Clara.

"I've been workin' for them from the beginning. I was their inside man, you might say. Heck, I knew Adie was gonna wear that necklace before she did."

"How?" I asked.

"Jerome. I was supplying him with opium, getting him drunk on rum. He knew everything about the necklace—even the combination to Dad's secret safe. Heck, he was the one who pulled the job for Dad in the first place. He had a peephole from his room into the old man's. He saw Adie sneak into his room at night and just stare at the thing. I knew she would be tempted to wear it, and I guessed the Governor's Ball would be the time. That's how the insurance dicks knew to be there, watching."

"But Adeline told me you were gonna blackmail your father," I said.

"Nah. It was never blackmail. Schiaparelli hired me to help him with the investigation. He had this feeling in his gut the necklace was still around. So he put me on retainer and offered me the hundred grand reward if they recovered the necklace."

"But what about Adeline? Did she make her getaway?" asked Aunt Clara anxiously. "Are the insurance guys chasing her?"

"She used the secret passageway to get her and the old man out of the house, so she had a big head start on them. In that car of hers, I'm surprised she didn't beat me here," said Albert.

Just then the doorbell rang. From upstairs, I heard Hattie grumbling, "Now what? What is this, Grand Central Station?"

"That's all right, Hattie. I'll get it," said Aunt Clara. She opened the door, and there stood Adeline and Mr. Keys, both looking much the worse for wear. Adeline helped her father, who walked with two canes and some difficulty. They were both covered in dark brown topsoil. "My goodness, whatever happened to you?" cried Aunt Clara.

I rushed over and put my arms around her. I was so relieved I kissed her in front of everyone, without regard for decorum.

"Aww, ain't love grand," said Albert. "So, what *did* happen?"

"Albert! You here already? Bet you're sorry to see me—alive!" said Adeline. "We were being tailed by the insurance guys. I was going rather fast. We were barreling down the big hill on Malibu Canyon Road, toward Pacific Coast Highway, when my brakes went." She gave Albert a significant look. "I'll bet you dimes to dollars *someone* cut the brake line, and all the fluid leaked out."

"What're you lookin' at me for?" said Albert.

"Who would have a better reason for wanting both me and Father dead? Why, then you'd inherit his entire fortune by default."

"That's a serious accusation, Adie. I hope you're prepared to prove it," said Albert.

"I'll try, Albert. I'll really try. Why are you all tied up?"

Albert looked at me sheepishly. "I had to take his toy away," I said, showing her the gun. "He wanted the necklace."

"Well," said Adeline, "while you're in this compromising position, I have something for you, Albert." And she walked over and slapped him hard in the face.

All the while, Mr. Keys slouched in an easy chair, nursing a small flask. "Masterful driving," he said, almost to himself, slurring his words. "You should have seen her, weaving in and out of oncoming cars. It was thrilling!" Then he noticed his surroundings, and his sister. "I don't believe I've had the pleasure, dear lady," he said to Clara.

"I'm Clara, Monty. Your sister."

"Clara? But you're so old!"

"We're both old, Monty. Finish your story, Adeline. How did you survive?"

"Near the bottom, the hillside is made of soft dirt. I just steered as gently as I could into the hillside, wrecked the right side of my car, got a whole lot of dirt in my lap, but it stopped the car."

"How did you get here?" asked Aunt Clara.

"We hitchhiked," said Adeline.

"Charming couple," muttered Mr. Keys. "I think they were on their honeymoon."

Meanwhile, Albert was glowering at Adeline and the adoring way I was looking at her.

"I wonder what your boyfriend would say if he knew what you really are, Adie."

"What do you mean?" Something about this guy made me really want to hurt him.

"Your girlfriend is nothing but a tramp, Larry my boy—a party girl. She and her pal Reggie throw sex parties—regular orgies. She does it with guys, two at once, girls, farm animals, you name it. Adie gets passed around like the church collection plate on Sunday."

"Why, you lyin'…" I tasted bile rising in my throat, and I was about to haul off on him again, but Adeline's voice stopped me.

"It's true, Larry."

I froze. I took one look at her tear-filled eyes and the shame on her face and knew it was so.

"I've been bad. Very, very bad. But I love you, and it will never happen again. Can you forgive me?"

I felt like I had turned to stone. Except for my eyes, which were filling with tears. I kept picturing her with all those guys. This explained why she repaid me by taking me to bed, when we hadn't known each other an hour. And I thought it was love at first sight. How could I have been so stupid? I said nothing.

"None of them meant anything to me. I was drunk. We were all drunk—and high on drugs. Reggie dared me, he taunted me, said I didn't have the nerve. Well, I sure showed him." She broke down sobbing.

Aunt Clara was clearly shocked and red with embarrassment. Even Mr. Keys snapped out of his stupor and stared, slack-jawed, at his beloved daughter.

Just then there was a loud pounding on the door. We all looked at each other.

"It seems they've arrived," said Aunt Clara. Then the front door burst open, with the two thugs in the lead, guns drawn, followed by Vincent Schiaparelli.

"Everybody, hands in the air...except you," said Rollo, noticing Albert. The insurance guys all snickered.

"Well, hail, hail, the gang's all here," said Schiaparelli.

"You. Drop that cannon," said Rollo, looking at me. I was still in a state of shock and didn't even hear him. I barely noticed the thugs enter the room. "I said drop it, buster!" I dropped the gun and put my hands up.

"Now you drop yours, boys!"

It was Hattie, the old housekeeper. She wielded a twelve-gauge shotgun. Schiaparelli and his henchmen had entered the living room and Hattie had descended the stairs behind them, ever so quietly. She cocked both barrels. "I've got one barrel for each of you two. And make no mistake, when I shoot, I don't miss. Now drop the guns, turn around, and hands up!"

I quickly retrieved all the guns, gave one to Aunt Clara, and put the other two in my pockets.

"Now, take the bag, Adeline, and you two make a run for it," said Aunt Clara. Adeline picked up the paper bag and headed out the back door that led to a rickety wooden staircase and down to the dock. I was still in shock. I followed her down there, slowly.

She looked back at me. "Are you coming?"

I just shook my head. I couldn't get the visions of her doing those things with other guys out of my head.

A mist had started to roll in over the Pacific. She jumped into the launch and cast off the bow line, then stood in the stern, looking back at me. She took the necklace from the paper bag and put it on, yanked on the cord, and started the engine. She was still wearing the silver satin gown, all muddied, with a black coat draped over her shoulders and a black beret. The necklace completed the picture perfectly. The little boat chugged out to sea. She raised her hand in a static salute of goodbye. I waved back, as if in a trance, and watched her recede, a frozen tableau, a bejeweled Joan of Arc, into the fog.

I didn't know what she had in mind. Would she go down with the necklace? Throw it overboard and sail off to a new life? One thing for sure: I knew I'd never see her again, and I'd live to regret it.

That's where the recording ended. And, I was pretty sure, the story as well. The thought that I would no longer dream in black and white, no longer dream of Adeline, was overwhelmingly depressing to me.

# VII

I went back to the life I'd known before Adeline, Larry, or Sharon came into my life. I had no regrets. I had one last unexpected hurrah. One brief flash of excitement and mystery before I took that inevitable slide down, down, down, to that last pathetic wheeze, that final whimper we all have to look forward to.

As before, I slept as late as possible and dreamed vividly— in color—mostly about times gone by. I was always young in my dreams, and so were the other characters, be they people I had once known or complete strangers. I got up, did my exercise routine, ate my cereal with blueberries, tried to do a little writing, tried to read as many great books as possible, watched the old movies even though I'd seen all the good ones dozens of times and, every day, I took my bike ride. Every day, the same circuit: up the hill on 16th Street, west on Idaho, north on Ocean Ave., and then east on San Vicente. I would take San Vicente to 26th Street, turn right, and go south to California (my street), then west back home.

It must have been four or five days after the last dream. I was stopped at the intersection of San Vicente and 7th. It was a Saturday, and there were a lot of people out jogging and cycling. I chanced to look to my right while waiting for the interminable series of traffic light changes: green for southbound but not for northbound, green for northbound, but not for southbound. Left turn arrows for all four directions. Then, finally a green light for me, going east. That's when I caught a glimpse of her. She was a beautiful blonde, no more than twenty-one, wearing a red jogging suit with white piping, straight hair pulled back into a ponytail, and sunglasses.

And she was a dead ringer for Adeline. If Adeline lived in my time, this is how she would look. For a split second, our eyes met, even though we were both wearing shades. And she smiled. Right at me. Even at my best, I'm no bargain to look at. But, in my cycling helmet, black kung-fu pants, blue-and-white three-quarter-sleeve T-shirt commemorating Creedence Clearwater Revival's fortieth anniversary, and the black-and-white low-top sneakers that resembled the ones I wore when I was ten, I looked especially dorky. And yet, she smiled at me. The light turned green, and I cycled on, certain I had imagined the whole thing. She was, no doubt, smiling at the young man on the bike beside me.

But then, the next day. Same corner. There she was again. This time I stopped and lowered my shades. I looked right at her. She smiled that smile that always dazzled me and lowered her shades. Our eyes locked. It *was* Adeline.

She crossed, against the light, to the southeast corner of 7th and San Vicente. On it stood a house that was at least eighty years old: a white, wooden craftsman-style with the classic California overlapping peaked roofs. Against that backdrop, she shed her red jogging gear. It turned into a black-and-white, forties-style frock with a short, tailored summer jacket over it, and a simple, broad-brimmed hat that dipped over one eye. Her hair was sculpted in permanent waves, just as it had been in my dream. She beckoned to me. I didn't hesitate. I started across 7th, paying no attention to the redness of the light.

An oncoming SUV, in a hurry to get through the intersection before the light changed, broadsided me without even slowing down. The bike and I flew halfway across San Vicente. A crowd gathered, and sirens approached. I felt no pain, just an incredible peace—and joy. Joy because I could still see her standing there in front of the big white house. But it looked a bit different. It didn't have the fancy brick gateway from a few moments earlier. She smiled and waved and, out of the crumpled heap of broken bones and bloody clothing of the old man lying lifeless in the street, rose me, Larry Holden. I was dressed in my usual trench coat and gray fedora. I walked across the street to her.

The crowd had disappeared. There was hardly any traffic. San Vicente had become a narrow, two-lane road. And it was all in black and white. She took my hand, and we walked through the gate of what I now knew was to be our house. Her Delahaye was all fixed up and parked in the garage. She looked up at me. We kissed. She asked me if I had forgiven her. I didn't know what she was talking about.

XOXOX XOXOX XOXOX X

# About the Author

After twenty years trembling on the brink of rock stardom and fifteen years working at record companies, Ted Myers left the music business—or perhaps it was the other way around—and took a job as a copywriter at an advertising agency. This cemented his determination to make his mark as an author.

His nonfiction has appeared in *Working Musicians* (Harper Collins), *By the Time We Got to Woodstock: The Great Rock 'n' Roll Revolution of 1969* (Backbeat Books), and *Popular Music and Society.* His short stories have appeared online at *Literally Stories* and in print in the *To Hull & Back Short Story Anthology 2016*. In 2017, his epic and amusing memoir, *Making It: Music, Sex & Drugs in the Golden Age of Rock* was published by Calumet Editions and more short stories appeared in *Iconoclast* magazine, *The Mystic Blue Review,* Centum Press' *100 Voices Anthology*, and *Culture Cult Magazine.* In 2018, his work appeared in *Bewildering Stories.*

# SPRINGTIME BY THE RAILROAD TRACKS

Ryanne Strong

We walked there together along the railroad tracks. The sun glistened in our hair and rested on our shoulders. Birds heralded the spring and its gentle breeze rustling through the brush all around us. The wind carried hints of wildflowers, raspberries, and old rain. In the distance, cars full of weekday warriors zipped by on the state road, eager to get back to the office in time to count the minutes until they could go home. In our cutoff shorts and tank tops, we could have been some of those workers skipping out on the routine to take a leisurely stroll on lunch break.

My knapsack was light, filled only with a sweat suit and a pair of gloves. But I heard something else clinking in time with Melinda's footsteps. It wasn't long before we came across a pile of old railroad ties left behind by some unknown work crew months, maybe even years, before. Stacks of railroad ties meant there were probably stray spikes. It might not seem like much, but the slivers of solid iron were always good for a few bucks at the scrapyard. There were never many, but that was all right with me. Old leather-faced Larry would get into a snit if you brought him more than ten at a time. I guess, technically, they were still the property of the railroad company even though they'd been left behind. Between the two of us, we only found seven— definitely a safe number, but not enough for Melinda. She pulled a crowbar out of her bag and set to work prying up one of the spikes from the track.

"Do you *have* to do that?" I asked. I didn't know what happened if you brought too many spikes to the scrapyard but getting caught pulling them out had to be worse.

"Like *one* really matters?" she said, plucking the newly freed spike out of the ground. "They only really need them when the ties go in new." Melinda tapped the plank next to the one she'd been messing with. "Now there's all those rocks and dirt to keep them in place. They aren't going to miss a few spikes."

They did seem to be packed into the earth, and there was, at least for the moment, still one spike left in each tie. Maybe that was enough. "Well, *I* wouldn't want to be responsible for a train going off the tracks. What if someone died?"

"Fine." She rolled her eyes, dropping two new spikes and the crowbar into her backpack. "But you know it's just cargo trains that come this way, right?" she added before slinging one strap over her shoulder. She was such a bitch sometimes.

I could see the old Whitney Box Factory poking out through the shrubs that had grown wild and unkempt in their decades without care. When we got close to the building, I stashed my bag behind a tree that looked big enough to provide adequate privacy for changing. Melinda had already snuck away to her own secluded spot. Sometimes we were totally in sync like that.

My foot hit something softer than the firm, rocky ground. It was cloth of some kind, maybe a T-shirt. You never knew what you'd find in the woods. Where there were clothes, there might be people. And people usually meant hassle. If it was some vagrant holed up on the outskirts, they might be too afraid to bother us. But if somebody was squatting in the building, they might see us as a threat. I did a quick sweep of the trees and didn't see anything—aside from Melinda prying away at a plywood sheet that had been attached to the frame on one of the huge industrial windows. I kicked at the crusty fabric again. I'd gotten worried over nothing: it was tattered and weathered, half buried in the dirt. Whoever had dropped it was long gone now. In the interest of time, I pulled the sweats on over my clothes and put the empty bag on my back.

"What took you so long?" Melinda said impatiently, without even looking up from the small crevice she was slowly making progress with. If it had been that old shirt's mysterious owner instead of me, they could've walked right up and clobbered her before she'd even had time to get snippy with them. I decided not to mention the cloth I'd found. She obviously didn't share my concern about interference from the local population.

As soon as Melinda got enough of a gap between the plywood and window frame, I shoved my gloved hands into the space and held it out so she could put her tool away. Wordlessly performing a ritual we'd repeated countless times before at old buildings just like this one in dejected mill towns up and down the coast, together we pulled until half the board was loose from its fasteners and there was enough space for us to shimmy into the dark unknown. Melinda went first, carefully avoiding the huge nails sticking out of the board.

She landed with a thump. "Shit!"

"Are you all right?" I could barely make out her silhouette in the darkness.

"Yeah," she grumbled a moment later. "It's like a three-foot drop, but…it's pretty clear." Once I let go of the board, it would probably snap back into place, so I really didn't have another option besides jumping down after her.

I waited a minute to let my eyes adjust so I could make a better landing. I inched inside, and the rotting wood of the window frame crumpled beneath my sneakers. I still couldn't see much, but Melinda was only a few feet back from where she must have gone down, leaving plenty of space for my drop. The window frame came roughly up to Melinda's waist. About three feet, just like she said. Not too far—so in one movement, I let go of the board and hopped down to the floor of the old wooden factory, grateful for all that tumbling I'd learned in drill team; it was better to roll instead of trying to land on my feet. I ended up on my side, catching myself just before my head hit the ground and putting me face-first in the filth and dust coating the floor. I could smell the familiar acrid tinny smell of rust and standing water, waterlogged floorboards just like all the other buildings, but also a faint yet dense odor, like pee. Not the sharp ammonia smell of wild animal urine, but the vitamin-dense kind that sometimes comes from people. Maybe we weren't alone in there after all.

"We should have brought headlamps," I told Melinda, making a mental note to get one for my kit before the next trip. I looked around as my eyes adjusted still more to the darkness. After years of weathering and deterioration, parts of the ceiling and most of the upper level had collapsed onto this one, which—where I was standing at least—seemed stable enough to walk on. I was glad we'd come in on the second floor. That was usually the safest bet; less stuff to fall down on us if something collapsed while we were inside. Although most of the windows from the upper floor had been knocked out by hooligans with rocks, they weren't much use for providing light; their angle seemed better suited for casting creepy shadows than for illuminating the next floor down.

Melinda scanned the room. "There's nothing good over here," she said, going farther in, limping toward the back of the factory floor. I stayed along the perimeter, where the other windows were, still boarded up like our entrance had been. As my eyes adjusted to the gloom, I made more sense of what I was seeing.

The thing about Melinda was that she was sort of greedy. Whatever the salvage hustler equivalent of *eyes too big for your stomach* was, that was her. If there were something valuable that the two of us would be able to carry out, Melinda would find it and more. Basically, there was no point in me looking around at all, so I let myself become distracted and just wandered among the forgotten mill's rubble.

Chunks of caved-in floor, barrels of old printing ink, pallets upon pallets of flattened cardboard boxes that had never been shipped out—all the stuff I'd expected to find. But then there was a calendar. The regular month-to-month kind you hang on a wall. Like everything, it was covered in a thick layer of grime, so I rubbed at it with my toe, revealing the date. 2001: not nearly old enough to been left behind when the factory closed. I was curious how it had gotten there, so I looked a little closer at the rest of the stuff around it.

A few bunches of the flattened boxes had been removed from a pallet and arranged on the ground in their own sloppy rectangle. On top was a tattered remnant of cloth, much larger than the T-shirt I'd seen outside, but just as crusty. Unlike all the other debris I'd seen in the building, the fabric seemed to have been placed neatly, like linen on a bed. The whole arrangement looked as dingy and dust-covered as the old building I'd found them in, the same inky smut blanketing the top in one even layer, except for the large lump near the middle.

Clearly, someone had been living here.

I was no stranger to hard times. I was rummaging through a building for scrap metal for gosh sakes, but even doing that, I managed to scrape together enough money for the little pay-by-the-week room I rented.

Finding little hints that someone else has been there before you is a pretty standard part of going into abandoned buildings. Not everyone went into them for the same reason me and Melinda did. Sometimes a regular person went out for a walk, got caught up in heavy rain, and ducked inside for a little bit of cover. Other times it was just somebody who got curious about the crumbling monolith they passed every day on their way home. This was different, though. It wasn't like somebody had left a blanket behind when they closed down the building, and anybody who was just passing through probably wouldn't have brought it with them either. Whoever set up this bed had intended to come here, and sleep…probably for more than one night. I was curious what kind of person would have needed to stay in such a dismal place. What brought them there? And what made them leave without their little blanket? Maybe their luck had changed, and they'd moved on to somewhere that the tattered shroud would have no place. And then there was that nodule underneath. Whatever it was had been important enough to bring into the factory, but not important enough to take with them when they left. I peeled back the cover to see what it hid. I thought it'd be another wad of old clothes or even garbage. Shielded there, from all the ancient dust coating everything around it, was a stuffed dog. Except for a few small smudges, the worn fur was still clean and white, which contrasted pristinely against the nastiness of its surroundings. It reminded me of the teddy bear I carried around with me when I was little. Whoever brought this toy in the building hadn't left it behind on purpose; they had protected it under the blanket. But what could they possibly be guarding it from?

Melinda screamed.

"Are you okay?" I called. I could see as well as I was ever going to in the near-darkness, but Melinda was nowhere to be found. I hastily placed the blanket back over the toy, sheltering its little plastic eyes once more from whatever unspeakable terrors its mysterious owner had been shielding it from.

When I reached the pile of debris where I thought I'd last seen Melinda, I was relieved to find a stairwell. "Melinda?" My voice echoed in the darkness, unanswered again. I heard sounds like something scraping across the ground. The stairs looked like they were still intact to me. Maybe her scream hadn't been out of fear at all. Perhaps it was just the excited shriek of finding our jackpot, perverted as it bounced through the musty walls carrying its echo. It *would* be just my luck if she found our big money item on the lower floor. I was not eager to lug whatever it was up those stairs.

My descent was uneventful until I got to the bottom, and my shoes landed in a cold, wet puddle. The old water seeped into my sneakers and drenched my toes. In front of me was the back of a pallid, inhuman creature. It loomed several feet over me, its opaque skin stretched too tightly across a rigid, macilent frame, so all the bones protruded menacingly from its body. The thing perched on reptilian haunches, tail scraping against unidentifiable debris as it swayed slowly back and forth—the way a cat's tail twitches when it's stalking prey. Cowering against the wall in front of it was Melinda, clutching one of the railroad spikes in a death grip. Her eyes found me where I'd frozen just beyond the stairs, then looked down, signaling me to follow her gaze.

On the ground between us was her backpack, shredded like the T-shirt I'd found outside and the blanket covering the stuffed dog on the makeshift bed, its contents scattered about. I spotted the crowbar at the edge of the beast's wrecking path and inched toward it between swipes of the treacherous tail. I couldn't tell if she wanted me to throw it to her or keep it for myself, but I was certain she wanted me to get it. Just before I was about to grab the tool, I looked up and saw Melinda's eyes widen as the creature turned its hideous head to me. The face was ghastly white and flat, like a human face, but in place of the nose there were just slotted nostrils. Its gaping mouth held pointed fangs, longer than my fingers and coated in dark slaver, which spilled over thin lips and down its chin. My heart recoiled as the crimson eyes glowered.

I snatched up the crowbar. Before I had time to fully consider if I should try tossing the tool to Melinda, the monster whirled to face me, its gargantuan tail whipping around in one smooth motion, landing across Melinda, muffling her shriek of agony.

It was just me and the creature then. It let out its own peculiar howl, bearing its dagger-like teeth and putrid black tongue. It lashed out with one gangly arm and nearly sliced me with one of its talons. The crowbar would never be enough. My only hope was to run.

I went as fast as I could up the rickety staircase. I ran across the debris on the floor. Past the bright white puppy stuffed with innocence, the only thing that seemed safe from the filth and evil corroding the building, tenderly hidden under its blanket. I was barely able to cling to the window ledge and pull myself through the narrow slit, finally outside.

I ran for as long as I could, until my heart was throbbing in my ears and the air burning in my chest. I collapsed with my back against the base of a tree at the edge of the clearing by the tracks. I scuttled around to see where I had come from. There was no sign of the monster on my trail; I could barely even see the box factory anymore. I stripped off my heavy outer layer of clothing—now drenched in perspiration—rested my head on my knees, and finally let myself begin to relax.

All I could think of was Melinda. We'd gone in there together, and I shouldn't have left her behind. She might have had time to find a better place to hide while the monster was chasing me through the building. But the image of Melinda's body, contorted under the crushing blow of the creature's tail, came back to me when I closed my eyes. If that hadn't killed her, the monster had probably gone back to finish her off. There was nothing I could do. It took hours before I could make myself leave the woods. I kept hoping Melinda would show up. Stumbling out of the brush, exhausted, terrified… still alive.

But she never came.

Not far from the clearing, there was a little river running alongside the railroad tracks. I was still sticky with the muddy mixture of black dust and my own sweat. The water was surprisingly clear. A school of tiny minnows swam just below the surface, zig-zagging arbitrarily in pursuit of unseen elements, oblivious to where I watched them from the shore. My reflection shimmered back from the water's surface, hair rumpled and face splotched with dark smudges. It looked like I'd been lost in the woods for years instead of just the afternoon. I longed to lose myself in the water's crisp, refreshing moisture and wash away the filth and sadness caked all over my body. I dipped my hand in the water, obscuring my reflection. The minnows scattered in all directions, desperate to escape the monstrous creature invading their home and shattering their serene existence.

### About the Author

Ryanne Strong's work has been published in *Tricks and Treats: A Collection of Spooky Stories by Connecticut Authors* (Books & Boos Press, 2016). She lives and works—but never sleeps—in Southeastern Connecticut as a stagehand.

# WHERE WERE YOU LAST NIGHT?

Jay Outhier

W here were you last night? Hiding in the lab, hunkered in a cage and huffing like a chimp so I wouldn't know it was you in the dark? In the wide white room of muscular pigs? Were you nestled in the straw, burrowing a warren when the fluorescents blinked on?

So strange to search for you in those sensor-decked corridors. I felt as if the laboratory itself conspired to assist me. It said, "Where are you, David? CAGEWASH? NECROPSY? Surely not beyond the bulky airlocks of QUARANTINE?" I took your lab coat from the closet, seeing as you'd forgotten it, along with the clip of keycards inside. Each door I activated triggered a chain of lights, one of which surely would flash on your whereabouts, but no, not a trace of Dr. Holawel among the rubber and steel, not even in the drains to which the tiles all sloped, down there in the glinting, sterilized wet. David? Hello?

I called your name until every animal was awake and every bit as worried as I was. You must have heard them clanging on the bars and the glass. The lights bore down on everything: on the rattling tubs and tanks and incubators and hutches, tables with empty straps looped at the head and feet, on the smeared basins beneath complexities of spigots and hoses. Light everywhere except those far corners of the cages, where rustlings stirred at the snick of my heels, the dragging of weight and the quick gleam of eyes. The most worrisome eyes, David. Have you ever held their gaze? Tell me, have you ever felt so worried?

There was something doing somersaults in the walls after you left. Something tumbling in the cavities of our blissful home where the studs and pipes and conduits live. Whatever it was had been there awhile. Dormant, I think, almost. The beams of your headlights must have knocked it loose when they waved over the yard. I turned all the lights out to watch you back out of the driveway. I held the heavy curtains apart with more strain than you might imagine. I have not been feeling well, not well at all. But I don't let on.

Maybe it was my shadow that set it off tumbling. For if your headlights swept the parlor, then, so too, did my shadow. They must have chased my outline like a bat across the room, from the low shelves of the china cabinet—where you stow your less *conventional* instruments—all the way up to the dusted cornices.

Something rumbled. Thunder, I assumed. Raindrops had clustered on the windowpanes, and there were winds, strong winds to spit them the full depth of our porch. But the sound came again, a descending thump and the strained whine of wood, and something above and behind me broke, deep within the wall, and set to rattling the picture frames as it tumbled about; only one row of them, so of course I knew it could not be the storm. I followed our clattering wedding portraits around the corner to the jittering figurines, those sorrowful stacks of exaggerated features you brought from the Congo—not the first instance I caught sight of them shivering—and on down the hall past your jangling achievements: your Overton Prize and NAS award in molecular biology, your Darwin-Wallace and Early Career Life Scientist medals dancing like spit in a ready skillet. The shaking rolled a few feet, ceased, and tumbled again until I faced the door of the east hall closet, the clamoring wall gone still as a stump. I was not afraid, David, since you always—fastidiously— keep that door locked, but I twisted the knob to be sure just the same. And the door swung open. And there, in the dark, the empty sleeves of your lab coat dangling.

Isn't it clear I was meant to find you? Isn't it palpable that, eventually, I will?

XOXOX

The noise in the house was of no concern to me, David, not when I saw your coat left behind; I only mention it because I know how you hate it when I keep things from you.

You are my sole, burning concern. Poor dear.

*He must be shivering in the rain,* I thought, *teeth chattering and his runny nose pressed to the windows, simply doleful for absorption in his research, eyes swollen up and round as a puppy's, and with no coat, no keys, no way out of the storm.* I know how staunchly you adhere to monitoring the test results, how it must tax your nerves to remain so secretive, to those outside the scientific community—that is, to people like your wife, who are better left unburdened, I know, by the import of some findings.

Such excitement and panic when the text alert rang! Nearly spilling your wine to swipe your phone off the table. I only leaned forward to smell your cologne—strange and new, when did you start wearing that scent?—I didn't tilt over the asparagus to ferret out the content of a private message. Of course, I know better than to nose around for details that might put me in danger.

*Needed at the lab immediately, an emergency!* But you were nowhere to be found at the front doors of the facility, not even in the car, *your* car, in the parking lot. Only rain scudding gold through the beams of the sodium lamps, splotches of oil springing purple and green iridescence between the dull white lines of the parking brackets. *He must be on the trails,* I thought, around back, the footpaths the university coiled through the woods beyond the laboratories so great men like yourself can stroll among the looming trees and think and converse with your contemporaries. It is important that you have your time alone. It is important you not be disturbed or depleted with the burden of jarring, importunate questions.

But the woods have been sealed away! Those forlorn, waving trees, wiping stars from the sky like mops across a floor, had all been corralled by makeshift blockade. A succession of barriers taller than the lampposts cordoned off the entrance as far as I could follow and terminated at a shipping container the size of a freight car, attached to the bed of a totaled semi. It seemed to have unfurled from the container as the truck sped along, and judging by the furrows in the mud and the grill of the truck smashed in billows against the facility, the barrier must have gone up in quite the hurry. A trench had been dug around it, steadily brimming with rain into a moat, the earth piled high into the hollows of the wall. The hooked arm of a track-hoe wilted above the segments, worms still wriggling from the mud in its teeth.

I hope you weren't back in those trees when the wall went up, David, because even I, with my slender frame—the frame I kept slender for your benefit, none other—can't crawl under the truck to start down the trails. Sand bags cram every inch from the mud to the undercarriage. And there is nothing out there for miles and miles, nothing at all in the woods, as intended.

Did you make a mistake, David? Is there something you feel you would like to tell me? For example, why didn't you tell me about the rats? Did you think I would sigh, disinterested? Did you think I might judge? Simply because they are slinking, deceptive vermin, gut-bags of disease with brains as flat and filthy as old pennies? Because they feed through the gaps to places they're unwelcome? Wouldn't I support that such creatures excite you? Row upon row of hairless, pink creases? Lusterless eyes, like blanched seeds of a watermelon? Neither muscled nor fat, but full, like sausages? Scurrying in a matrix of cribs down the holding table, eager to dart icy tongues on your cheek?

I take no issue with the rats at all. Except, maybe, that they would speak to me, David. Not in squeaking and hissing and grinding of teeth, but speak to me, succinctly, so I might understand.

And how outlandish is my desire, really? Are we close? Might it happen? One had an ear, nearly human, not unlike my own, protruding from its back, the cartilage straining against the skin as if one of your protégés—Elizabeth, was it? Lillian, Lila? With the daffodil blonde frizz budding sprigs from her surgeon's cap?—as if she, that girl, you know the one I mean, had tucked the cup of a sea shell underneath, snugly there, just between the flesh and the spine, and stitched the incision with such skill and attention that even I couldn't manage to locate the cut. I upon whom nothing is lost; I, who, in time, notice everything.

Lily is her name. Yes! Lily! That gamine little puck! Where did you find gloves to fit such exquisite hands as hers? Special ordered from the boys in synthetics, no doubt. Such peculiar, pretty little hands…you must know their dimensions. Must have studied them closely, buffed the exalted pearl of each knuckle, pressed the rose of each nail until it bleached and blushed again at the fleeting pressure. You must have splayed her fingers with two of your own, far as they would spread, and with another traced the curve of that web, the *plica interdigtalis* (I've been perusing in your study, as much as you're away) testing tensile limits and the arc of its curve.

You have always been so dedicated to your work, always so available to your students, especially the timid, the malleable, the naive. You've earned a reputation with the more talkative graduates as a man whose office hours extend well into the night and who may even be summoned to quell small curiosities. Those small curiosities can nag at one, can't they? Especially at the girls. Though I've heard a few boys have sought your input as well.

Night after night, tearing napkins at the barstool in the bottle-lined mirror, I hear many things. Enough that I do wish the rats could speak to me. Especially the one with the ear on its back, as I'm sure it's heard everything that happens in the lab and would rush to give testament, its life being so short. I'd jabber like a loon if I thought my life nearly over. The lights stammered on in every chamber. But where were you, David? Where were you last night?

It's your judgment, isn't it? Just as you feared, your discernment has atrophied. For wasn't it you, more than any other, bent at the fountains of mutilated sheep? *The disheartening side effects of the trauma training prototypes*, as lamented in the margin of your leather-bound journal, two pages prior to the resting gold ribbon. Is that why you didn't simply return home for your keys instead of fleeing into the night, just as the soldiers on the blast course sewed the eyelids of the goats instead of stanching the wounds, joined the stumped thighs of two macaques instead of reattaching the limbs? Marvelous that the animals felt no pain and would rush the minefield again, if called upon. Still, if contact with the animals ignited such distortions in the medics, then I cannot blame you for being so hastily rid of them. But I wonder, did you dispose of them correctly, or have you, as Field Medic Alvarado so vividly performed in your records, *fashioned a tourniquet from the maimed beast's intestines*, so to speak?

And this is but one of your groundbreaking experiments. I've read the whole journal, David. No wonder you have been so absent, so stressed! It must compound your worries, numerous worries, concerning every project, knowing something from the animals leads the mind astray.

Obviously, you haven't been thinking clearly. Why else would you reassign Lily and her skillful hands to another facility? Such a bright student, and you find her suddenly unsuitable to the project? And why would she agree to forego your oversight? The esteemed Dr. Holawel! Is she insane? Or was she exposed, too? And to what degree? Surely the two of you didn't carve into the mutants as nakedly as those soldiers. That is the point, isn't it, of soldiers? I imagine the work you and Lily did together as much more cautious, more gradual, though that poses a series of insidious risks of its own. And surely David, the two of you wore protection?

The suits are not so difficult to slip into, and the laboratory even tells you when. Is it something in the air that triggers the sirens, a mesh in a vent with a taste for contagion, or something rudimentary as the automated chimes, like the kind in the doorways of boutiques or gas stations? The pods extending from the walls, the rotating warning lights, the helmets rising on pedestals theretofore concealed in the countertop, it all gives one the venturesome feeling of all of a sudden becoming an astronaut. Hurry! Hurry! Become! A scientist and an explorer! Hundreds of thousands of miles from home! But you are already a scientist and explorer and maintain an orbit nearly as far. Tell me, are you warm there?

※※※

Even with the directives from the loudspeakers and step-by-step instructions printed on the display, I can sympathize with why you and Lily may not have worn the suits. The excitement of discovery can carry one away. I know this for a fact, because I, in my own excitement, only haphazardly donned mine. I did not attach the air hose to the mouthpiece or turn the respirator filter three times until it clicked. I didn't so much as disturb the gloves from their handcuffs in the pod, knowing the first thing I would want when I found you would be to reach out and caress your rough cheek.

There are nights I awake and reach for your cheek, and sometimes I find you through the folds of the bedspread. You sweat as if your pipes had burst. I walk to the foot of the bed, trailing the blankets behind, until you writhe uncovered and wet in your underwear, the hair on your chest and belly matted flat, your limbs splayed horribly and a darkness spread beneath as if you had fallen from a treacherous height. You lay so still I would think you had died of fright in your nightmares if not for the querulous motion of your lips, pantomimes of a defensive murmur, and the sweat, spills of it still running from your temples and wrists. I watch you, and wonder where you are. But more often my hand falls only on sheets, soaked and rippled like sand pressed by a tide, and I know where you are. You're in the lab. You're working. But where were you last night?

I think I know.

Down the corridor to the partitions of intubated steers, down the stairwell to the aviary—why underground?—its hexagonal netting gone frantic with wings, through the tunnel of colonies ticking pincers on the glass, through the gurgling aquarium and vivarium stacks, I searched for you, opening every latch and cubby until creatures swarmed and nipped at my feet. But in the room with the pigs…it was there, I think, that I faltered.

In that wide, white sty—you hid from them, didn't you? Not from me! From the pigs! Hulking, vigorous slabs of brawn, as white and as hard as if carved from marble. The painted snouts and long-lashed eyes, blue sacks of vein coiled under the lids. Almost like clowns, nostrils honking. I ran my fingernails in the grooves of muscle as I stumbled through the straw, the straw I know, now, you were hiding beneath. The one obstruction I failed to check, even though I realize now I heard your voice. It was you, wasn't it? But through the straw it sounded strange, strained and chopped through the piles of stalks, that when I turned and saw the largest of the pigs smiling at me, its red lips curled over those teeth—so human—and the muscle at its throat flexing like a fist, it was the pig that spoke to me, calling me Lily, telling me to go back to my house, to hurry, and its eyes so wet and rimmed with blue and the flesh of its chest so stretched atop the muscle that I thought less of clowns than of whores, all them grunting and staggering my knees as they rooted and swarmed against me that I struggled to break free for fear they would devour me with those perfectly aligned teeth.

I rest on faith that they didn't get to you. I know you wouldn't let them. Those horrible things. That's why you burned the lab to the ground, isn't it? Once I was safe and away? Those things tried to gobble you up, made you confuse Lily with your own wife as you trembled there beneath the straw; that's why you destroyed them and everything, because, like me, you are faithful.

But even the faithful falter, don't they, David? There is a bad persuasion in the air of that lab. I hope you have burned it all away. For as afraid as I was of that clown-whore pig, even though I had to kick in its blue sack of an eye to escape through the door, even though it spewed my leg with something awful when it broke and its snout tore at my shin, gnashing, I did precisely as the pig said to do.

I drove straight to Lily's house. Straight to where she lives.

I hurried. Tires spinning spray from the road as I scanned the bushes and mailboxes for sight of the pigs peeking out at me, following. Scrawls from your journal singed into the high beams of rain. Numbers. Dashes. Letters. Echo Drive. Lily's address. Or was it from your Rolodex? Or scratched into the wallpaper? Her address. Yes. I feel I have seen it everywhere. It steadied my shaking hands on the wheel to know where I was headed, that the person there, so close to you, your confidant, would know where to find you; that if there was anyone in the world I could trust other than you, it would be her. I knew I could trust Lily.

And I needed someone I could trust, because something else written in your journal sent my blood racing into a headache of fear, something suddenly pertinent, and deadly—that the medics, the soldiers whose minds had fouled when they rushed to the animals, that several had slunk out of the hospital only to show up in the oddest of places: as valets at a fundraiser, as a caterer at a symposium, and one, still in his gown, his hand held to the glass of the cafeteria window, watching you fumble with a carton of orange juice. His forehead hard against the glass when you felt his gaze and looked up. The spiderweb of cracks. Gunfire. *Dissatisfying sweep by decontamination squad.*

*They know,* you wrote, *how to find us. Locked on scent, a specific heat imprint. Something in the shifting of their perception. Some kind of homing. Bent on violence? Revenge?* Your journal is filled with so many question marks, more on each page, as if they were breeding or spreading like a mold.

The pigs. Were they following me, too? I hurt its eye, David, gouged it with my heel. Are they coming for me? Those huge muscles churning as they gallop through the rain, little ears flapping over those grotesque, clown-whore eyes?

I shuddered at the thought of it, powerful shudders wracking my composure, though only for a moment, my hands on the wheel and holding my head, striations of light narrowing to a white-hot point, even as I squeezed my eyelids shut…and I wrecked the Lexus, wrecked it into her house.

Strange to see such a serene young woman in a state of distress, almost as strange as a car with its hood pouring steam into a living room. I reached for the door handle to find nothing there, only space, and I scrambled out through the wreckage over scattered glass to console her.

Her steady hands shook, David, and I held them fast to the couch to still them. But the fingers still curled, and the eyes spun about as if looking for something, and holding her there, I looked around, too, wondering what it was she needed—the clothes she'd been packing? Her ringing phone on the end table? I released her hands to reach for it and found, along with the fact that it was you trying to call her, that what she wanted was a shard of glass. She slashed at my face, but my legs carried me down and out of the way of her strike, pulled me to safety without my even trying, and my arm extended to pin her hand to the wall as she strained against me until blood ran from her palms. I couldn't stand to think of those hands damaged, so I whipped my neck and butted her head until my ears rang and my mouth gushed with the bright taste of copper, and she slumped to the floor in the wash of my headlights. Maybe it was the injuries marring her complexion, the stains, the swelling, but I thought it strange that I had thought her so flawless, that tumid face of hers broken under lights.

The phone rang again, and I did not answer but thumbed *accept call* and held it to my ear.

"Lily?"

My dear. So confused!

I said nothing but listened, and you told me where to meet you, which city, which bar, which booth, the importance that we take separate flights on separate days, and not direct flights, apart for a time then back together at last. But you never told me where you were last night, and I have to wonder. That's what confuses me.

Sure enough, there were tickets in her wallet. Not the real one in the leather clutch, but the e-wallet on her phone. I had only to press her thumb to the button, the limp hanging hand, to find them. Then on to the clutch for the passport, the driver's license. You know, we don't look so dissimilar, Lily and I; perhaps that's why you saw so much in her.

I don't doubt for a second I could have used those pictures to board the first flight, but they noticed the hand, and suddenly, there was gasping all around me, and I was pinned to the ground, my own wrists going into handcuffs. The whole time I was thinking *if only there had been time to print the tickets*, or if only I had taken just the thumb, opened the phone that way, perhaps I could have done it on the sly. But the hands, David, I knew you would want those delicate hands, thought even you may be able to interchange them with mine. I thought, *yes, I wouldn't mind having them*. But they noticed, David, and even took the prints. They think I have something to do with this thing the two of you have done, this thing you are running from. And I would, David. I would, if only you would let me.

If I had those hands now I could surely pick these locks, could stroke the ears of the guards until their spines went loose, and they acquiesced to let me back into the night. I could drive, David, for days and days, the numbers and letters flashing in my vision, and, eventually, find you. I could rent another car and drive to the glow of the lab, the same I saw burning on the horizon on my way to the airport, and some scent in the air there would tip me, I know, in your direction.

But please do not worry, darling. For however long they hold me, I promise you, I'll come. And it may not be long. Because if anything escaped that lab, it will come for me, too. I'm waiting for the screeching and lowing of animals, the squeal of those pigs, hundreds of strange, perturbed beasts, and the guards' guns all distractedly blazing and the bars swinging open like the closet with your lab coat and your keys, and I know there will be more to be found and that it won't be long until, love, I find you.

XOXOX XOXOX XOXOX X

## About the Author

Jay Outhier is a waiter and musician living in Princeton, New Jersey. He plays bass with his band Essie & the Big Chill on weekends, waits tables at the brewery on weeknights, and writes horror fiction and poetry much later at night.

# GUEST EDITOR

## Stacey Longo

Stacey Longo is an award-winning author and editor. Her books include the Pushcart-nominated *Ordinary Boy*, a dark fiction novel, and *Secret Things: Twelve Tales to Terrify*, a short story collection, among other titles. Her book *My Mom, MS, and a Sixth-Grade Mess* won Best YA Novel of 2017 in the Preditors & Editors Readers' Choice Awards. Her most recent release is the YA horror mystery, *My Sister the Zombie* (Storyside Press). Longo is a former humor columnist for the *Block Island Times* and writes a weekly humor blog at www.staceylongo.com.

# WANT MORE
# FREE BOOKS?

Join our mailing list to learn about freebies, giveaway contests, and new releases. Sign up at **www.darkalleypress.com.**

# AUTHORS WANTED FOR

# INK STAINS
## ANTHOLOGIES

We are looking for unique dark fiction submissions for upcoming editions of *Ink Stains Anthology* from Dark Alley Press.

Submissions are now open for pieces 3,000-15,0000 words for all works that fit under the Dark Alley Press banner, including those in the following categories:

- Dark fiction (including lit fic)
- Gothic fiction
- Supernatural/paranormal fiction
- Horror
- Steampunk
- Black Comedy
- Fantasy

Authors of acquired pieces for Ink Stains Anthology will receive a flat fee payment upon publication. For more information, check out our website.

# www.inkstainsanthology.com